Praise for Jem

Pretty/Ugly

"More than a simply a fine horror fantasy, this is a highly polished psychodrama exploring early trauma, identity, life's exigencies, and fates – all woven together in a stunningly creative tapestry of a unique novel. Jennifer Anne Gordon is on the ascent as a literary figure of stature!" – **Grady Harp – Top Shelf Magazine**

"Pretty/Ugly is a lyrical, hallucinogenic train ride through the end of the world. It's the story of two people falling in and out of loneliness as the end draws near. Each moment is more beautiful and terrifying than the last. Pretty/Ugly is the combination of Contagion and Lost in Translation I didn't know I needed. It's Lost in Contagion" – **Allison Martine (Author of the Bourbon Books)**

Beautiful, Frightening, and Silent

WINNER KINDLE AWARD FOR BEST HORROR/SUSPENSE 2020 - Finalist for American Book Fest's Best Book Award Horror 2020

"The writing is incredibly beautiful, rhythmic, and precise, and Gordon's use of objects laden with emotion is masterful… This is horror in love with life, and an author in love with language. You will encounter scenes you won't forget. Be ready." - **Diane Zinna author of The All-Night Sun**

"Dark, twisted, and lyrical. This book destroyed me, and I couldn't put it down." – **Kassie Romo – Reedsy**

From Daylight to Madness & When the Sleeping Dead Still Talk (The Hotel Series)

"This hallucinogenic novel reads like 200 pages of pure nightmare" – **Michelle Hogmire – Reedsy**

"Gordon proves herself an astute observer of a social era, especially in her portrayal of the gender disparity and prejudices of the American Victorian age. Gordon's impeccable writing, mesmerizing prose, and pitch-perfect pacing bring an immediacy to her protagonists' struggles with their personal traumas. She adds tantalizing scares throughout, and her world building is electric as she transforms a familiar Gothic setup into a twisty roller coaster heavy on foreboding." – **Book View Gold Seal Review**

ISBN- 978-1-7354021-7-8 (ebook)
ISBN- 978-1-7354021-8-5 (paperback)

Cover and Interior design by: Books and Moods
Printed in the United States of America.

A NOVEL

JENNIFER ANNE GORDON

pretty/ugly

JENNIFER ANNE GORDON

part 1

DAY 1

A thousand little cuts.

Tis the tempestuous loveliness of terror;
For from the serpents gleams a brazen glare
Kindled by that inextricable error,
Which makes a thrilling vapour of the air
Become an ever-shifting mirror
Of all the beauty and the terror there
—Percy Bysshe Shelley

Prologue/

As Most of You Know, My Name Is . . .

She was barely able to drag her ass out of bed today. She felt it; she was destroyed. Last night's drinks left her with a throat that felt like it was filled with cat hair and dried grass. The rest of her just felt a little raw. Her lips were swollen, and her mouth felt tender and chapped. She remembered Kim. She reached up and touched the back of her head, it was sore. She remembered it had hit the wall at one point. She tried to smile, but even a smile hurt.

She hadn't had that much to drink, just a few fruity concoctions with the girls before the slow, smoky, and sad descent into whiskey . . . *Girls.* That stretched the truth. Girl. last night it was just *a* girl. Only a girl. Girl.

This morning she felt like she was still there in that stupid bar, Lampadario; the music seared into her skin, eighth grade razor blades. Her eardrums hurt. It was too loud to have a conversation. She spent the whole night sipping 18-dollar Cosmos as she screamed, "What?" every time someone tried to talk to her. She only remembered one of her conversations from last night, but maybe it's not that she can't remember the others, maybe she never even heard them. She only heard one. She half-remembered it was about love languages and buildings that collapsed against you . . . and at the end of the night, it's not conversations that matter anyway. The thing that mattered now was how the world saw it. Fear of Missing Out. FOMO is what she had tried hard in the last ten years to build her life on. Building blocks like this are precarious and, in the end, even memories felt like falling downstairs.

It's the photos and selfies she got when she was there, when she felt her life through anyone else's eyes. She posted a few to her Instagram earlier and the hearts started coming in almost right away. She knew they would. She knew her audience.

She shied away from the windows like a vampire and swished some room temperature water around in her mouth. She looked out the large windows near her bed, all the buildings on the other side of this city looked like empty picture frames. She was lucky; the renovated mill building where she lived had high ceilings and huge windows. The bottom floor and the two sub basements of this building were filled with sand to kill the Anthrax. The building was once a slaughterhouse. It killed herbivores, cows, sheep. Some of them had been sick. This is why this apartment building started three floors up; everything else was sand, and on top of that, expensive apartments.

The Merrimack River, which during early spring ran high when the snow from the White Mountains melted, made the river sound like an ocean squall as it barreled through Manchester; it cut the small city into two parts. Omelia could see across the river to the *West Side* of the city. She saw the steeple of Saint Marie's Church as it tried to fight against the earth and reach out almost touching the sky. When she was a little girl, she went to school close to there. It was a sprawling Catholic school that somehow seemed in her memories to be made up almost entirely of basements. That building is empty now and does nothing besides take up space and hold squatters in what has become, in the years since her childhood, a sketchy drug-filled collection of scraps. Now it is called a neighborhood.

When she was young, there were little worlds and small communities in that part of "Manch-hattan." They all lived in shabby houses and in three floor walk-ups. They were mainly French-Canadian speakers. She and her classmates all had parents who had thick French-Canadian accents, their voices sounded like work boot leather. They mangled the word order in most of their sentences. She remembered her father screaming up the narrow stairwell in her childhood home how he was able to scream and be exhausted as he said, "Throw me down the stairs my slippers." No matter how many times she tried to correct him he never seemed to get it right.

She ran her hands through her hair; it still had enough product in it from last night that she thought she could get away with not doing anything to it at all. Her face was free of makeup as she needed to be, and she was lucky enough, even now as she barreled towards thirty, that even without makeup she was what most people would call *striking*, not *pretty*, and thank God, not *attractive*. When she had makeup on, she was more than striking she was a work of art, a small, framed portrait in a gilded frame that hung on a museum wall. She was the Mona Lisa; except she was hot.

Today she saw that there were shadows under her eyes. Her delicate, papery, thin skin had a blue tinge to it, and it darkened to an almost plum in the corners of her eyes. She leaned in closer to the halo mirror that was set up with her light and phone. The camera settings were perfect. They took at least six years off her skin. Even so, she thought she could see little veins; they reached though her eyelids like famine and hunger. She looked at herself, and all she could think was that she looked like the worst kind of Dickens character.

Without makeup, she was the laundress, at best.

Maybe she looked more scrounged up than she thought she did. Maybe she was tired. It didn't matter though—at least it wouldn't soon. She changed the setting on her halo light to the rose gold setting, and she noticed an immediate change in her appearance. Her mirror saw her as healthy, vibrant, and effortless. If she faked it long enough it could almost pass for happy.

ROSE GOLD.

She smiled, she could do that now, her real life, her make believe life only started when the camera was on. Her hand tousled her perfect messy bedhead in place. Everything before and after this didn't matter.

She knew when she genuinely smiled that her mouth was crooked, and she felt it made her look like the worst of Picasso's paintings—the ones he did on plates and napkins when he could not afford the check. She also knew that when she smiled, she looked like her mother; her father used tell her that when she was a girl. His eyes would grow cloudy and unfocused. They would brim almost to the surface with tears. He went quiet after that and would stare out the kitchen window for hours. He never spoke; there was nothing to say. She tried to understand his grief over losing his wife, not to death but to indifference, but she was so little and understanding someone else's sadness was impossible. It was easier for her just not to smile.

To not remind.

She checked her Instagram one more time before she switched her camera on. She is close to 1400 likes on a selfie from last night, in less than two hours; it's not bad, it could be better. She smiled again, her real smile, her crooked one. She knew when she wore a corset made of book covers that it would be a hit. She switched over to her camera and placed it in the stand. She switched the filter to vibrant, and that filter and the rose gold light combined with the natural light from her windows would be perfect. It changed her dull green eyes to an almost emerald with specks of gold. Her dark auburn hair shined with a vibrant red in this light. This is who she is now, who she was meant to be the whole time. She started up her live stream. She was barely done waving at the camera and she saw there were 447 people watching already.

Her laugh was deep and throaty; she had taught herself to do this without letting out a natural smile. She glanced at herself one last time in the mirror; the blue shadows under her eyes were not noticeable in this light. She breathed in and exhaled slowly.

"Hey everyone, thanks for joining me today, as most of you know, I'm Omelia."

Chapter/
ᛒᚾᛖ

OMELIA
Sugar and Spice and Everything . . .

For the first few months that she was doing her live streams and makeup tutorials, Omelia would often stumble when she said her name; her voice would catch a little in her throat, her body fought against the lie. You see, Omelia was created to be simply that, just Omelia. Someone new, someone who was not her, just an idea of her. When she was asked about her unusual name, she would laugh and tilt her head, so she could feature the left side of her face, which was always more prominently featured. That was her better side. The right side of her face had a small half-moon shaped scar on her chin from the time she was bit by a baby chipmunk that she picked up in the parking lot of a corner store. With her head tilted, she would tell the story of her name. "You see, my mother is a yoga instructor, and my father is a pilot, and he always said his first-born daughter would be named Amelia after Amelia Earhart." She would always pause here in the story, waiting for the "whomever" asked really to hear what she was saying. She would continue, "My mother, being a yoga instructor and very into New Age meditation wanted me to have the name of a goddess, or something more mystical yet earthy. They fought for months, they probably both wished I was a boy at that point, but they finally settled on Omelia." She would make a little shrugging motion and then usually say something like, "It was hard growing up; I always wanted a normal name."

It was a lie. Not the part where she had said, "It was hard growing up," that part was true. The rest she had made up during the sleepless nights in group homes, the places that always had green painted walls in one too many shades. There was that time she made it into a foster home—but that was just a wound that never healed over. In her mind, she always picked at it.

Her mom, she thought, might still be alive. Her dad had gotten a letter from her a few times over the years. There was never a return address, but they were all postmarked from Florida, which as a child felt like the other side of the world from what she considered home. There were a couple from Miami, and then one came in from Clearwater, and then eventually Tampa. That was back before Omelia was Omelia, when she was just Nicole from Manchester, New Hampshire. Nicole's father never let her see the letters from her mother; those were for him, they were private, he said. He did, however, let Nicole keep the envelopes the letters came in. One time when Nicole was about five, she pried the stamp off the envelope pressed it to her lips, and she could feel her mom's kiss and she thought for a moment she finally felt love, all the way from sunny Florida.

She had lived in a little bungalow house with her father in the poor section of a rich town. It had low ceilings and crooked floors, and the walls smelled sour with cigarette smoke. She would go to school and the other children would laugh at the smell of it radiating off her. Sour smoky sadness. Her father . . . he tried; he really did try for years. He worked as a plumber, and he paid the bills, and sent little Nicole to a private Catholic school where they wore uniforms and learned French so the children could communicate with their parents and the people that worked at the corner markets.

School picture day had always been Nicole's favorite. It was the one day of the year that they didn't have to wear their school uniforms. Nicole loved clothes, she loved playing with makeup, which her father let her do, if she didn't leave the house "painted up like trash." So, on picture day Nicole would dress up; she was the prettiest girl in her class, she knew that. However, when the photographers would try to get her to smile, she would not. She would stare straight ahead into the camera; she would make her eyes wide and filled with emotion. She thought that was better than smiling anyway, it was more honest.

Year after year, Nicole would bring home her school portrait, her green eyes wide, her mouth unsmiling. Her father would put the portrait up near where he sat at the kitchen table. It would hang next to him while he read the paper and watched the news. It hung there, held to the nicotine-stained walls with a thumbtack. He would be able to see it out of the corner of his eye as he stared out the window, waiting for his wife to come home at long last. The year Nicole turned 13 she was finally allowed to wear makeup to school for the first time and on picture day, she wore a deep burgundy lipstick, and her eyeshadow made her eyelids look like burnished bronze. The gold flecks in her eyes, which were normally unnoticeable, popped. She sat down in front of the photographer. He was a new one, younger than the old man who had been taking her photo since she was small. He looked at her and said, "You belong in front of the camera, you're the prettiest girl I've seen in my life."

Nicole laughed, and she smiled. She really smiled. The flash went off on the camera and for a split second, she was blinded by it. "Wait, can you take another one? I think I was making a face . . ." her voice trailed off. Her regret sounded like a moth's wings.

"Nope, you weren't making a face, you were smiling, and it was beautiful. Don't worry." As the photographer said this, he already looked past her to the next girl who walked awkwardly towards the camera, and the stools that wobbled if you were not sitting just right. As Nicole walked out of the room, she heard the photographer as he said to the next girl, "You're the prettiest girl I've seen in my life." His words stung; she felt betrayed by a generic compliment and felt foolish that she had believed him . . . yet he did not tell that other girl she belonged in front of the camera. No, he said that part only to her. She held that inside of her, close to her heart.

When Nicole brought her school photo home a few weeks later and handed the large envelope to her father, her hands shook, her knuckles were white, and she realized that the envelope felt damp and curled around the edges from her nervous sweat. Her father slid the photo out of the envelope and stared at it. His fingers traced her face. His thumb lingered on her smile. She knew he could see it, the smile that reminded him so much of her mother. He whispered his words barely there against the deep wheeze of his breath, "You really do look so much like her." He stared at the photo for a few more minutes. Nicole stood in front of him, her hands clasped behind her back. Her heart tickled in a bad way. She stared at him silently. She watched as his hands began to shake a little, and he slid the photo back into the envelope and then gently placed it on the pile of that week's discarded newspapers.

It did not hang on the wall. When Nicole went to sleep that night, her kitchen wall still looked like last year.

The next day when Nicole came home from school, she found a note written on the back of an old electric bill on the kitchen table. It was written in her father's slanted handwriting, a combination of half cursive and half printed. It said simply, "I want you to know that I tried, I really did, for as long as I could. Do not go upstairs, just call 911 and tell them that your father is dead, and you have been left alone. I'm sorry. When you are older, you will thank me for this."

She never did thank him.

These were the thoughts and memories that shifted and switched like a kaleidoscope in her head that constantly arranged and rearranged all the time. The pictures, the memories, they were beautiful, and they were awful. Her childhood was a bruise as it changed from dark purple to yellow. But you see, Nicole or rather, Omelia, couldn't say any of this. She could not talk about the kaleidoscope, not when she chatted away on her YouTube channel; in fact, she could not even say these things to herself. She said them once or twice to her shrink, that's when he gave her the meds. After that, she didn't have to say it at all. All she had to say was, "They're not working," and then there were always more. They helped, but only to a certain extent. She made her *living* by doing makeup tutorials based on whatever vintage book she had read in the past few days. She couldn't talk about being Nicole when she had to pretend to be Omelia, hell; she had pretended to be Omelia for so long now that she almost forgot that Omelia didn't really exist.

Being fictional was much harder than anyone could know.

"Ok everyone, I know you have been dying to know what we are doing today." The comments rolled in so fast she could barely even read them anymore. Omelia held up a worn and tattered copy of *The Conjure Wife* by Fritz Lieber. The cover had always been one of her favorites, done by Jeff Jones. It featured a beautiful woman, running from a castle, her hair long and loose, and her eyes smoky and kohl rimmed. It looked like a silent film if it could scream in terror. She put the book in front of her face and let her viewers soak it all in. "Friends," she said, as she moved the book off to the side of her makeup table, "you all know how much I love these Gothic Horror covers, I'm obsessed, obsessed." She did her version of her new Omelia smile, even though the memory of her buying this book at a flea market when she was young played in her head like a movie.

A Kaleidoscope.

A book peddler with a green parakeet on his shoulder sold her ten gothic horror paperbacks for two dollars. She was in heaven. Her dad had thought she was reading books about princesses in castles . . . they didn't have money, but there was always money to make her happy.

"So today we're going to do a look that's based on this, the pale face overall, not a lot of contouring, and we will accent that with a dark smoky eye, almost a cat eye, so we need to use our liquid liner today." She saw the normal comments pour in. People feared liquid eyeliner. "Don't be scared everyone, we'll get through this together."

Omelia had been live streaming makeup tutorials and book reviews on her YouTube station for years, had over 300,000 subscribers, and was sent free makeup and books all the time, though to be fair, she still preferred reading used books like the vintage ones with yellowed paper that are just on the verge of going brittle. Sometimes she found an old book that smelled like stale secondhand smoke. She always bought those, and if they smelled like birds, it was even better. These scents would cloy her nose and make her feel sick, but she bought them anyway.

Sometimes at night, with the lights off, she would sip straight vodka still cold from her freezer, and she would take her books out, along with the brittle, empty envelopes from Florida. She would smell each one of them; they smelled like home.

"Okay everyone, I know a lot of you like to do your foundation with a sponge but remember your face is a canvas and you are the painter, and you are the art, so I like to . . . paint with a brush." She saw all the comments as they came in, they all said, "paint with a brush," and some had smiley faces and hearts after them. It was one of her phrases, and her followers commenting it at the same time she said it, well, she was sure it made them feel like part of a secret club. She gave that to them. What she did was more than just makeup and being pretty, she gave them a home; this was her version of empty envelopes and the smell of secondhand smoke.

Parakeets.

"So, because we are going for a slightly gothic look, I am going to use my palest foundation, my winter foundation. I'm going to put this all over my face, everywhere except my eyebrows, I'm even covering my lips. Now, I already used a face primer before we went live, but if you haven't done that, make sure you do that now. You don't want your makeup to look like it's going over the texture of an orange; this will smooth everything out. Remember, artists prime their canvas." She saw the comments come in as she said it. *Prime the canvas.* This feels like home. *This* feels like love.

Omelia pumped her liquid foundation onto the top of her left hand and dipped the tip of her brush in it. She turned towards her mirror and put a dot on her forehead, nose, chin, and two tiny dots on each cheek. She saw that maybe she thought too soon about the blue tinges under her eyes; in the few minutes she had been live they seemed to have carved blue half-moons under her eyes. As she moved her foundation brush over her face in circular upward motions, she saw most of the imperfections start to blur away. All except one.

She leaned in close to the mirror as if she were going to give her reflection a kiss; she stopped short when she noticed a small red patch near the corner of her mouth. She touched the spot with the tip of her pinky finger and could feel a pain that crackled like fire and radiated through her face. The back of her eyes hurt. It throbbed all the way down into her jaw and shot down into her neck like whiplash. Jesus, what the fuck is this? She winced, she knew she did, and the comments showed that everyone else noticed too.

"OMG GURL U OK?"

"AGH OMELIA what's up?"

"Shit Om. Do you have mouth herpes? Lol"

"Oh, looks like someone's breaking out, LOL!!!!!"

"Yikes Omelia, maybe you shouldn't put makeup on over that."

There were too many comments to count; she read them while she still held her foundation brush. It hovered just above her face. She had no idea how she didn't see this before she went live, she would never go live if she were breaking out, it's a cardinal rule. Especially since the advertising money started rolling in and she was being paid to go on a European tour, doing her makeup in some of the fanciest bookstores all over Italy, Portugal, and Spain. She knew she couldn't back out right now; she had to finish this makeup tutorial. For some reason, the longer she sat there the more live viewers she had, it was closing in on 900 . . . wait now 914, 935 . . . what the fuck? She worried they were tuning in to see her melt down, to see the ugly behind all this pretty.

"GROSS Omelia, looks like you're not so perfect after all… :("

When she saw those words, she knew what she had to do. She put on her best Omelia smile, her head tilted, and she showcased her right side to the camera. The little half-moon scar was now on display but luckily that thing, that stinging red, blight was hidden. She did her best throaty Omelia laugh, and then made a face that she thought screamed 'sincere'. She looked into the camera and said, "Thank you so much for caring, friends. THIS IS WHY WE NEED TO CLEAN OUR MAKEUP BRUSHES!" She yelled this with frivolity that bordered on mania. "I won't lie to you, as you know if you follow me on Insta you've seen I've been out a lot over the past week, and every night I tell myself, your friends can wait Oms. You need to take care of yourself, you need to clean your brushes, you need to catch up on your reading . . . but I failed at that. I failed for me, and now I know I failed for you." With that, she continued to apply the winter shade of her foundation. The circular motions and the makeup that hit that red spot on her face made her eyes water and her jaw start to throb, it ached going down her neck. But she kept going—one eye on her mirror, on her once again seemingly perfect face and one eye on the comments.

"You didn't fail us Omelia."

"We love you Oms!"

"I wish I had your social life, LOL. Brushes can wait!!"

"Take care of yourself gurl, the way you take care of all of us."

Omelia smiled her fake smile past the pain, "Okay everyone, now that we have the foundation set, let's make sure we apply our setting spray." She closed her eyes as she sprayed herself. The pain had seemed to crawl from that small red spot down into her stomach. It made her ribs ache and her throat feel even rawer as it made its way down her body. When she opened her eyes and looked at herself, she looked pale, but perfect. She was a blank canvas. No one, no one understood just how hard all of this really was.

Chapter/ two

THE EAGLE
Sam

He didn't know how he got himself into this situation. When he looked back on his life, his choices . . . he shouldn't be here. He knew that. He was playing a part, the part of a dutiful son, the part of someone who was a leader; Jesus he wasn't a leader. "FUCK!" He screamed this at his reflection and pounded his fist onto the wall next to the mirror in his bathroom. He was a theatre major once upon a time . . . he never should have let his father talk him into law school. He hated law, the weight of it, the responsibility of it, but what was he supposed to do, *NOT* go? Was he supposed to say no to his father? That was before his father was the Vice President, when he was just Senator Santo Alberti, but still, his father somehow always managed to get what he wanted. He wanted Sam to be a lawyer, and now he was a goddamn lawyer. Worse than that was the fact that he had somehow become the Democratic Candidate for Governor of Massachusetts.

He opened his medicine cabinet and his long fingers wrapped around the bottle of Adderall. He popped one in his mouth and took another two over to the coffee table. He ground them into dust with the meaty part of his hand and then divided the powder into lines using the edge of his phone. Residue of the powder caked between the phone and the case. Shit, he didn't think this through, it wasn't his fault though, and his thoughts had been fuzzy for the past 12 months. He had been forced to give up the coke when he announced his intention to run for office last year. He didn't think he would win the primary, he thought he could say he tried, he would disappoint his old man, but he would be done, he would have done his part in politics. But fuck, he won.

He leaned down, pressed one finger over his left nostril, and snorted the Adderall. It burned and dripped down the back of his throat. It tasted bitter. As he did the last line, he could feel that he hadn't crushed the pills well enough and felt the little chunks of the orange tablets as they scraped the inside of his nose. It was as if he had snorted sand. As he leaned back on his legs, he almost felt like he would be able to get through this nightmare of a day. Jesus, this was not how he wanted to spend his Friday, doing some PR stunt where he read Shakespeare to kids at some inner-city school in Roxbury. At least it was Shakespeare; he could finally pretend for a minute that he was playing Henry V.

He glanced at his phone and realized that he was already late; his car was probably downstairs. George would be pissed, he knew it; he had been trying to get Sam to be more punctual for years, hell, since he was a little boy. George had been the family driver since they moved to Boston. Sam always wondered if George had come with the historic brownstone in Back Bay, that perhaps the realtor had boasted about the arched windows, the four floors, the two fireplaces, and the servant's quarters, which came complete with their very own servant.

George waited outside the car and gave Sam a wide smile that showed too many teeth. His eyes didn't crinkle when he smiled, so Sam knew that it wasn't sincere. "Morning George," Sam said as he ducked into the backseat of the black Mercedes. He tried to stretch his legs out as much as he could, but at 6'4, there never seemed to be enough room for him anywhere.

When George started the car, he gave Sam a quick look in the rearview mirror and said, "You know Eagle, you really need to work on your punctuality, you can't keep people waiting all the time, especially those kids you're reading to today. And, if you keep playing your cards right, soon you will have the whole state counting on you."

"I know, I know, I'll try to do better George, for you." Sam smiled and he meant it; at least he meant it every time he said it.

"Thank you, Eagle." George said with warmth in his voice.

George was the only person that still called Sam by his childhood nickname. Everyone else had stopped when Sam's twin sister Shannon died of leukemia when they were eleven years old. He could never hear that nickname without Shannon's voice in his head, and the relentless way she teased him. You see, Sam's father had named him after Sam the Eagle, from the Muppet Show. Shannon told him it was because Sam the boy had the same aquiline nose that the big blue bird had. He hated her for that. But he would do anything to be able to hear her say those words again; he would give anything to have been able to grow up hating her. Instead, he had grown up with a Shannon-sized hole in his heart.

As Sam reached up, his hands started to shake a little from the Adderall as it coursed through him, and he traced his finger down his face from forehead to chin. He felt the slight bump on the bridge of his nose, and the little horizontal scar that was there. He closed his eyes and all he could see was that damn Muppet. He knew because he finally asked his father if he was named after the bird because of his resemblance to him; no, it was because Sam the Eagle was a Republican, just like his father.

Sam was glad he could still hate him for that.

He popped his ear buds in and pulled up a playlist of dark ambient music. It wasn't really music. More like the sounds a haunted house would make if it became sentient. The ride to the Hudson school took about a half hour, and Sam didn't know if it was the music or the fact that it was early for *him* to be up and about, but by the time he got there the initial burst of adrenaline from the Adderall had already begun to fade. He saw the camera crews from 60 Minutes were already there. They chatted with his campaign manager; all of them clutched large Starbucks cups as they waited outside on this chilly October morning. They had been following him around for the past few days, getting behind the scenes footage for a feature they were doing on him called, "The New JFK." When they pitched the idea to him, he said no. Actually, he said, "At this point I wish someone would shoot *me* in the head." Then he laughed. Later that day his campaign manager called him and said he was doing the interview. Gretchen was a political machine, and his father swore that he never would have become Senator, or now Vice President without her machinations.

Sam's door opened and George said, "Knock em dead Eagle. You'll do well with that speech. I remember when you worked on that in college, that Shakespeare."

"Thanks George. Hopefully it won't take too long in there."

"Oh, you know me, I've got nowhere else to be." George wiped at his eyes, which were glassy and teared up from the cool damp air. Sam noticed that George had dark circles under his eyes, and his lips were dry and cracked; his bottom lip looked as if it had split open and scabbed over. He seemed to look *smaller*. All the countless errands, Sam's need to be shuttled to and from campaign events, fundraisers, and the liquor store, must have gotten to him too. He looked terrible.

"Where the fuck have you been?" Gretchen hissed these words as she walked towards the car; no, not walked, *stomped*.

"Sorry ma'am there was a lot of traffic on the way here, it's not Eagle's fault he's late."

Sam reached out his large hand and gave George's shoulder a squeeze, and leaned into the man, and whispered into his ear. "Thanks. I owe you.

Maybe you should take a little nap while you wait for me. Stretch out in the backseat. The rest will do you good."

With that, Sam turned and walked towards the camera crew. His hand swept back his raven- dark hair that had just started to silver at the temples. He smiled and started to play the part of the "New JFK."

"How long is this going to take?" Sam asked Gretchen as two other people orbited around him; one attached the lavalier microphone to the inside of his blazer and tucked the mic pack into his inside pocket. The other person fussed with his hair and brushed his angular cheekbones and nose with a sheer powder, so he didn't look too shiny under the camera lights. There was no makeup or powder to cover boredom.

Sam had whatever the male equivalent of *resting bitch face* happened to be. He was often accused of looking angry until the moment when he turned on his smile; it was in that instant as if everyone in the room was drawn towards him. He radiated something that, while it was not quite happiness, was something close to it. On the other hand, when he was not being watched or expected to shine, his face wore a serious and drawn expression, and his already dark eyes would seem to blacken completely, like a shark. This was the look that he gave Gretchen now. His smile faded, and she was met with dead-eyed coldness.

Gretchen had also known Sam since he was a child, though she'd never endeared herself to him to have called him Eagle, the way George did; no, she called him Damian, but never to his face. "We've gone over this Sam, you are reading the Saint Crispin's Day Speech in the Honors English class, you will then eat lunch in the cafeteria with the kids, don't worry, you won't really have to do it, we just need a couple shots of you waiting in line with the kids for the hot lunch. People will love it; it will make you seem more . . ." she paused not knowing exactly what to say here. "It will make you look more *human*. After that you will have a meeting in the teacher's lounge with a small group of the staff, including the principal, the vice principal, and the custodian."

"The fucking janitor?" He sighed and wondered just how this all happened.

"All total you should be done in two hours. You can do that right? Pretend to be a good fucking person for two hours?" Gretchen adjusted his suit jacket and reached up to straighten his hair again. He flinched away from her and ran his hand through his hair in the opposite direction, giving him a tousled look. He glared at her long and hard before he responded.

"I don't have to pretend to be a good person Gretchen, haven't you heard?" He gestured towards the camera crew and the intern holding two cups of coffee, "I'm the New JFK." He sniffled a little and though it had now been a little over an hour since the Adderall, he still felt like he could feel it scratching at the inside his nose like a rat trapped in a wall, and with each scratch the pill melted a little more and dripped down the back of his throat, searing it like acid. He started to feel a little woozy and flushed.

Before he could say or do anything, the makeup person was back at his side and re-powdering his face. He was about to ask for a glass of water when the bell rang; the sound was so shrill that the room began to swim in front of his eyes and there was a brief but very noticeable moment of vertigo combined with an ocean wave of sound as the blood rushed in his ears. The kids swarmed out of the classrooms; some took notice of the well-dressed man and full camera crew, but most of them just buzzed past them all. They barely looked up from their phones; their fingers moved fast over the screens as their bodies shuffled almost mindlessly to their next destination.

The only one who seemed to take notice of him was a scrawny boy, on the small side for eleven. This one wasn't texting, he was talking on the phone, and Sam could hear him saying, "I don't know Mom, I just don't feel well all of a sudden." The boy wasn't really keeping track of where he was going, he only noticed Sam because he walked right into him. "Uh . . . sorry dude." The boy barely glanced up at him before putting his head down. Sam was overwhelmed with a feeling of pity for the boy; he saw that the side of his face was badly broken out, down the side of the nose and creeping into the corner of the boy's mouth. It must be terrible, Sam thought, to have skin like that. He had always been lucky; he always had money and doctors, and never had to feel the sting of embarrassment about being an ugly kid.

There was a feeling inside Sam's chest, and his heart skipped and tumbled. His breath started to get shallow and uneven, this couldn't be nerves could it? No, it couldn't be that. No, Sam the Eagle only got nervous when he cared about something, and this school, these kids, this day, hell even this election . . . he didn't care about any of it. Right?

He was ushered into a classroom, where the small desks that took up most of the room were lined up like sandbags holding back a flood. They were almost on top of the teacher's desk, which itself was nearly sandwiched to the blackboard. Sam smelled the staleness of the air, the cloying hot dusty smell that was plaited with teenage hormone-scented sweat. There was something else though that lingered in the air, something that reminded him of when he was little and would get sick and would stay under the blankets for days on end. When he would finally rise from his bed, the room would be filled with a musky sick smell that was reminiscent of sour milk and saltwater.

This classroom, it smelled like that.

The room began to fill; each desk housed a little hormonal freak child. The kind that was both too poor and too smart ever to have an easy life, the kind of kid that had to work hard, the kind of kid that cared. Not like Sam, hell, not even like "Eagle." As a boy Sam never cared. He didn't have to. The back rows of the classroom filled in first. The teacher who was barely over 23 and still had large, scared doe-eyes, leaned towards Sam and Gretchen, and said, "I don't believe in assigning seats, so the back rows fill up first." She paused, looking at Sam for just a beat too long before she continued, "Don't worry, the latecomers and the eager ones will fill up the front desks." She smiled and the corners of her mouth curved down. It wasn't pretty. *She* wasn't pretty.

Sam looked down at his script, the typed-up Saint Crispin's Day speech in a font large enough that he would not have to squint to see it. He had rolled the paper over and over again in a *not nervous* fashion, so it looked like a scroll. When he unrolled it now, he realized that the paper felt damp. His palms were more than clammy; they seemed to be dripping with sweat. When he looked at the words, they blurred and waltzed in front of his eyes. He couldn't understand them. It was as if he were trying to read in a dream. Somewhere in his memory, he knew the words but not how to say them or feel them. He breathed deep. The bottoms of his lungs ached, and his ribs began to squeeze tight, making it hard to breathe. The skittering heart, it was back. The room was hot, too hot, that he was certain. He felt his papers ripped from his hands even before he heard Gretchen's words, which hissed into his ear. The sound was dry, and hateful. "You don't need this shit; you have been practicing this speech since you were in college."

The words sounded harmless enough, but it was the inflection in the word *college* that stung. The implication that Columbia's Musical Theatre Program was not valid. Look, Sam knew how people looked at him when he had said he was a musical theatre major . . . but what those people didn't understand is how much he could get laid if he did musical theatre or danced. Being a straight white guy was easier. Fuck, if Sam could have been a ballet dancer he would have. He loved sex, he did. He loved fucking girls with low self-esteem and daddy issues. He loved all of that. But what he would not let anyone know is that he loved theatre; he loved being someone else, even more.

So yes, maybe . . . maybe he was a little nervous, not about being the "New JFK" but about the speech, about Henry V, about Saint Crispin's Day, about the role he would never play because at best he would be the 'conservative' democratic governor of Massachusetts, and at worst, he would be a failed politician, and lackluster halfhearted ACLU lawyer.

"How the fuck did I get here?" Sam whispered this to Gretchen, but she had already walked away. His speech rolled in her hands and then tossed into the wastebasket by the door. The room was almost full; only one lone desk, situated on the stage left side of the classroom, right in front, remained empty.

"Has anyone seen Simon?" the teacher's voice screeched out, sounding more like a petrified possum than a human. No one responded to her, and Sam understood of course, it wasn't that they didn't hear her. They did. They just didn't give a shit where Simon was. She began to close the door in an overly dramatic way. It was then that the too small for an 11-year-old boy with the bad skin snaked his way into the room as the door slowly slid shut, and drowned out what was left of the hallway chatter. "So glad you could join us." The teacher's voice sounded like underripe grapefruit, the way it pinched your jaw with every word. The boy, Simon, smiled, or at least tried. He slid into his desk, just shy of center, stage left, the best seat in the house.

Simon's eyes were more bloodshot than they were before. This was not, as anyone who bothered to look, out of sickness alone; it was also out of sadness. His eyes were swollen, tinged with a deep red. They looked like eyes that had spent the day fighting three ways: sickness, sadness, and allergies. Right now, the tears had played their strongest part. The conversation that Sam had collided with in the hallway was a now four minutes in the past. Simon, who was not allowed to leave school early, was here, and he seemed too close. He sat in his chair and tucked his old pay-as-you-go iPhone into the grungy army bag he used as a backpack. A bag that had belonged to his father who had come back from the second Gulf War more bruised inside than broken on the out and had eventually left them with just this bag as a reminder.

Simon's head tilted as he looked up at Sam. His eyes took in the tall figure in front of him with an earnestness that could not be faked. Sam realized that the boy's expression looked the same way Sam always hoped love would feel. This boy, this ugly little stranger looked at him the way Shannon always had. As Sam took another deep breath, he felt his lungs begin to relax. He missed Shannon, and somehow as he allowed himself to miss her, he remembered the words, and he knew he would get through this speech.

Simon smiled, and was excited finally to be able to hear Shakespeare's words spoken aloud. Maybe part of him was glad that his mother had refused to let him leave school early. She probably thought he had faked being sick; he had done that sometimes, but today was different. While Simon sat there in the front row, eager to hear the Saint Crispin's Day Speech, he had started to feel chills run through his body; he had a fever of 101 and it was climbing. He had the sensation that his guts were being split in two and his body was being run against the ice coating on a railroad track. It cut cold one way and screamed bloody raw the next. He saw the tall man from the hallway staring at him, and Simon felt self-conscious about his bad skin, how it seemed to get so much worse just this morning. He reached his hand up to hide the worst of it, nearest to the corner of his mouth. His fingers barely grazed his reddened skin and he had to stop himself from screaming out loud. His body broke out into a cold sweat and the room around him seemed to make a high-pitched buzzing sound, like cicadas on a hot summer day. His vision blurred for a moment and by the time the buzzing and the blurred vision had stopped, he realized the tall man was already finished the speech.

He had missed it, somehow.

The cramped room filled with lackluster applause when Sam had ended the soliloquy. Only the boy in the front row clapped with some enthusiasm, though even he had not started to clap right away; he looked like he had been asleep with his eyes open, and the sounds of his classmates had startled him back to reality. Sam gave a small head bow to the class; he tried his best to look humble and fulfilled with their attention. He was able to get through the rest of the class, taking questions from some of the children. He was good at this part, not the children, but talking about Shakespeare. For twenty minutes, he could almost remember who he was, who he was supposed to have been. The *him* before law school, before this sad attempt to become governor, and before he let his father make his decisions for him. He had no explanation for that; his shrink had said it was repressed guilt over Shannon's death. Shannon had wanted to be a lawyer; Shannon had wanted to be president someday . . . Sam looked down at the faces of these kids; they all looked the same. He could imagine Shannon in the back row of the classroom, he imagined her attending school, and he imagined her being the girl with the brother who had died of cancer.

Yes, that would have been better for all of them, certainly better for the State of Massachusetts.

When the bell rung the room emptied out, the kids reached into their bags and pockets and were on their phones before they had even finished standing. Everyone filtered out except the scrawny boy in the front row, who once again looked like he didn't realize things were happening around him. His close-set eyes seemed to be unfocused, and tired.

"Ok, it's lunch time now, so they want to get some footage of you in the lunch line with the kids, maybe even sit down with some of them at their table, laugh, look personable." Gretchen was whispering all of this to Sam. She had a way of talking that sounded like her voice was barely attached to her breath, a whisper that she'd perfected over the years, and she had said was the only way to talk to someone who was wearing a microphone. She had a whisper that couldn't be picked up. "Oh, and for fuck's sake try not to look bored."

Sam doubted Gretchen would go to the cafeteria with him, Gretchen never seemed to eat, and she survived on a combination of gin and making his life miserable. Sam looked at the scrawny boy who had slowly gotten up and out of his chair; his little hands shook as he put his giant three ring binder into his bag. When he slung the bag, heavy with books over his shoulder, he looked like he would collapse right on the spot. "Hey, can you tell me where the cafeteria is?" Sam asked the boy.

"Um . . . yeah, you can just follow me if you want, I have lunch now." Simon's voice was in the tender stage at the beginning of puberty, he mostly croaked now, and his voice was combination of his former baby voice and something strange and new. It was the voice of a stranger. That was what Simon's mother said to him when she had been drinking Peach Schnapps straight out of the bottle the other night. The boy walked a few feet in front of Sam, and then the camera crew followed both. Simon called over his shoulder "You're lucky, it's pizza day." He said this and found that it was hard to breathe. The words 'pizza day' left him winded the same way running the mile in gym class had. Every time he inhaled, he felt little knives slicing into the bottoms and sides of his lungs. His pace slowed a bit and he found that he now walked side by side with the tall man. "Why is there a camera crew with you?"

Sam smiled at the boy. "Oh, you shouldn't have reminded me, I keep trying to forget about them. They're from 60Minutes; they are doing a story on me." He tried to give the boy a conspiratorial look but was afraid that instead it had come off as a leer.

"Oh, is that why you're here, so it looks like you do stuff like this?"

"Yeah, pretty much." Sam smiled, and if he was not mistaken, the smile felt real. "What's your name?"

"It's Simon."

Sam heard the cacophony of sound as it roared from the cafeteria as they approached the first set of double doors. The wall of sound was both high-pitched and strangely rhythmic. Sam, of course, had never attended a public school. He never experienced the strange excitement in the air when it was 'pizza day' Instead he had been sent to the European International School of Boston; it was his mother's idea. Sam could hear Simon struggling for air as he walked, and he thought he should offer to carry the boy's bag for him, but then thought better of it.

"So, am I going to be on TV?" Simon asked, his voice creaking with nervous excitement.

"Yeah, yeah you might be. I'm not sure how much of this they're going to use." As Sam said this, his eyes scanned the noisy room. He looked instinctually for the hottest teacher he could find. Simon had walked to a table in the corner of the room and dropped his bag. It was clear to Sam that Simon was used to occupying the end of that table by himself. He looked at the boy again, and saw that his face was shiny with sweat, and his skin had a gray-tinged pallor to it. The only color he had was due to the sores on his face. Sam noticed that mingled with the sweat was a little bit of blood, which seeped from the largest and likely most painful area closest to his mouth. "You're bleeding a little." Sam gestured towards his own face as he said this. He also made sure to use his most 'Gretchen-like' whisper when he said it. He hoped the kids at the other end of the table had not been able to hear him. Sam had forgotten about the microphone.

Simon used the cuff of his shirt delicately to blot the blood away. What Sam did not know or understand was how painful that was for the boy. That the soft cotton of his shirt as he dabbed his face felt like metal slivers. The pain was so bad that Simon felt the floor tilt under his feet. He stumbled a little as he felt Sam's large hand reach out and steady him before he went down. His eyes were unfocused, and his expression dazed, but he recovered faster than he had in the classroom. He hadn't lost more than thirty seconds this time.

"You okay?" Sam asked this, but to Simon's ears, the voice sounded like an underwater scream.

"Yeah, I am, I just didn't eat breakfast, I knew it was pizza day. It's my favorite. Even the tater tots are great; I mean they taste more like grease that potatoes but they're still good." He smiled and a little more blood collected at the corner of his mouth. Instead of wiping it away like he did before, he snaked his tongue out of his mouth and lapped it like a cat. It was gentle, like a wounded stray. It was far less painful than touching it would have been. Simon did have the thought that there was something wrong with how it tasted. It was bitter, and earthy. He was suddenly not as excited about pizza day as he was pretending to be.

Sam followed Simon to the hot lunch line. He noticed that no one spoke to the boy; they didn't even bother to look at him, he moved among them unseen as if he were nothing more than an apparition, and not really there at all. In the boy's presence, Sam, for the first time in maybe his entire life also felt invisible. The camera lights on his skin, and the ever-present 60 Minutes crew barely seemed to register. If no one saw Simon, then no one saw Sam, and invisibility had a certain intoxication that he could get used to. He wondered what it would be like, to go through life unseen. A ghost.

The hot lunch line shuffled forward, a few kids shambled in, several at a time. Sam thought about pizza day, thought about the tater tots that tasted like grease . . . he couldn't remember the last time he had carbs that didn't come in the form of alcohol. He glanced at Simon's shiny face; his skin was the color and texture of boiled potato skins, ones that went into the water green, shriveled, and already sprouting spuds. As they began to approach the first of the lunch ladies, the one that was in charge of *vegetables*, in this case it was corn, Simon careened his neck to look past Sam and saw that the camera crew was deep in discussion about how they could all fit inside the lunch queue.

When he knew no one was paying attention Simon said, "It's too bad I look the way I do; maybe if I cuter and I was on TV then I could get a girlfriend." Simon smiled. The blood pooled once more near the corner of his mouth. It looked darker than it should, almost like syrup. His tongue snaked out again and licked it away. Sam could feel the bile heat up in his stomach and throat. It burned like cheap scotch and under-crushed Adderall. It felt hot in this little queue, and he didn't know if it was the chemicals wearing off or if it was his anxiety, but when he heard Simon and lunch lady number one both shout in unison "pizza day!" all Sam wanted to do was run as far as he could away from them, and away from this school. He felt overwhelmed with a sudden bout of homesickness, not for a place though, but for a time and a person, a person he lost, and the person he failed to become.

As Simon turned to Sam, there was a little bit of dark blood near his mouth, and a second trickle that had started from a patch of sores between his eyebrows. There was a dark stream that snuck down the bridge of the boy's pug nose and a little more that had collected near the corner of his right eye. Without hesitation Simon reached up to wipe it away, but instead it smeared into his eye. Sam could see him as he blinked a few times, his eyes were irritated and started to look a bit seepy. This is when Sam said, in a non-Gretchen whisper . . .

"Pizza Day."

Later that evening, little Simon would have a fever of 103 and be enveloped in an unwanted fifteen minutes of fame, and then in less than 24 hours he would be admitted to Boston Children's Hospital, and Sam, well Sam would be just another disgraced politician by then.

Chapter/ three

OMELIA
Mirror Mirror

She had spent the better part of the afternoon sitting there, in front of her mirror. She had left her makeup light on and her phone's camera was still pointing at her even though she had ceased her live stream what seemed like hours ago. She had been slumped there for close to four hours. Truthfully, she had barely made it through her show, each layer of makeup made the room grow blurry, and in her head, there was a noise and energy that sounded like a swarm of grackles *grackeling*. It almost overpowered her. After she had ended, she tugged her chair away from her makeup table and put her head between her knees, her body soaked with a thin sheen of flop sweat. She sat doubled over with her cheek rested against her right knee for what seemed like hours but was only a few minutes. She needed air; she needed to cool down. She was unsteady on her feet when she got up from the damask velvet upholstered chair she got at Target when she moved in here a few years ago. She held onto the table and used it to pull herself forward towards her wall of almost floor to ceiling windows. When she got there, she tried to open the large center window, but it was too heavy for her. She had never had a problem with it before.

Today was different. She placed her palms on the glass and tried to open it, even just a few inches. She bent her knees and tried with her whole body to push the window up, but it was no use. Her only relief came when she felt the cool glass against her skin. When she took her palms off the window, she saw the steamed-up handprints linger there like a dream before they faded in the sun. There were only a couple hours left of daylight, and the sun made her entire apartment glow a deep orange. She thought about how beautiful the light was when she decided to rest her face gingerly against the glass.

She breathed in, one, two, three, and then out, her breath slower, one, two, three, four, five . . . she repeated this until she felt like she could move again. "I need to get a wet cloth," she whispered to herself as she pushed away from the window. She saw the glass now, the little spot where she had allowed her cheek to kiss the cool glass of the windowpane. It was smeared with foggy sweat, with dark, mottled brown blood, and a small chunk of skin. Omelia always had a queasy stomach and when she saw the blood, and whatever else that lingered on the glass, she doubled over and vomited. She had not eaten anything yet today so the only thing that came up was the sour remnants of last night's cocktails. It left an acidic tear in her throat that burned when she tried to swallow. The front of her shirt was coated in her own sick. She was able to wrestle herself out of her top as she stumbled back to her chair. She sat there in her bra, feeling completely incapable of getting to the sink to get a wet cloth. She tossed her kimono robe on, not bothering to tie the front; she had no energy for that.

In lieu of being able to get to her bathroom, she settled instead for a makeup wipe. She used this on the back of her neck. She closed her eyes and remembered when she was still Nicole, and her father held a wet rag to her neck as she spent a night throwing up after eating a handful of raw ground beef that was supposed to be for *cheeseburger Friday night.*

Omelia didn't have anyone to hold a cool cloth to her neck now. She was alone. It was her own fault; she knew that. She didn't *have* to be alone;

she chose it. She had always chosen it. There had been people that she had become friendly with over the years, but she had no real friends. She hooked up a lot with girls and some guys she met but she had never let them in her apartment and she never spent a whole night with anyone. It was just how she had always been. She had never been able to fall asleep being near someone. She blamed the group homes for that; too many bodies, too many smells, too many beds in a room with too little love to go around.

Omelia knew she had a fever.

She could tell by how quickly the cucumber water and tea tree oiled makeup cloth had dried out as it rested against her skin. She also knew that any time she was sick with a fever that her past and her present would dance together until it was impossible to tell them apart.

Omelia or Nicole. It felt the same right now. She remembered why she ate the raw hamburger; she wanted to feel loved and even way back then, she was confused on how to make that happen.

But today, in the present she didn't need love, she needed to get the makeup off her face; she could feel that red sore near her mouth as it screamed and throbbed. She could feel her heartbeat in her face, it sounded like her name, Omelia. She could feel the ache of it as it crept into her mouth and made the back of her tongue feel swollen and her jaw ache. She felt her pulse as it hammered away inside of her. Omelia, Omelia, Omelia. It raced one moment and slowed down with irregular beats the next. Ommmm-e—lia. It felt like someone was inside of her, tapping away at a secret message. With a new makeup wipe, she very carefully started to wipe away her 'Gothic Horror' makeup look from earlier in the day. When the little damp towelette moved over the red sore on her face she gritted her teeth and let out a deep guttural sound like an animal giving birth, it was strained and painful. The wipe didn't just take a layer of makeup off, but a part of her skin had peeled away too. Her eyes filled with tears and as the salty water traveled down her face, she felt the sting, over and over. A thousand angry hornets. It was then that she looked at herself, in the rose gold light that normally flattered her.

She saw that the one red sore on her face had turned into two, and a third smaller one had started; it created a terrifying constellation that she was sure she would be able to see grow if she stared at herself long enough. The skin around it all was stippled with what looked like road rash.

"Jesus fucking Christ." She leaned in towards the mirror to take a closer look at herself. This was not just breaking out, or infection from a dirty makeup brush or sponge. "Fuck, fuck, fuck, fuck . . ." She whispered as she reached for her phone and went to her camera roll. Omelia had made sure that over the last year or so she had snapped a photo of every person, every fuck and down to every intoxicated make out fest at the bar. She couldn't always remember names, and she definitely could not remember usernames, so she always liked to have a visual reminder of every person that she had been with, just in case one went full internet troll on her. Now, she was a woman on a mission. Her hands were clammy, and it was hard to get her phone to unlock, as her fingers shook and slid over her screen like a toddler who had not mastered fine motor skills yet. Once it was unlocked, she was able to quickly swipe through her pictures; she zoomed in on everyone's mouths. She knew she had to have caught this from someone, someone recent. She scrolled back through at least four months of one-night stands, and while she saw a few people with red mouths and swollen lips, she thought that was most likely caused by Omelia's own deep raisin colored lipstick.

What Omelia failed to see when she swiped through her phone so quickly was that there was a photo of a woman from last night. A pretty blonde with skin and a smile like sunshine. Her name was Kim. Omelia had gone to high school with her, way back when Omelia didn't exist and she was just Nicole, a girl in search of her next foster family and living in a group home. Kim had not recognized her at all last night, not when they *met*, not when they danced, or when they had a long conversation that rambled into beauty spoken in half-screams and intimate whispers. Nor did she recognize her when they kissed against the back wall in the basement of the bar, the one closest to the bathrooms with the dim lights and low water-damaged ceiling. Now, it was time for Omelia not to recognize something. While it was true, Kim's mouth was smeared with Omelia's dark red lipstick, what Omelia failed to notice was that next to Kim's beautiful blue eyes, on the deep sunshine of her face, there was a small red spot. Had Omelia spent the whole night with Kim and woken up in her sunshine, she would have seen that the one red spot on Kim's normally perfect face had spread down from the corner of her eye and traveled to the crook of her nose. If Omelia had spent the whole night with her, they both would have been on their way to Urgent Care now. As it stood, both women were unfortunately alone. One was sitting in the waiting room of a Convenient Care, and the other was in her beautiful studio apartment as she faded in and out of time.

The wave of disorientation began to overtake her again, and she felt her body as it burned from the inside. She needed water; she knew that. She needed a doctor; she knew that too . . . but if she could not even make it to the sink, she understood that there was no way she would be able to call an Uber and have her taken anywhere. She needed to cool down somehow. She grabbed another of her makeup wipes, slid herself down off her chair and onto the hardwood floor under her table. Omelia thought somehow that the shade that the table would afford her would be better than the burnished orange light that filtered through the windows. She was confused for a moment when she unfolded the wipe and held it against her bare stomach . . . *where was her shirt?*

Then she remembered the sour smell, and she remembered how her throat burned like lightning when she had gotten sick. At the memory, her room smelled like electricity and greasy hair. She thought she might get sick again, but no matter how many times she gagged, nothing came up. All she felt was the skin by her mouth coming apart, like a poorly sewn doll. She reached for her phone and found the contact that said, 'Doctor Paul' and hit the green phone icon.

It rang three times before she heard "Doctor Nadeau's Office?" It was both a statement and a question. Omelia knew that the woman answering the phone was his new wife . . . well, she was not new anymore, she should just think of her as his third wife. Omelia could hear the woman's bracelets as they jangled against each other.

"I need to speak to Doctor Nadeau please."

"I'm sorry he is with a patient at the moment may I take a message?" Omelia could hear the woman as she flipped through the paper message book looking for a blank space. For a moment, she almost felt a sense of nostalgia before she felt the sickness overwhelm her again.

"Um, can you interrupt him please? It's, um, I think it's an emergency." She paused and she felt the tears fight against her pride. "Can you tell him it's . . . Nicole?" And with those words she cried, her sobs were ugly as they raced through her body, each shudder broke another part of her that was already broken.

"Nicole . . . He hasn't heard from you in almost a year, sweetie, what's wrong?"

"Can you just get him please?" Omelia knew she *should* have or at least *could* have been nicer, but the truth was she could not remember wife number three's name on a good day, and she certainly could not remember it now.

"Okay honey let me see what I can do. You just sit tight."

Omelia could picture this wife, number three. She wore Rose Quartz Crystals, had a collection of 'energy rocks' and always smelled like sandalwood. She was just a shade older than Omelia herself. That thought should have sickened her, but it didn't. I mean she thought it made Doctor Paul seem lame and gross, but she wasn't sick about it, just snobby. She remembered having met wife number three at some awkward 'meet the family' dinner. She had not and did not understand how she and the new wife could be the same age. Doctor Paul had explained that *she*, the new wife, had been the oldest of seven children, and in many ways, she had been born a forty-year-old woman. Omelia had laughed it off and said, "I don't judge," but she had, and she still did.

Omelia laid on the floor, her phone next to her was on speaker, and she heard the easy listening music as it warbled out of the other end of the line. Her brain could not understand what she was hearing, was it George Michael? Was it Mariah Carrey? She had always thought Doctor Paul was gay, and these music choices were not changing her mind. She closed her eyes, and in a half dream state, she felt her father place a damp cloth on the back of her neck. She heard him whisper *"why did you have to go and eat all that raw meat . . ."* then he chuckled a little, but it was the kind of half laugh that just makes you sadder when you hear it, and sadder even still when you remember it.

Omelia half mumbled, and half whispered the words, "I didn't know if you would come back, I didn't know if you would come back . . .." She had almost forgotten she was under her makeup table, one half of her mind listened to *muzak* and waited on hold while the other half was being cared for by her father, a cold cloth on her neck. *"I just got stuck late at work kid . . ."*

"Nicole . . .? Nicole?" His voice always crackled with concern for her; every moment since the first moment. Doctor Paul, he had tried to love her since she was fourteen.

"Dad?" She knew her mistake right when she said it "Oh, no I'm sorry . . . Paul . . . Hi . . ." she started crying again. "I'm sorry to bother you at work, I know you said after the last time that I could only call if it was an emergency . . . but I think . . . I'm sick." She said the words and then dry heaved again a few times. No, not exactly dry, there was a little blood this time, it came out of her in a brilliant crimson and landed on the floor not as liquid but as waxy shavings like a sharpened red crayon. She gagged again and a little more blood came out, this time it was dark, almost black, this time it was liquid. It tasted like a damp towel left in the drier too long. "I need you, can you come here? I can't leave."

"Nicole, honey did you take something? Do you need to go to a hospital?" There was a pause that ached for the longest four seconds of Paul's life. "Nicole?"

Her voice was quieter now, halfway between a whisper and a dream. "Do you still have the emergency key I gave you?"

"Yes, yes, of course I do . . . but honey."

"And you still know my security code to the front door?"

"Is it still the day your dad died? Or did you change it?"

"No, it's still the same." Omelia hung up then; she didn't wait for him to respond, she had to trust he would be there, he was her favorite former foster father for a reason . . . it was just a shame everything that had happened with that situation. It was never his fault; if it was anyone's, it was hers.

Doctor Paul Nadeau called Nicole's name a few times, each one grew a shade more shrill with panic as if he were a parent losing at a game of hide and seek. He realized the phone had gone dead after the fourth reiteration of her name. He had already grabbed his keys and had shaken one arm loose from his white coat. In between the third and fourth time he said Nicole's name, he had exited his office. He shouted over his shoulder to Heather, wife number three, "You need to cancel everything, tell them it's a family emergency." He still held the dead phone to his ear as his hand touched the door handle and he left his small office, which was housed in a strip mall in the affluent suburb of Bedford, New Hampshire. He thought that the door handle felt sticky, and hot. He never noticed the faint sheen of deep red liquid that got onto his hands. He did not notice anything wrong and wiped that onto his dark pants.

All he could think about was Nicole, the little girl that he failed, or so he thought, in every way. As Doctor Paul started his car, he felt a rot gut of fear. If she were sick, how could he help her, really? After all, he was only a dermatologist.

Chapter/ Four

SAM
The Once and Future King

Sam left the cafeteria and the inane hum of puberty's crescendo behind him as heavy wooden doors closed behind him. He left the 60 Minutes Crew to scramble to keep up with him after he had grown too pale and bored to keep up pretenses. He'd gotten up from the table and left Simon there, mid conversation, his mouth stuffed full of tater tots and French bread pizza. The remnants of 'pizza day' were now his only companions. The smile the boy had plastered on his face while he talked to Sam faded as the camera lights abruptly turned off and the heat that had radiated from them finally ceased. Simon felt a moment of relief, as if he had stepped out of the hot sun on a humid Boston day. The sweaty sheen on his face had not dissipated before the fever made itself known again.

Sam leaned against the door; the little plaque labeled "Cafetorium" dug into his left temple. The hallway was empty except for Gretchen, who stood in the middle of the hallway; she was vaping and blew the smoke down the darkened hallway to her right. She turned around to face him as she heard the door's squeaky hinges as it closed. "You can't smoke in a school Gretchen." He said this as he walked towards her.

"It's not smoking you dumb shit, it's vaping." She paused and looked at him, and in a deadpan tone she said, "You have blood or something on your face."

His hand reached up and wiped it away. He smeared the red liquid onto the nearest locker and grimaced as he did this. "It's not blood, it's tomato sauce. It was *pizza day*". He said the words 'pizza day' in an angry singsong way. He hated everything right now, he hated tater tots and the lockers, the greenish sickly lights from the fluorescents, he hated himself and he hated, — "Did you see that fucking kid I got stuck with? Are you kidding me? Was that a set up? Is this something you orchestrated? There is no way he was really that pathetic, so sad, and just— gross." He forced himself to chuckle a little before he kept going. "Did you see his skin, Jesus I almost felt bad for him a little bit, at first, but he was just so disgusting. There was like, blood and pus. Gretchen, he was licking it and smearing it away. I almost puked. And then there was the food, fuck, you know, I'm glad I was rich because if that is what they actually get excited about then the public school systems are more fucked up than I thought." Sam whispered this; his words were fast and sharp like the battle in West Side Story. Unlike Gretchen, who had mastered the art of *how to whisper* in a way a lavaliere microphone could not pick up, Sam's voice was still loud, they were the stage whispers of an actor playing Iago in a thousand seat house, a whisper that even theater goers in the cheap seats could hear. "And I had to sit there, and eat pizza with that kid, that little gremlin in front of me, oh and the cameras . . . Jesus the fucking idiots at 60Minutes, this can't be what they wanted, God, the lights were so hot, and it was just making him sweat more, and bleed more. Fuck, I mean I started to feel sick, really sick because of it." He finally stopped his rant. He felt some moisture that had built in the corner of his mouth like a rabid raccoon. When he reached up to wipe away the saliva, he found that he had missed a little bit of the pizza sauce on his face. This time he didn't bother to wipe it on a nearby locker, he just smeared it on his pants as he let out an overly dramatic sigh of exasperation and boredom. "I don't feel up for a meeting with any of these low-rent teachers or the guy that cleans the fucking toilets. Can I just leave now?"

She did not bother to answer his question. Gretchen stared at him; her eyes grew colder as she said, "Are you still wearing your microphone?"

Maybe Sam had forgotten that he was mic'd up. Maybe Sam had, in some way, decided halfway through *pizza day* that he just couldn't be the "New JFK" anymore. Maybe he looked out across the crowded cafeteria, had hoped to see Shannon, and was deadened inside once again by her absence and the inane buzz of all the incessant chatter, all the kids that got a chance when she never did . . . and maybe part of him had decided to blow up his whole life.

Or maybe he just forgot.

When he turned to see the camera crew of 60 Minutes still huddled by the doorway of the cafetorium, he knew they had heard everything he had just said; all the cruelty and the hate that had just come out of his mouth. And soon, the world would hear it too.

Chapter/ Five

Omelia and Her Favorite Former Foster Father

er apartment appeared empty at first glance. He called her name out and it sounded somewhere between a whisper and a song. It seemed to echo back to him off the large glass windows on the opposite side of the high-ceilinged studio. "Nicole?" When she didn't answer him, his first thought was that she was dead. He was too late; she had overdosed . . . It flashed through his mind like heat lightning before it faded away into nothing. There was tension in the room. The air was close and stagnant, like a cave. It felt like waiting . . . No, she couldn't be dead; she was probably asleep. Hell, maybe she wasn't really sick at all, maybe she was just drunk; it wouldn't be the first time he tended to one of those calls.

"Nicole?" His voice was a little louder this time as he stepped into the apartment and closed the door behind him. That was when he smelled it. The air was musty and sour, like rotten fruit. He expected to see fruit flies or those dusty moths that nest in bags of birdseed or cereal. The smell was both disgusting and a little comforting. It smelled somehow familiar.

The afternoon sun still shone above the steeple of the church across the river, but it was not the bright yellow of midday anymore. The sun had ripened as the day moved into late afternoon. Nicole's apartment was bathed in dark orange light and the shadows of creeping dusk were textured like old blankets. The only place that was well lit was her makeup table, with the halo light still shining bright. That was when he saw her; she was crumpled under the table. Her body was a tangle of sinewy pale limbs and a silk kimono-style-robe. The robe was the same deep orange as the setting sun, and the fabric had a Japanese pattern of swans or maybe they were egrets. Her face was hidden, tucked into the far corner next to the leg of the table. She was in the shadows. The way her arm was draped up over her head and face reminded Paul of when she had first come to live with him and Meredith. Nicole would hide from the sun and feign sleep when they would try to wake her up for school. "Nicole?" He squatted down and reached out tentatively to give her leg a shake. She rolled over a little, and he saw that she had gotten sick all over herself, and there was a small pool of dark liquid that she had been practically laying in. "Nicole, sweetheart, you need to talk to me. What's going on? Did you take something? Or did someone give you something?"

"No, no, I was fine. I was going live and doing my makeup and I started to . . . I don't know.'" her voice was small and childlike, slightly higher pitched than her "Omelia" voice.

"We need to get you out from under that table okay Nicole?"

"It's Omelia. I've told you that. Nicole's dead." She whispered this as she tried to push herself up with one arm; her hand landed in the puddle that was near her head where she had gotten sick the second and then the third time. Her hand slid out from under her and slipped back down again. She still had not looked at Doctor Paul; she kept her face turned away from him. She was, on top of everything, embarrassed for him to see her this way. She thought that even though her name has changed, she was still the fourteen-year-old that had gone home with Doctor Paul and wife number one. She was the same girl that got drunk on Mad Dog 2020 with some guys she met at the coffee house on poetry night a half hour from their house. She was the same girl that had passed out during that night and woke up to find that one of the guys was jerking off on her and the other one was holding her down with one hand heavy on her chest; his other hand held a cell phone and was filming the whole thing. She had decided to fake sleep and wait it out. Whatever had been happening to her was terrible, but it was better, she thought, than being raped. Later in the night, she had tiptoed down the stairs and walked out the front door. She was able to stumble her way to a nearby gas station and found one of the city's last functioning payphones. She had no money, so she called Doctor Paul collect. Her voice had lowered and was heavy with teenage shame as she said, "I need you to come and get me" . . . and he came to her rescue, then, and now. So, when she said, "I need your help getting out from under here," her voice crackled with the same shame it did on that dreary early morning almost fourteen years ago.

He reached under the table for her, and awkwardly tried to find a way to help her. There seemed to be nowhere *safe* for him to touch her. Her satin robe was open, and underneath she was wearing just a bra and silky black pajama bottoms that hung low on her hipbones. He darted his eyes away from her as his hands connected under her arms and he tried to slide her towards him. He saw her robe dragged in the puddle of her vomit and it left a trail that led back to him. He felt her ribs as they pressed into his hands with each breath; they were shallow, almost nonexistent, until she gasped for air. But even more than her breath, he felt the heat as it rose off her body. "Nic . . . I mean Omelia, I think you might have a fever." He said this as he propped her against the little white bureau that had belonged to her way back when she belonged to him, well, to them. The little bureau that had once held all of Nicole's belongings now held just her makeup.

She was slouched forward; her head throbbed, and she could feel her erratic pulse as it played in staccato rhythm in her chest as it reverberated through her skull. It was difficult to catch her breath. She felt the cool metal drawer handles through her silk robe. They felt so cold she could imagine the handles leaving a branded mark against her skin, so cold it burned. It reminded her of the New Hampshire beaches, with water so cold it felt like it would eat through her skin when each wave came in and made her bones ache.

"Do you have a thermometer? We need to see how high your temperature is." Paul said this as he stood up; his knees creaked and his left one seemed to make a groaning sound like ice before it calves and falls into the sea.

"It's in my medicine cabinet, and I need some water, my throat feels like there's broken glass in it."

"Water, after we take your temperature, we need it to be accurate." He walked into the bathroom and opened the medicine cabinet. He saw at least a three-month supply of her Prozac, the bottles positioned neatly like little watchful toy soldiers. The bottles were unopened and still full. He checked her Xanax and her Buspar; lifting the bottles he noticed that at least she had been taking those. As he closed the medicine cabinet, he called out to her. "Are you still taking your Prozac?" He knew she hated it; she had always said it made her fat, and unable to dream.

"No, I don't need it anymore, and don't snoop through my stuff." She sounded the same as she did when she was a teenager. Except this morning, her voice was weak and the way it trembled reminded him of Katherine Hepburn in *On Golden Pond*. He could hear from across the room that her breath had begun to gurgle and wheeze. She sounded old and waterlogged.

He walked back into the main room of her apartment. It was an open space, and had everything she needed; her bedroom, her bookshelves, her makeup station and a small kitchenette, which he was sure she never used. Nicole's body was faced away from him. "Alright let's get your temperature." It was then that she finally turned to him and he saw her face. "Jesus, Nicole . . . what happened here?" He knelt on the floor in front of her and with his gentle dermatologist hands, tilted her face so he could see it better. She flinched when his fingers brushed against the skin near her jawline. She sucked her breath in as he moved his hands again. The skin underneath his fingertips had all but disintegrated. "Does this hurt, just having my fingers here?"

"Yes, goddamn it! Be careful." She snapped at him, but before she had finished the words, her lip began to tremble, and her face crumpled into tears.

Paul moved his hands off her face but continued to study her. He had never seen anything like it before, except perhaps in medical school when he had seen case studies of patients with advanced AIDS who had contracted Herpes Simplex. The virus would attack their immunocompromised body and ravage it, cause Meningitis and cankers that could eat away the skin around their mouth and nose; even their eyelids were overtaken and eaten away with cankers. That was what this looked like. "When did this start?"

"It happened out of nowhere, I felt fine this morning, and I looked fine. I was doing a makeup tutorial and then one my followers mentioned it in the comments . . ." She spoke through tears, and her voice made choking sounds between some of her words. "I covered it with makeup. I know I shouldn't have, but I had to, I was in the middle of something. I think I made it worse, that's when it started getting hard to breathe. Can I have water now?"

At the tail end of her words, she began to cough, and Paul saw a trickle of blood peek out of the side of her mouth. He could not tell if the blood was coming from her lungs or if it was coming out of the new crack that had formed at the corner of her mouth. It stretched out in a deep maroon line that seemed to stretch into her cheek; it branched off like shallow roots of a willow tree. "Here, let's see how high your temperature is." He handed her the thermometer and stood up, but not before he checked under her makeup table one more time and saw the dark red lines of blood splattered there as well. "We should bring you to the hospital."

"No," she mumbled as she struggled to keep the thermometer in her mouth and balanced away from the left side of her face. Paul grabbed a coffee mug from her dish rack and turned on the tap. Even though her studio apartment was expensive, the pipes in the old warehouse still rattled and knocked when the water ran. She always thought that the water tasted like rust, so she never drank straight from the tap. She wanted to say that to him, to remind him to get the sparkling water from her refrigerator, but the pipes clanged, and the sound made her head swim, and the room around her grew a little darker. She tried to press herself once again into the cool metal of the drawer pulls. She did not know if she closed her eyes, or if the room had just gone full dark, no stars. The thermometer beeped for about fifteen seconds before her eyes opened again. By then Paul had knelt in front of her. She could hear him saying her name, but it sounded like he was speaking a different language.

Paul reached out and placed the back of his hand against her forehead. He thought he could hear the hiss of steam as his hand brushed against her skin, but then realized the sound was coming from Nicole, she was hissing and pulling away from him like a scared cat. Her mouth slacked open, and the beeping thermometer fell into the bunched-up fabric of her robe between her legs. As he reached for it, she reached for the glass of water that he had placed down at her side. Her hand aimed for and missed the glass three times before she finally connected with it. As she brought it towards her mouth, he saw that she was holding onto the mug with both hands as if it were a soup bowl. Her fingers shook so much that the water lapped over the sides of the mug and down onto her bare stomach as she tried to bring the mug to her mouth. She looked up at him with her big eyes, and for a flash, she looked the same as she did when he first met her. He looked at the thermometer, and at first the numbers did not seem to register with him, it couldn't be right, it couldn't be 105.3. He didn't have time to raise his head to see her before he heard the coffee mug shatter on the hardwood floor followed directly by the sound of Nicole's head when it hit the ground a moment later with deadweight.

Chapter/
six

SAM
Cherry Bomb

60Minutes had it up on their website by the time George had pulled up alongside the curb in front of the family home. Sam would not know about it until after he made his way to his bedroom, did a few lines of Adderall, and began to sip the Old Fashioned he made before he headed up the stairs. He thought he would be able to let the day fade away as the sun started to set. He picked up his phone, which he had silenced hours ago before he entered the classroom. He knew right away there was trouble when he saw that there were seven texts from Gretchen, and one from his father, which simply read, "Call me." He could not remember the last time he had a conversation with his father that Gretchen had not facilitated as part of an elaborate PR event. He made a conscious decision not to call him back.

Gretchen's texts were more *colorful* and included, "You're dumber than I thought you were," "You fucked us, you dumb shit," and "Call your father." Sam of course knew what the story would be even before he pulled up Google on his phone and searched his own name. The 60Minutes website came up first with a headline of, "Another Politician to Break Your Heart."

The next website was TMZ, which stated, "Politician Demolishes Young Boy for Being *Ugly.*" The third one was from a local television station and that one read, "Boston's Prodigal Son Disgraces Family and Dashes Political Dreams."

"Fuck," Sam whispered to himself as he clicked the screen off. He pressed the screen of his phone against his forehead as he relished the cool glass. He felt feverish and anxious. He allowed his eyes to close; he was exhausted and had begun to regret his decision for more Adderall. Sam wanted to shut down, to turn off. His heart pounded in scattered bursts, like a runner that always tried too hard and never found any joy in it. That was his heart; it beat without joy. He suspected this frantic rhythm in his chest was equal parts nerves and amphetamines. He made the conscious decision to unclench his jaw and lower his shoulders, which hovered close to his ears. As he felt himself start to relax, he was immediately pulled out of his reverie by the shrill, startled scream of his ringtone. It was his father. He hit 'decline' and then tossed the phone onto his bed. He finished the rest of the old fashioned in two large gulps. His mouth and throat were dry and ached as if he had been singing all day. *It's the Adderall,* he thought, or maybe it was his nerves, hell, maybe he was even a little scared; he might even have started to feel guilty. When he closed his eyes, Simon's face was there. His eyes were wide with attention and veiled in sadness. Behind Simon was Shannon . . . but she would not look at him.

Sam had wanted to be a better person. He just didn't know how even to start. It seemed like so much work. When Shannon died, his father had gotten publicly drunk for the first and only time in Sam's life. At the memorial service, he pulled Sam into the kitchen and slurred that, "Shannon took the best of you with her when she went . . . your mother and me, we both know that. She was the heart of this family. Now we're just a man, a woman, and a kid." Gretchen of all people was the one that coaxed the rocks glass from Santo Alberti's hand and steered him away from Sam. She had tried her best to usher him up the back stairs. Sam didn't know where his mother was when all of this had happened. He supposed it didn't matter; it was always Gretchen who had been more hands-on. She played the role of disgruntled campaign manager and part-time unpaid nanny to the best of her ability, yet even with Gretchen, when Shannon died there had been a drastic change.

They had all changed.

Sam's phone started to ping; a couple messages came in rapid succession. He lazily went to the bed and checked his screen. One text from his father, which read, "I am getting on Air Force Two; wheels on the ground in about 2 hours." The next message was from Gretchen, "Your father is on his way." Then a second message from her, "He asked me to be there, your mother won't be coming." The final one said simply "My advice is to be as drunk as you need to be for this. I have taken an extra Xanax." Then there were a series of smiley emoji and some sort of laugh/cry emoji, followed by three frowny faces and then the poop emoji.

"Fuck," he said again, the word dancing on his breath, coming out like a sigh. That simple thing made him realize once again just how dry his throat was. He stared at his phone as he walked into the bathroom. His fingers moved over the screen; he checked Google again, and hoped to see that in the forty minutes that he had been drinking and doing Adderall, that the story had blown over already. When he checked the local news station there was a headline that a local reporter was going to be speaking with, "The Broken-Hearted boy: Boston's Saddest Middle-Schooler," on the six o'clock news. Shit that can't be good. Sam thought for a moment about who he was and how he wanted to be remembered at the end of the day . . . was it too late for him to change this scandal around, to have it not be about him destroying a young boy's self-esteem on a hot mic? Maybe he should text Gretchen, ask her if he should do something even worse, and spin the story away from the boy and onto Sam.

He thought about sending dick pics to all the women in his contact list. Would that do it? Would that save the boy from more heartache? It was then that he raised his head and stared into his own dead-eyed reflection in the mirror. A shark. His skin seemed unnatural in color—like plastic coated with chalk dust. His body had begun to move on autopilot. He opened the medicine cabinet and popped a couple Adderall in his mouth out of habit. He knew it was a mistake as the pills sharp edges seemed to scrape his throat as he swallowed them. There was one still stuck in his throat. The pill seemed to cling to the raw parts of him and not go down. When he found himself doubled over, he threw up onto the closed toilet seat; it was probably for the best. He leaped back just in time as the sour liquid splashed onto the floor, narrowly missing his Gucci shoes. He saw the two still-undissolved tablets clinging to the edge of the toilet seat, and without thinking, he reached for them and almost put them back in his mouth. He caught one whiff of his fingers, which smelled like bile and orange bitters. He gagged again and instead of putting them in his mouth, he tossed them onto the floor, where they scattered and got lost somewhere under the shaggy bathmat. He rinsed his hand and tried to get the sticky residue of the pill's coating off his fingers. He dried his hand on his pants, and an orange sherbet colored smear appeared next to the crusty remnant of the red *pizza sauce* from earlier in the day.

Pills were not the right choice today. What he needed was another drink.

If Sam had to say what his best skills were, he would have to say that besides having a smile that made the recipient of it feel like they were the only person in the world, he knew he could make a killer Old Fashioned. When he and Shannon were kids, his mother and grandmother would spend Saturday afternoons sitting in the study, playing cribbage, and drinking until one or both of them would have to *take to the bed*, skipping dinner and saying they had a *migraine*. For whatever reason they liked the silent company of Sam and Shannon, who were required to sit in the room like two decorative lion statues. The twins liked it as well even though silence was required. They had to remain mostly still, except for when one of the women would raise her glass and shake the melted-down ice cubes around; they made a tinkling sound against the glass that always reminded him of forlorn scenes in black and white movies. That clinking sound beckoned the children, who were to take the glass, run over to the bar, and fix their next drink. Their reward for this was that they got to eat the garnish or fruit that had been in there, soaking up the booze. Sam always made sure he garnished the Old Fashioned with an orange rind, cutting it so it curled like a spiral and held onto the edge of the glass with just its edge. Shannon preferred to make her version of the classic cocktail with a Luxardo cherry. The women did not prefer one garnish to the other, they only cared that the twins made their drinks strong, fast, and very well.

That was how Sam got his taste for bourbon but lost his taste for the gourmet cherries.

When he got to the bar in the study, he made his cocktail with an effortlessness that was akin to breathing. He carved the orange rind into a perfect spiral, just as he did when he was a boy. He used only the finest bourbon that they had in the house in his cocktails. However, before he sat down with it, he pulled a shot glass out of the drawer and shifted the bottles until he found the Jack Daniels. It's what his family had always considered *hobo bourbon*. He poured a shot, and drank it down, then another, and then another. He knew the rules; you never waste good liquor on a shot. Now, three shots and a couple cocktails would be enough to derail anyone, but Sam was a pro. At six foot four, combined with the fact that he had been drinking bourbon since the night of Shannon's funeral, he knew he and his liver could handle the alcohol.

He never hoped for oblivion, he only hoped for numbness.

After the three shots, he decided on a fourth, that decision made when he raised his eyes and saw the little jar of Luxardo cherries tucked in the corner. It was the same jar that they had had for years. No one in the family had the desire for that particular garnish anymore, and each one of them was too scared or superstitious to throw it away. He reached his hand up and touched the jar. The glass was sticky with splash-over from the other bottles near it and thick with dust from the years of silent life between them all. With his fingernail, he scraped at it a little. He thought he was just running his finger over it, but when he pulled his hand away from the jar, he saw that he had carved a very distinct S in the sticky dust, allowing the grime to carve away. Inside he could see the dark red liquid; it had mottled and gone bad years ago. Its three-year shelf life already gone by when Sam was just fourteen, and that was a little over twenty years ago. He closed his eyes and saw Simon smearing the blood against his mouth by accident. Sam felt his stomach flip again, and he felt like he was on one of those pirate-ship rides, during that whisper of time you have no gravity.

He heard a brass bell ring; the sound came from somewhere upstairs, from the room that smelled like Baby Soft Perfume, and dust. It also smelled like two kinds of lemon, a juice box, and disinfectant.

The room. The shrine.

Sam opened his eyes and the bell stopped ringing. Its echo filled the room and pressed against his body before it released. The smell traveled downstairs and found him there, Baby Soft perfume, and hospital hallways. It smelled like Shannon during the last year of her little life. He fought to smell something beyond that, anything . . . He brought the Old Fashioned up to his nose, and the orange bitters and brown sugar made the smell of her phantom Baby Soft fade away, but Sam couldn't smell the bourbon. All he could smell was a childhood gone missing, and disinfectant.

Two kinds of lemon.

He smelled grief, and a house turned into a hospital.

The drink went down easy. Sam shivered as he checked the grandfather clock that leaned against the wall; that clock, and clocks in general always made him nervous. Maybe this was why he was always late. He would have to bring this up to George; he hoped the old man would get a kick out of it. He did not know how much time he had wasted or how much longer it would be until Gretchen and his father arrived. He assumed Gretchen would be first; she would burst into the room, like a tornado in a power suit. She would force some mints into his mouth and a cup of coffee in his hand. Until then all he had to do was wait . . . and drink. Numbness. He needed it to creep in from the edges, come up from the floor and down from the ceiling, like light fingertips over his skin until they finally got to his heart.

He sat down or tried to sit. He realized it was less of a sit and more of a heavy collapse into the chair, his father's chair, the one he was never allowed to sit in when Santo was home. He placed the rocks glass on the table next to him. He did not care about using a coaster or leaving a ring on the mahogany. All he cared about was the uncomfortable relaxation he felt that came with this chair. The deep maroon velvet chair with stately arms that made whoever sat in it feel like a king. He faced away from the bar and turned his head away from the hallway that led to the entryway. He would not look at the Luxardo cherries, no matter how much he wanted to.

Exhaustion. He felt it now. The Adderall was gone; all he was left with was the memory of this day. He rubbed at the space between his eyes and let his hands press against his forehead above his eyes. Everything hurt. He pressed harder and felt the strange kind of pain that borders on pleasure, like peeling a sunburn or putting a terrible case of poison oak under scalding hot water.

That's when the thought of Simon came back to him. His skin, which seemed to turn gray as the lunch period droned on. With his eyes closed, he could see Simon; he could remember the boy's face, which had been slack during the Saint Crispin's Day speech but had come alive at the very end. There was a light in his eyes; it looked like fireflies in tall grass. A light that was both beautiful, and delirious. Feverish.

That was when he heard it again, the bell, as it rang. It was faint at first but it grew louder and more frantic as he sat there. Someone was trying to get his attention. *She* was trying to get his attention.

"Shannon, stop it, I'm not in the mood." He knew he didn't have to yell to make sure she heard him, but he did yell, because that was the kind of day it was. The sound of the bell ceased, and the air pressed against him. Like low pressure, like weather changing in the air around him. It was a hospital hallway. The air changed again, this time it smelled like gourmet cherries, and two kinds of lemon. He finished his drink. Simon then raised his glass and tinkled the ice cubes against the sides. Part of him hoped she would be there, that Shannon's little ghost would run to him; he would've loved her to have made a drink for him. She could use the mottled and rotten cherries from the jar; he didn't care.

He waited.

He raised the glass again and tinkled the ice a little louder, a little ruder. He had channeled his best impersonation of his mother, who was a woman made up of equal parts Grace Kelley and prescription pills. The room didn't press in on him this time; he was met instead with anger, the air pulled away from him in disgust. The brass bell that would always start so far away, and so timid, instead seemed to scream through the air. Each ring was a demand, and then a question, then a demand, and then a question . . . he knew the question, he could hear it in the way the bell tolled. It screamed into the room, the room that now seemed to smell sour the way Simon did, and like Baby Soft, the way Shannon did before she was sick. The bell screamed its questions, its demands.

Sam didn't realize that his rocks glass had collided with the grandfather clock until he heard the glass shattering like ice across the floor. He also didn't realize he had shouted until it was too late. "Fucking Shannon, I told you, I am not in the mood today . . . What? Are you pissed because today is not about you? For once in my life today is about me . . . not you, not your cancer, not your death . . ."

"Son."

Sam turned to face his father; disgust radiated from him as he stood in the doorway. He wore his camel-colored cashmere trench coat, and Gretchen was standing unnaturally close to him, her head peered over his shoulder like a devil just waiting to whisper.

Sam made eye contact with the man he had not seen in person since the announcement of his intention to run for governor. That was over nine months ago. His father frowned. "Oh Eagle, what has happened to you?"

Sam threw up for the second time that day, this time on Santo Alberti's favorite chair. What erupted out of Sam was the color of spoiled Luxardo cherries . . . but it tasted like bronchitis, and rotted leaves.

Chapter/
seven

How Do You Solve A Problem Like Omelia?

OMELIA AND PAUL

t was the side of her skull that hit the floor first, and then her body was wracked with unnatural shudders. Paul had never seen a seizure, but he did know that when she rolled onto her back and began to gurgle and grunt that he needed to turn her back on her side. Her mouth seemed empty at first, but he heard a rattling that started in her lungs and gurgled out of her like the little girl in The Exorcist. The liquid that bubbled out of her mouth was a deep maroon. It was a mixture of blood and something else. As he turned her over onto her side, he reached his fingers into her mouth; he scooped the thick liquid out and he had to turn his head, not able to look at her like that. Even the liquid that came out of her was hot, and it made his fingers burn and seem to go numb at the same time. It made his hand with a strange pain that throbbed as it traveled up his arm.

No, that had to be his imagination.

"Nicole, honey, can you hear me?" He reached under her arms and tried to get her to sit up. She was deadweight as she flopped awkwardly in his out-of-shape arms. Her eyes were closed and when he tried to pry her lids open, he saw that the rims of her eyes were swollen and red; her eyes that he had seen for only a second before they rolled back in her head were pale buttery yellow. They were not yellow before; he would have noticed that; he was sure. "Hey, hey, hey . . . you need to wake up okay. Sweetheart, your fever is really high, and we need to get you cooled down fast." He tried to lift her, but her body was limp, and her slender limbs were like sticks in a bag. He pulled her against the hardwood floor, her beautiful silk robe dragging itself once again through a puddle of bile and vomit, what looked to him like blood, and tangled weeds. The sun was starting to go down and the room had darkened into a burnt sienna hue. When he got to the bathroom door, he heard her bony hips as they made a *ka-thud* sound as they bounced over the rim of the door. Her knees banged against the doorjamb, yet she never stirred. Paul thought of her legs and hips that by tomorrow would be covered in deep purple bruises. Nicole had always been sensitive; she would complain that the stiff cotton sheets that covered her twin bed in their house would cause her skin to bleed as they chafed against her every time she moved.

So sensitive. Too sensitive.

He remembered the first winter that she lived with them, a time when she lifted the arm of the heavy Irish wool sweater they had bought her and showed them that her arm was covered in what looked like a downy layer of bruised skin. He could not see where the bruise stopped, and the color of her skin began. He remembered thinking that he did not know anything about being a parent to a fourteen-year-old girl. He could not even keep her safe then; when it was just a sweater that had harmed her. What could he possibly do now? He leaned her body against the tub; the cool porcelain must have been startling to her in a way that her body banging against the floor and walls had not been. She made a low noise; she mewled like an orphan cat in a cardboard box. The noise was everything to him right now. It was hope.

He used what he could muster of his strength and imagined himself like one of those mothers who was able to lift a car off their child trapped beneath. He felt like that now as he bent over and was able to get her to a half-standing position. Her body slumped heavily over his shoulder. He stepped over the rim of the deep tub and heaved her in there with him, one leg and then the other. He laughed a little, out of fear. Nicole had reminded him of a marionette with tangled strings.

Once she was in there, he eased himself back a few steps, and tried to get her to sit up and lean her back against his legs. It was hard not to drop her now; his arms shook, and he knew he had used the last of his strength. He was not as strong as a mother lifting a car. He was just a man lifting a girl, no, a woman who was not even his daughter. Everyone in his life over the past thirteen years had always reminded him of that, but he never listened.

Nicole was hunched over, her knees up by her ears, her head dangled loose between her legs. He could see a slow-motion bloody stream drip from her face, or inside her mouth, he could not be sure. It made a little pool between her feet. He thought she was unconscious, but she made the same noise as she had before and then leaned her left side against the far wall. He was able to step out of the bathtub as he said, "I know you are not going to like this, but we need to do it okay, I need to get your temperature down. Nic, can you hear me?"

She mewled again; it sounded mournful, and holy. She said, "It's Omelia, I told you, Nicole died." She managed to eke out the sounds without moving her lips at all.

"Okay on the count of three I'm turning the water on okay; it's going to be cold." He didn't wait for a response from her. He had his hand in his pocket and he grabbed his phone as he said, "One, two, are you ready? Three." Halfway through three he had turned the cold water on full blast. The pipes made a clanging sound from deep in the belly of this old factory and the water sputtered at first onto her, each sputter a little more powerful than the one before it. Each one lasted just a few seconds longer before it evened out and the water fell on her like a heavy cold rain.

The first few bursts from the showerhead had barely touched her, but the third one landed right onto her face and filled her mouth, which was hanging agape with cold water. She coughed the water out; with it, there were veiny red clumps, and what can only be described as a black spindly vine that she had to reach up and pull from her throat as she coughed. It seemed to disintegrate in her hand as she placed it in the pooling water at her side. It looked like a liquid shadow by the time it washed down the drain. The part of Paul that remembered he was a doctor had wanted to reach into the water, pull that black barbed wire-looking thing from her hands and study it. The other doctors, the *real* doctors, they would need to know, they should see whatever it was inside of her. They would have to find out how it got there.

It was too late; he had watched it swirl into nothing and then disappear. He dialed 911. He tried a few times and each time his hands shook more and more. When the call finally went through, he took one last glance at Nicole, who had her arms wrapped around her legs; her hands moved up and down her shins and her toes scrunched in and out, like a girl trying to warm her skin inside damp winter boots.

"911 what's your emergency?"

In a little voice, he thought he heard Nicole say, "The water is too hard, it's going to bruise my skin." Paul blinked slowly, and he saw her in his mind. He remembered her turning towards him at the beach; her feet barely touched the water. The gray waves came in with force and hit her shins. She had refused to go any further that day. He hoped now, that in her head she was there, on that early July day when she was fourteen. The only time they had gone to the beach as a family.

"911 what is your emergency?" The voice startled him, and brought him back to this bathroom, on this day, as it darkened into evening.

"Um yeah, hi . . . Um my daughter, I mean, my foster daughter, she was my foster daughter. She's sick, really sick. She has a fever of 105, she is throwing up, and there's blood, she coughed up blood, and . . ." The room darkened around him and he heard the water roaring like a jet engine next to him. He could hardly breathe now; he could hardly think. "There was something else, it was, it was black, like a vine, no, no, not a vine, like barbed wire, but it's gone, and it went down the drain . . ."

"Sir you are going to need to calm down, you need to tell us where you are." The dispatcher's voice should have been nicer, but it wasn't. He heard that, he heard the disbelief in her voice; he heard the doubt. He had sounded panicked, and neurotic; he knew he had. He should have taken one of Nicole's Xanax . . .

"She has sores, on her face, those just started, but they've spread just since I got here, I don't know what it is. I'm a doctor, I've never seen this." He glanced at Nicole again. Her hands still rubbed against her shins, but now she used her nails. Her perfectly French manicured nails tried to dig little ditches in her legs. He couldn't look at her. As he turned away from her, he caught his reflection in the mirror above her bathroom sink. His skin was pallid, a pale grayish yellow. He saw a little patch of something close to his mouth, red, flakey. He bit and chewed at his lower lip when he was scared, that's all that was, right? Paul reached up to touch it, but his fingers still felt numb from before, when he touched *it* . . .whatever it was that had come out of her mouth before she got in the shower.

"Sir we need to know where you are."

"When you send people, you need to tell them . . ." He leaned into his reflection and looked at the spot near his mouth, the spot that he could swear was pulsing erratically with his heart. "You need to tell them that I think it's contagious. Tell them they need to wear Hazmat suits. I think—I think I have it too . . ."

"Sir, I know you're scared but we need an address."

He couldn't remember it; his brain was busy, it unpacked boxes of memories and facts inside his head, but there was no address there. "We're in the mill yard. The condos with the clock tower, I can't remember the address . . . if you look out her window you can see across the river. You can see Saint Marie's Church. I . . . I don't know . . . I can't remember." He started to cry. He cried for Nicole, and himself, and he cried for Heather, whom he realized that he really did love very much; he hadn't realized it until now even though they had been married for almost two years. "We're on the fourth floor, apartment seven." The room darkened again, and began to swirl around him, dark and light, dark and light. His heart beat like a war drum in his chest. He wished he had learned to dance. He looked over at Nicole; she had laid down in the tub, her body no doubt being bruised by the water's little fists. The room had grown darker as he said, "You need a code to get in, but you remember it don't you? It's still the same; it's the day her father died."

And with that, Doctor Paul collapsed.

Chapter/ eight

The Bells

SANTO AND THE EAGLE

Santo Anthony Alberti was a man whose name and title preceded him into any room he entered. This was a fact, even before he was a state Congressman and then a Senator for the State of Massachusetts, and finally the Vice President. He was not a large man, but he wore the mythology of his life around him like a shroud. As he moved through space, a person could hear Da Vinci's paint strokes as they echoed through the years and miles. These phantom sounds left a breadcrumb trail all the way to this man, and then later, to his twin children Shannon and Santo, who always went by Sam. His hair was salt and pepper, and at his age, it was both startling and intimidating that it was much heavier on the pepper. He was a man that when you met him, you loved him . . . well, strangers loved him. His children, the twins, had loved him in a way that favored fear and respect over affection.

Though he never talked about it, he knew he was a man that had a hole in his heart, carved out by his daughter Shannon, who was named for his wife's Irish roots. That hole grew larger over the years and was shaped and carved by his wife, Erin, who had for many years lived like a haunted porcelain doll. She was either at his side, or on a shelf. The love he had for her had ruined him for years and was now neatly tucked away . . . wherever her mind chose to reside. There was something that *ailed* her. He did not have the time now, or the patience to understand it. Whatever it was, it was something beyond grief. Grief had only woken something up inside her; his wife was turmoil inside, and cold veneer on the outside.

"Son."

It was not a question; it was a statement of fact. As his son turned towards him, Santo began to say the words . . . the echo from a life that barely seemed like theirs. "Eagle . . ."

It was then that Sam got sick all over his chair. He saw the sickness, and then the color registered and he thought at once of sour cherries. He saw Shannon's sticky fingers reaching into the jar. He remembered her putting each cherry in her mouth as she sucked the juice out of it, the sweet and sour luxury of a gourmet cherry. He would always give her a wink and try to be a cool dad and shoot a finger gun at her, or an awkward point. She always would wink back and place the cherry, with all the best parts sucked away, back into the glass of whichever pale blonde alcoholic was drinking her cocktail. Santo smiled in his memory, and it entered the room where he stood now, in front of his son, like a sneer.

Sam, the Eagle . . . he'd never taken the time to notice the softer side of his father. He never saw the camaraderie between Santo and his daughter; Sam never saw the love pass between them like a secret code. Sam, the Eagle was too busy making sure he carved the perfect orange rind to place on the glass. Sam never saw the fatherly love; he never saw the game. He only had ever seen melted ice cubes and the perfect cocktail. His sole focus had been on what he could do to make the women in his life smile, if only for a moment.

As Santo looked at his son, he realized now that nothing had changed.

Sam was a hollowed-out version of who he was as a boy; one-half of a very full whole.

Sam and Shannon.

"Dad . . . I'm sorry, Father . . . I meant to say Father," Sam said as he peeked over Santo's shoulder and glanced at Gretchen. She whispered into one cellphone while she frantically texted into another with her left hand. Sam had always hated people who were ambidextrous, it seemed unfair to him that there were people who could access each part of their brains and bodies, while he, a dyslexic, fought every day of his life to read and memorize the words he was supposed to know, whether for theatre or this other new game. It was no wonder, he thought, that he had been destined to fail. He had played the game backwards. He thought of JFK, and his political career ending with death, and then he thought of his own *career*, starting with death. He looked at the vomit on the chair, the thick viscous cherry colors.

Sam wiped his mouth. He saw the abstract painting that splashed from his gut and landed, haphazard onto the velvet chair; he thought of JFK's brains splattered all over Jackie's beautiful Chanel Suit. He felt the end of something.

His father's chair and a family dream shot down.

"Sorry, I've had a bad day . . ." He tried the smile that made news cameras light up. His father would have none of it. He was stoic, like a blank-faced beautiful statue in a second-rate museum.

"You've made a mess, you know that. I don't want to waste my time, or Gretchen's time going over all this again. I think at the end of the day you will need to sit with what you have done and who you are, and the disappointment that you have caused not only our family, but your staff, and the people of this state."

Gretchen nodded. Her eyes lingered on Sam's, not in camaraderie but instead in damnation.

"I heard the footage on the hot mic, and Gretchen informed me on the way here about what state you were in when you got to the school, that you showed up late, and your pupils already dilated—"

"Wait, Gretchen told me she was meeting you here, you already talked to her?"

"George picked Gretchen up and she met me at the airport. Oh, and by the way, you owe an apology to George, he has the flu or something, he looks terrible and he was still willing to go get her and bring both of us here." There was a pause then. "Do you know why he did that? Do you? He did that for you, he did that out of some misguided belief that you are the same boy he knew years ago." Santo took a breath before continuing. "You know you fucked this up, not just for you but for everyone . . . I mean Jesus, Sam, what the fuck were you thinking? Could you not hold it together for two goddamn hours? You just *had* to prove to me, to the world once again that it should have been—" Santo stopped, but he had not stopped soon enough.

"That it should have been me that died," Sam whispered. He had not wanted to say it aloud, but he knew he had to say it before his father did.

"That's not what I said." Santo had a way to turn his hateful words into honey and olive oil dripped onto sweet bread. When he spoke, if Sam closed his eyes and kept them closed, he could taste the olive oil, and feel the Italian sun shining in through the windows of a train. He could see them; two children with legs like doughy pretzels, he could hear their laughter. That summer, their skin had smelled like basil if they spent more than twenty minutes in the sun. They were somewhere south of Rome headed towards his Nonna's house just outside of Palermo. Sam remembered looking at his mother, and he wished now he had memorized her genuine smile, the one that made the space between her nose and her lips disappear into laughter. She had looked like a movie star; every man in Italy had fallen in love with her from afar.

He did not know he would never see her genuine smile again.

"Gretchen and I have prepared something, a statement for you to deliver tomorrow." Santos shoved some already yellowed and wrinkled index cards towards Sam. "You will need to memorize it and use your damned theatre degree for once to make this believable."

Sam held the index cards in his hand; he was sweaty the way he was when he was eight years old and had given an unprepared oral report about Helen Keller. The moisture from his hands made the paper cards curl in like palm fronds. His voice was monotone, stilted, and awkward as he read the words aloud. "I have been unwell. I know that you all know the struggles I have had in the past with drinking, and with drugs. I hate to let you all down, but I have not been able to overcome them . . ." Sam sighed and looked up at his father. He met his eyes and then turned his gaze towards Gretchen and aimed his words at her. "So, the story is that I am a drug addict? Is that what we are going with?"

"Sam, it's the best narrative we could come up with, it's one that rationalizes your behavior without it being forgiven. What did you want the statement to say? Did you just want to stand up in front of the world and tell people you are just a spoiled rich man-child? That you are a narcissist and the only reason you bothered to run for governor is because you were bored? Is that what you wanted?"

"Does this end with me going to rehab? Because if that is the case then fuck that, no way."

"This all ends," Santo interrupted, "with us telling people you are entering a facility. You are a grown man, and we can't force you, but what will be required of you is that you get out of the public eye for a while. You can go to Nonna's. We will have the caretakers get the place ready for you. You could be there in a few days."

Sam stared silently at Gretchen the entire time his father spoke; he watched her face, and it was frozen like a pantomime mask. He wanted to see a flash of humanity in her, but he saw nothing.

"Now," Santo continued, "you will read what we have prepared for you. You can rehearse it tonight. I would like you to cry when the time is right; I will tell you when that is, but for most of the speech I want you to sound sorry, act sorry. Do you understand me? Nod if this makes sense to you."

Sam nodded. He found his father's eyes. He realized every time he looked at him that they shared the same dark eyes. Shannon had them too. Sharks. "Yeah, I understand."

"Good. Now, we have been in touch with the boy's family, and he will be there as well; if you look on the last of the cards that is where you will find the personal apology to him. After you apologize, you will say the words, 'Do you forgive me?' The boy will be instructed to stand and then approach the podium, and he will say 'I forgive you; none of us is perfect.' He will then put his hand out to shake your hand that is when you will go to him, get down on your knees and give the boy a hug. That's when you will cry. Got it?"

"There is no way the kid is going to do this, it's bullshit. His parents won't subject him to this."

"That's where you're wrong," Gretchen said. "I did a little research, and the boy, Simon, comes from nothing, his mom is a single mom. The dad came home all fucked up from the Gulf War and no one has seen him in years, he's probably homeless or dead. The mom's on food stamps, they live in Section 8 housing, she works mostly daytime hours stripping at The Full Spread. The place is a rattrap. She'll make sure the boy does what we want him to do. We've offered her fifty thousand dollars."

"If we have to, we can go up to seventy-five," Santo leaned over and whispered this to Gretchen, his lips brushing against her ear.

"We won't need to, I promise you. Hell, I think she would bring him there for as little as ten thousand, or less." Gretchen's hand reached up, squeezed Santo's shoulder, and then lingered there for a moment before she removed it. She let it trail part way down his back before she took her hand away, and awkwardly brought it to her hair and pretended to fix it.

They were fucking, of course they were. Sam had often suspected it, but he never saw any actual proof, until that moment. When he saw her hand on him like that it made him feel like he was going to be sick again. There was an uncomfortableness inside his body; his bones were starting to ache, and his stomach burned. The air smelled like sour cherries. His eyes started to burn, and without him even realizing it, Sam fought back tears. He turned away from his father and Gretchen and he felt a hot tear slide down his face. It almost stung his skin. He wiped it away, but as he did, more had begun to fall. He wiped them away with his knuckles, and it looked more violent rather than soothing, as if he had punched his own face.

He looked at the cards to try to busy himself. He saw the words, "I really did want to do my best for all of you, but I realized during this journey, that the pressure was too much for me. I was never deserving of the trust you placed in me. I can only hope that one day I will be able to make the people of the State of Massachusetts proud of me once again. I know I have disgraced myself, and my family who has stood by me through all my problems; to them I am sorry. I am also sorry to my sister Shannon, gone from us too soon. I am sure she is looking down on me in every possible way. I'm sorry Shannon; I wanted to do this for your memory . . ." As he read this to himself, he thought he could hear it again, the faint sound of a bell as it rang from upstairs. It was asking a question.

"You should probably consider checking yourself into someplace though. You don't look good, son." His father had practiced his patriarchal voice for his entire career, but Sam could count on one hand the number of times that it was aimed at him and not at the populace at large.

"Yeah, I don't think that's going to happen," Sam mumbled more to himself than anyone else. He turned back to face his father again, and his eyes were red, and started to feel swollen and raw. He used the cards to gesture towards the maroon chair, his father's former throne, and said, "I'll pay to have that cleaned. Don't worry about it."

"I appreciate the offer, but I will have the chair removed tonight. I realize I no longer car for it anymore. Now, you should get yourself cleaned up. Go over the cards some more. Gretchen will be here for dinner and after we eat, we will want to hear your statement. Memorize it if you can so it looks like you are speaking from the heart."

When Sam had returned to the room, he was met with the overripe sour smell of sickness and a cabin at a boy's sleepaway camp. In the hour and a half that it had been since he got sick, the walls had soaked it in and it would probably be impossible to ever air out. He thought the smell had come from his bathroom, but then was quick to realize that it had begun to seep from his skin as well. He needed to shower, and he knew the mess that was waiting for him in the bathroom, and he didn't want to deal with that, but he had to.

He clicked the light on in the bathroom that he had once shared with Shannon and grabbed some towels from the rack and did his best to soak up the mess from the toilet seat and the floor. As he did this, he realized that he had no memories in his life of ever having cleaned something up on his own. Even when he was away at college, he had rented an apartment in the city, and had a cleaner come in a few times a week. The way he mopped up the mess only made it worse, as he seemed to have smeared it everywhere, rather than disposing of it. He did not understand how people knew how to do things. Was cleaning self-taught, or were kids taught to clean messes when they were children? Was this like cooking or baking? Was there some secret class that people took for all of this? Had he missed a class in private school or was this something he had never been expected to learn?

How could he be 36 years old and have never managed to figure out how to live a life? The bell rang again, quietly, almost timidly at first, but then with more force. It came from behind Shannon's closed door, the one that adjoined the bathroom. She had tried to get his attention for hours.

He always tried his best to ignore her, the way he did *that night*.

He could hear it in between each ring, the silence sounded like she had whispered his name. He left the wet towel on the floor; he shoved it further into the corner and tucked it between the toilet and the tub. Sam walked towards the closed door and placed his hand on the wood. He could almost feel the memory of that night, as the memory vibrated under his hand; it tried to get his attention. He waited, and then he heard it again. "Shannon, please, I'm not in the mood for this tonight."

Silence.

He thought perhaps she would be quiet now; it usually worked, if he just talked to her, she would settle down. This had been going on throughout the years since she died. It was almost nightly at first, in the years right after her death. It only started to calm down a little when Sam finally went away to college. But this, the bell, this was the reason that he would come back home on the weekends, this was also the reason he had chosen to live here, even into his adult life. This is where the bell worked. He had tried a few times, bringing it with him places, but it never rang. Shannon was here, in this house, and behind this closed door. The strange part was no matter how loudly she rang the bell, Sam was the only one who ever heard it. He exhaled and felt his shoulders drop a few inches. He had not realized he was holding his breath. It felt like he had been holding it for years.

He backed away from the door a few feet. There was a silence in the air that now seemed unnatural. This silence, it ached. It wanted to whisper his name, but it didn't. The air pressed in around him, and he felt a headache starting somewhere in the back of his head. It would travel to the backs of his eyes until he was finally able to sleep.

He closed his eyes, and his head rested against the door. There was something beautiful, and awful, in these moments, when he was alone with himself, and the part of him that was dead.

The bell rang again, this time it was louder, more determined. "Shannon." He said this and there was a warning in his voice, but it was not just a warning, there was something underneath it too, there was fear. It rang again, louder, angrier. It sounded like the brass was hitting against the table by her bed. He pounded against the door, in the same way he used to when they were children, and she would lock him out of her room.

The bell just rang and rang. Each clang seemed to grow louder and expand into the silence of the rest of the house. "Knock it off Shannon, I'm warning you." Gone were the staccato pauses in between the clangs, the bell just rang without pause, it just screamed for his attention. He did not know what he had expected when he opened the door. He did it with such force that it hit the wall. The bell finally stopped. Had it happened the moment he had wrapped his large hand around the delicate carved glass of the doorknob, or did it stop the moment when he stood, framed in the doorway with the bright bathroom light behind him. The light shone around him and it created a little pool of safety and normalcy that only reached a little over a foot into Shannon's room.

Two different kinds of lemon. Dust. Hospital hallways.

He saw the bell where it normally lived, on the little table by her bed. It was where it had stayed throughout her illness, and even now, in the years since her death, it always remained there, standing up straight, her little night watchman. Yet now he could see that the bell had been knocked over, it lay there wounded, tipped over on its side. He walked towards it, as if it had called his name. He was careful when he picked it up, not to let it make a sound. He felt the brass handle, and it was warm, as if it had spent the day in the sun or clutched in his sister's sweat-covered boney hands. Piano hands, too weak to play.

The rest of the metal was still cool to the touch, only the handle was still warm. He traced his fingers around the inside of it and felt all the little dents from each collision of the clapper. He wondered how many of these little divots had been created before Shannon died and how many since? He traced them now, his fingers read each little dent as if were braille. He wondered what she had been trying to say to him. What was the story these little divots were trying to tell?

If he counted them, how many would there be? A thousand . . . a thousand little deaths?

"I miss you kid," he whispered as he put the bell back in its rightful position. He hated to turn his back on it, to leave the room. His life was a list of all the times he had abandoned her. He felt this way when he was young, and he felt a burning relief to be able to go to school, alone. Throughout his school days, he would drown in guilt, in pleasurable terror of what happened to her when he was gone. The pressure of this memory felt like heavy water on his lungs. It was the same when he eventually left for college, though by then he knew to return home before the pressure on his lungs became too much to handle. He always came back here to this room, to her bell. He stared at it, on the table in the dark room; the light from the bathroom did not reach here but he could still see a dark shadow around her bell, he saw it, it breathed with him. He kept his eye on it as he backed away, as if it were an angry dog. When he finally turned and left the room, he closed the door just as he heard the bell fall over onto its side.

He stood there, leaned his back against the closed door, and held his breath. He hoped in his own way to hear the bell again; he waited for it, and it never came.

He decided against going down to dinner that night. He read and re-read the index cards until the words would be able to play off his tongue with earnestness. As he studied them, he began to believe the words. And that night, after the Adderall and alcohol finally wore off, he closed his tired eyes, and as he drifted off to sleep, the room started to smell like cherries, Baby Soft, two kinds of lemon, and dust . . .

He was asleep when the bell started to ring again. He woke for a moment, and then closed his eyes. Just like the final night of Shannon's life, he chose to ignore it.

DAY 2

Interitus

Masculine noun ruin; rot, violent/untimely death, extinction; destruction, dissolution.

Because I could not stop for Death –
He kindly stopped for me –
The Carriage held but just Ourselves –
And Immortality.

We slowly drove – He knew no haste
And I had put away
My labor and my leisure too,
For His Civility –

We passed the School, where Children strove
At Recess – in the Ring –
We passed the Fields of Gazing Grain –
We passed the Setting Sun –
                                    - Emily Dickenson

Chapter/
nine

OMELIA
Sweet Dreams Seem to Whisper . . . ICU

There were big hospital clocks that were interspersed throughout the ER. They all clicked at different times, each secondhand lived in a different reality than the one, just one patient station over. Time is fickle, even here as this day slowly bled and wheezed its way into tomorrow.

The Code Blue Trauma Team was set up when she arrived. The paramedics, though they had been advised to, had not been wearing Hazmat suits, and the immediate diagnosis had been an overdose of some kind; the sores on her face were "probably meth related". They had found her, half-drowned in her shower, a fever spiking; infected cankers had spread over her face. Doctor Paul had also been found unconscious when the paramedics and the police were forced to break down Omelia's door. She did not worry about the damage done, or her security deposit that she would never get back.

Omelia wasn't worried about anything, not anymore.

The little curtained off section that her gurney was taken to had a fluorescent light that flickered overhead, like a convenience store in a David Lynch movie. It did nothing to show the attending physician the true color of her skin, which in this light, looked pale like the underside of a mushroom. Her skin looked like mud season in New England woods. In this light, they couldn't really see the gray color that edged closer to blue death. They did not notice due to her French manicure that her fingernails had also turned a pale white, and underneath the acrylic gels, the tips of her natural nails started to flake away. Her nails had turned ephemeral like the ragged edges of a moth someone tried hard not to harm as they pinched their wings and lifted it out of the house.

The big clock over her bed in the ER clicked just past midnight, and in Omelia's world, it was already tomorrow. It is already the future turned sour. Turned wrong.

In Doctor Paul's curtained off area, he had regained consciousness, and felt foolish. His fainting spell in Omelia's apartment is what they were saying was just part of a panic attack. They gave him a sedative in the ambulance ride to the Catholic hospital on the other side of the river in Manchester. There were closer to better hospitals in Omelia's neighborhood, but he somehow understood that they were overrun, and all new traumas were being sent to the other side of the city, in the hospital that was settled in the shadow of the beautiful church that Omelia looked at every day.

In the ambulance as the sedative started to work, Paul chuckled to himself, about 'new trauma' being sent to the 'Catholics.' Whatever they had given him was making him feel good; he tried to make a joke to the paramedic who was now in the front seat, and who looked bored as his partner drove at a normal speed towards the hospital.

A part of Paul understood that Omelia had been taken in a separate ambulance. A part of him remembered that he saw them work on her body, which appeared lifeless at the time; the doors of her ambulance had still been open. Part of him remembered that the ambulance started moving, as it screamed its way towards the bridge across the river, and it did this before the back ambulance doors had even closed. He saw the paramedic lean out and shut the door. He did this with one hand, the other hand held a cloth over his face.

Yes, they should have listened; they should have worn the Hazmat suits.

The ambulance that took Nicole away had its siren on and swerved through the parking lot as if it were in a British road race. The ambulance Paul was in drove smooth and steady like a Sunday drive to a 'pick your own blueberries' farm. He heard one of the paramedics play music on his phone; it was that shitty new country, always songs about bars and beer . . . what had happened to old school country? The stuff his parents had listened to, Johnny Cash, and Merle Haggard . . . songs about prison and loneliness, where were the songs about mama? Where were the songs about a good first love gone badly? Where were the songs about . . .?

He must have been talking out loud. He heard laughter in the front seat, and he could have sworn he heard one of them say, "I don't know, he has whatever the balding middle-aged man version of female hysteria is . . ." Then they both laughed, and it was a slow motion underwater garbled sound that made his heart tickle and then ache with embarrassment.

Maybe none of that happened. And even if it did, did he care? He started to understand why people did drugs. What was that they gave him? A needle in his arm 'of temporary happiness. A needle in his arm full of yesterdays . . . A needle full of times gone by' ". . . like that song on Archie Bunker." he mumbled. His words were half inside out like an old shirt.

He looked up now and was somehow out of the ambulance, transported through hallways that seemed too wide and too tall. He was now in a curtained-off alcove, tucked in tight in a gurney next to trauma three; he heard the whispers of "Code Blue." His body was there, and his mind was dream casting. Paul looked up at the clock on the wall; he saw that it was still a few seconds before midnight. He heard the ticking and watched the second hand catch in place a few times before it moved onto the next second, he watched it again . . . there was something that tried to trick him with this clock.

The curtained-off area where they had taken him didn't really exist in the world around him. Here, behind the curtains, time was moving so much slower. Each second was three, then four, then two . . . maybe it was the clock, maybe it was the drugs. Maybe he was dying; maybe he was dead. He didn't know. All he knew was that it was still today, and if it was still today, then maybe there was time for Nicole.

Tomorrow, and Nicole . . . maybe those two things didn't go together. Maybe they were never supposed to.

He thought of Heather, he should have loved her more, and then he thought of Meredith, wife number one, and thought that maybe he should have loved her a little less. Wife number two was Candace and technically that one did not count, married on a Carnival Cruise and annulled a few weeks after they returned to dry land.

Next to him, shadows moved in frenetic motion against the curtains of the trauma three section of the Catholic hospital. The lights just one bed over had pulsed in uneven beats. The words that came from the space next to him were going too fast, and then too slow. He heard the word overdose, and then people asking about the fever . . . and then, "What about her face?"

He watched the clock in his room again as the second hand finally made its way just past midnight, after laboring for so long. In his bed, within his curtains and under his non-flickering light, it had finally become tomorrow; he had no idea what day it was for Nicole.

He closed his eyes and he saw Nicole as a girl; she was the oldest and youngest 14-year-old he had ever seen, though admittedly he had not seen too many. Her eyes had always been wide, haunted, and sad like an owl. He saw her the day he met her, and he saw her the day that he and Meredith, wife number one, had watched as a social worker had walked her out the door. Nicole had turned back one last time to look at him. She clutched her blue suitcase to her chest like a life raft. She left the white bureau behind. It was years before he was able to give it back to her.

His hand reached up and his fingers brushed against the curtain, and it was only that, and the lighting, that separated him from trauma number three. His fingers wrapped around the divide in the curtain; he was about to lean over and open it when he heard someone rush past his bed and pull the curtain on the other side. He heard her say, "PPE NOW. She has what they have, the same thing that closed the Elliot, they're dying over there, get your gear on, and get whoever came in with her in isolation now."

He heard a nurse from behind the curtain, her voice was small but brave as she said "I'm covered in her blood, I had my fingers down her throat already, and it's too late for me. Jesus, just let me help her if I can." There were more mumbled sounds, and people crashing into carts filled with medical gear.

He heard the rest of the medical team scurry like crabs. He tried to pull the curtain open and before he was wheeled away, he saw people in masks and goggles. They barely touched his gurney as if it would burn their skin even to touch it. He felt a pin prick in his arm. It was another needle full of happiness, another needle full of yesterday afternoon. The room started to get dark around him. He looked back at the big clock on the wall above his bed; it had somehow gone back to right before midnight. He remembered saying, "Don't worry, it's not tomorrow yet, and I'm not sick, I just have female hysteria."

Paul thought he was laughing, when in fact he was just sleeping.

Her body was awake as it twitched in a half-dream state. There was a shadow woman, she moved quickly, and was a blur of bright blue scrubs with pugs on them. Her hands wore red gloves that melted and dripped onto the floor. She could see the bright blue stiff cotton fabric and the little homely faces of the dogs as they blurred in and out of her vision. Their eyes were big and frightened. The woman in the scrubs had her fingers in Omelia's mouth, and she pulled something out of the back of her throat. She shook her hand and whatever it was fell to the floor, it sounded solid, but wet.

She had the thought that it was a child, but that didn't make any sense, she wasn't pregnant, not now, and babies, they could not come out of your throat, could they? Maybe they could come out of her stomach, yes that seemed right. They could come out of the stomach.

She remembered the miscarriage she had when she was seventeen when she was forced to go back to the group home again; that time all she brought with her was her makeup and the crowns and sashes she had won as Miss Strawberry Festival and Winter Ice Princess, her books, and her empty envelopes. She remembered herself in the bathroom there; she placed a tiara on her head and doubled over as she bled. The *thing* coming out of her sounded like that.

Wet.

Solid.

That was a long time ago.

She heard Nurse Pugs whisper to her; she said her name over and over while everyone else in the room filtered in and out of her vision. The lights strobed on and off and she realized maybe she was still in the bar the other night, as she sipped cocktails that tasted like laughter. She wanted to close her eyes and feel herself kiss Kim, the girl who smelled like sunshine. Her eyes had been bright blue, like these scrubs, like these pugs . . .

The pugs were talking again, they whispered in her ear, "I think you can hear me, if you can hear me squeeze my hand . . . good girl, I knew it."

Omelia was confused. Maybe the blue pugs had been talking with someone else; she did not remember having squeezed anyone's hand, but then her eyes trailed down her arm and she saw her hand, recently orphaned on the bed. Her fingers were coated in secondhand blood. She moved them a little and she felt something sticky like milkweed in between her fingers. Oh, yes this must the baby . . .

Babies come from the stomach. That's what happens when you kiss boys.

She wondered what happened to her tiaras. Winter Ice Princess was her favorite. She had always been allergic to strawberries. For a long time, the different crowns were on a shelf above her bed. Were they still there? She tried to picture her apartment, but it looked empty, and all she could see was the church across the river, the late day sun, as it made the green copper steeple start to glow.

"I am going to need you to breathe out everything you can, okay? Breathe out five, four, three, two, one, we're going to do that, and then once we get to one, we are going to take a big breath in, real big okay? I know you can hear me." The pugs sounded less like a nurse and more like a preschool teacher.

Omelia didn't say anything but she moved her fingers as if she was twirling a baton; she spun her hand and felt the green light from the flickering fluorescent play between her fingers like music. She groaned, and it sounded like sandpaper as it scraped against the jagged edge of a saw. The pugs didn't know that Omelia was asking about her old crowns, she wondered where they were . . .

"Okay here we go. Breathe out 5,4,3,2,1 . . . AND in 1, 2, 3, 4, 5 . . ."

When Omelia had gotten a little past two on her inhale, she felt someone else that she had not seen before start to push her forehead back; her head tilted, and her mouth was forced open. She felt fingers and cold metal bang against her crooked back wisdom teeth that she had never had the money to get removed. The cold metal did something to the back of her throat and then she felt a snake slide down, all the way down until she felt nothing at all. Except pain.

"She's still awake." The pugs said, over their shoulder to a man who was made of shadows. He was backlit with flickering green light behind him, and he was covered completely as if Omelia was radioactive. The pugs didn't wear a mask or goggles; she held Omelia's red-streaked sticky hand in hers. The pugs wore red gloves that looked terrible with the blue scrubs.

Scrub pugs.

Milkweed and blood.

Something on the floor.

Solid.

Wet.

She wore her crown then, but not now.

"She can't be awake, it's impossible," said the shadows.

"I think it's the fever, it's burning the sedatives off. Look at her, look at her eyes."

The shadow man leaned over her and made noises like he was chewing a roast beef sandwich. He shined a penlight in her eyes; it hurt. It made the back of her skull ache and caused a shooting pain from the soles of her feet and up into each of her legs; the pain died down as it passed her knees. It got lost somewhere before it reached her uterus.

This is what happened when you kissed boys. She wanted to say it but trying to form words made her mouth hurt.

The man of shadows left for a moment. Omelia was flat on her back and she stared at the ceiling light as it flickered. She worried about the hue of the fluorescents on her skin. The pugs had said something, but she had forgotten to listen. "We're just going to give you a little more, alright Nicole? We need you to be able to sleep now. You will be asleep for a while, but don't worry. There will always be someone with you."

Omelia's eyes were able to dart to the right, and she saw the pugs' face for the first time. She was a pretty brunette with a sensible bob haircut. Her eyes were kind, but behind the eyes was resignation, and regret. Omelia felt someone move her other arm and suddenly felt a cold shock in her veins. It felt the way ice sounds when you press your ear to it on a frozen lake. It sang to her.

"See Nicole, you're going to be okay."

Omelia tried to form the words around the tube in her throat, she tried to say her name was Omelia, but the only thing that came out was a wheeze. Before her eyes closed, she looked at the pugs, she saw her face, and saw the red blister, just starting to form near the crook of her nose; it had little black veins that crept towards her eye like a child's excited hand.

The pugs looked at her one last time; regret, and resignation which clashed with the pretty, hopeful sky blue of the scrubs and the eager little faces of the funny dogs.

Neither of them knew that Nurse Pugs would be dead in three days.

Chapter/
ten

SAM
I regret to inform you—

The brass bell, with all the divots inside, had continued to ring throughout the night, and finally settled down just a little before 4am. Sam, in a state of emotional exhaustion, did not hear any of it after the first tentative ring. It was quite different from the time, over 20 years ago, that he and Shannon had fought like cats throughout the day. He never understood how someone who had shrunk so much and had started to collapse in on herself like a dying star, could fight as hard and in such an emotionally vicious way as Shannon had. Even consumed with sickness, she had always somehow known the words to use to be able to creep under his skin. She could press her finger on the soft parts of his psyche with all of her weight. Shannon, as much as he loved her, always had known how to make him feel like shit.

The night after they fought, he had heard her bell; it was anxious at first, and then sometime after 1am, it had rung with a fervor that Sam did not know she still had in her. He ignored her. She deserved that; she had been a bitch to him for days. His parents had tried to explain that the chemo and the claustrophobia were turning her into someone that even she didn't like. He got it, *she was sick*, but being sick and being mean didn't have to go hand in hand. He knew that the way the bell had rung that she just wanted attention, hell, maybe she wanted to say she was sorry . . . but she probably just wanted him to go down to the kitchen and get her a sugar free butterscotch pudding cup. It was all she was eating these days. She had said swallowing regular food made her insides bleed.

For once, Shannon would not get what she wanted. Not that night.

The bell rang at an even pace for a little over 40 minutes until it began to slow down. After that it rang off and on, and Sam could almost imagine Shannon having fallen asleep with the bell still clutched in her hand. He could see her startle awake when it would clang as her arm finally relaxed against the bed. He could almost see her barely awake for a moment; her eyes already heavy as she gave the bell a few more lackluster rings. He thought she was doing this out of spite, not out of need.

"If she needed me, she should have called out for me." He could still hear his words, the way they crackled with guilt as he had said them to his parents; his voice was shaken, small, already aged with regret.

He could not tell them that he had heard the bell on and off until a little before 4am. The same way he would never tell them that there were many sleepless nights he'd spent in that room even now, hearing the same bell, the same pattern, the same sleeping and waking, only now when he heard it, he only heard the need, not the spite.

But he did not hear anything last night. He worked to memorize the script his father had written for him until he fell into the emptiness of his life, the comfort of the great alone.

When his eyes opened at a little after 10:30am, he was confused that he had been able to sleep for over twelve hours. He could not remember the last time that had happened. Not since he was a teenager, he thought, and he had gotten mono from that Goth girl who played third chair violin in the school orchestra. She had been homely, albeit *talented*, in every way.

When Sam tried to heave himself out of the bed, his fingers were hard to move and everything from his wrist down seemed to pull him back into the bed. His hands felt like they were filled with small stones, collected by a water's edge. He thought of Virginia Wolfe as she filled her pockets with rocks. He had a strange sensation that sometime in the night Shannon had snuck into his room, sliced open his wrists and stuffed smooth stones down into the very tips of his fingers. He tried to open and close his hands, but they still felt the same; they were heavy, and swollen. When he swung his legs out of the bed and his feet hit the floor, he had a similar sensation. There was heaviness, and weight. He felt as if he were about to be pulled down through the floor. He thought he would find himself in his father's study downstairs. His body would fall onto the damask chair that was now stained and reeking of sour cherries. A pungent childhood memory come to life.

He was already late. The press conference was set for 11:30 am, and that gave him a little less than an hour. When he walked to the bathroom, each step landed heavy on the cool floor, and even though he could not see it, he could feel the chandelier downstairs rattling with each step he took. He was a heavy walker, every step a stomp. When he got to the bathroom, the smell hit him first, yesterday's sickness, still ripe in the closed-off stale air. He saw that the adjoining door to Shannon's room was open, and there was light pouring in from her windows. Her curtains were open, as if Shannon, wherever she was, had already been up and out of bed. Shannon had *already* started her day; she was not late for the press conference. No, Shannon was always early. Sam walked the few steps to close her door and block out the morning light. He caught a glimpse of himself in the mirror; his skin was gray, with an undertone of yellow. He didn't need the natural light to pour in the room for him to know that he looked like shit. His hangover was a death mask.

There would be no 60 Minutes makeup crew today to powder his nose and give him a faux healthy look. He splashed some water on his face.

He didn't bother to wait for it to get warm, and he also didn't bother with his $70 cucumber and Dead Sea salt face scrub. Fuck it. Who was he trying to impress? Who was he trying to fool? He opened the medicine cabinet and grabbed the bottle of Adderall. He popped two in his mouth, but instead of swallowing them, he chewed them like a Flintstones Vitamin. He wanted it to taste terrible in his mouth, he wanted this to be just the small price to pay for yesterday, for all the days.

He had ignored Shannon.

He lifted the toilet seat and poured the rest of the pills in the water. Sam flushed the toilet right away, before he changed his mind. He was afraid he would reach his hand into the cold swirling water, try to pull the pills that had already started to disintegrate out of the water. He made his choice. They were gone, at least for now.

No, not for now, forever. There. That was his choice. He knew there were hidden bottles in three different spots in his bedroom, but this, he wanted to take the win. He got rid of the pills. That was a start.

By the time he was dressed and headed out the front door he knew that he would be, at best, ten minutes late for the press conference, which was being held on the front steps of the school. When Sam approached the car, he thought that George was not in there, as he glanced in the front seat and it appeared empty. It was not until he got a little closer that he saw that George was leaned over on his right side, his body curled in an awkward and uncomfortable snake position around the stick shift. His head rested on the passenger seat, his eyes half-opened, but vacant. He didn't move as Sam approached, and it wasn't until Sam rapped lightly on the driver's window that George sat up. He looked at Sam; his eyes were soupy and disoriented. They were red around the edges as if he had been crying. He had a blank look on his face as if he did not recognize Sam. The driver looked a little lost; he made eye contact with Sam, but luckily for both, he snapped out of it. George's eyes went through a series of emotions in just a few seconds: confusion, recognition, followed by the one that broke Sam's heart the most, love.

George opened his door and mumbled an apology. "Sorry Eagle, had a restless night last night and I just need to get caught up on a little shut eye. I thought you may be out earlier today, so I've been here a while." He opened the back door of the car. When Sam slid into the back seat, he realized that the car smelled a lot like his bathroom did . . . sour cherries. "Don't you remember what I told you yesterday Eagle? You promised me you were going to try and be better about being on time from now on."

Sam tried to hide the disgust from his face over the smell of the car. He tried his best to smile as he met George's eyes in the rearview mirror. "I think I'm scared of clocks, I realized it last night."

"That's a poor excuse Eagle, you just need to promise me you are going to be better."

"You're right George, I promise, I'll try to be better."

"I forgot my index cards," Sam whispered to Gretchen as he turned his head away from the crowd, the camera crews, and reporters from countless television stations that had been camped out in front of the school since before sunrise that day.

"Didn't we tell you to memorize them?"

"I mean, I did, or I . . . Ugh . . . I tried, I did, but I wanted to have them here just to make sure I said the right thing. Do you have a copy of my statement?"

"No, Jesus Christ Sam . . . You had one job last night, memorize the script. Fuck. FUCK." Gretchen saved her swears for when her back was turned to their audience that had grown in number with Sam's arrival. People from the houses that surrounded the school, who had spent their morning glued to their windows, had finally started to meander in a forced suburban casualness onto their front lawns and over towards the crowd in front of the school.

All of them had noticed that twenty minutes ago a limousine had shown up with several dark cars full of Secret Service flanked around it. Vice President Santo Anthony Alberti had arrived but had not gotten out of the car. He remained out of sight even when his only child had finally shown up. Santo's plan was to stand behind his son, with a look of worry and sadness on his face, and he hoped he would be able to work up a few tears that he could hold in when Sam got to the part about his struggle with drugs. Santo planned that he would let the tears fall at the moment when Sam invoked the name of his dearly departed long dead sister.

"It's okay Gretchen, I know what I am supposed to say, I remember most of it. Whatever I forget I will just talk from the heart."

She rolled her eyes, and that said everything she needed it to. Sam thought he heard her whisper in a sarcastic tone, "your heart," as she turned away from him and walked towards the limousine. Santo opened the door to a wave of applause, his eyes squinting under the glare as all the cameras flashed at once. Sam, at that moment, went completely ignored. He felt a tide of relief wash over him as he felt all eyes from the ever-growing crowd leave him and go to his father.

All eyes, except of course for Simon, who continued to look at Sam; the pomp and circumstance of the Vice President never distracted the young boy's gaze. His hazel eyes swirled with confusion, hate, hurt, and fever. No one saw the fever, not until it was too late.

Sam felt Simon's eyes on him before he bothered to look around the crowd and really notice who was there. Sam realized once he saw the boy, that for him, there was no one else there that day, not his father, or Gretchen with her whisper that hissed in his ear, unable to be picked up on a microphone. There was just Simon, and a woman that Sam had to assume was the boy's mother. She ironically wore acid washed jeans and a yellow hoodie with Tigger and Pooh Bear embroidered on it. She flashed a peace sign as she tried to take some selfies. Her hoodie was unzipped halfway and even from 40 feet away, where Sam began to slowly inch towards the podium, he could see that under the hoodie she wore a tight-fitting red V-neck T-shirt.

Showing more unfortunate cleavage than a distressed mother should. On the opposite side of Simon, there was an empty chair. This was the chair where the missing father should have been, or the friendly "cool aunt." Instead, it was empty.

There are always things that people cannot see. Not even Gretchen, who prized herself on her incredible knack of observation. Even the staff of Secret Service did not see what, or who, was really in that empty chair next to Simon.

While Simon's focus was entirely on Sam, who now held onto the podium in front of him, as if he were about ready to faint, there, in the seat next to him, was a thin ghost, with limbs like dried cornstalks. Shannon, for the first time in over twenty years, she wasn't focused on her twin, her severed limb, her Sam . . . She was looking at this boy.

As the television cameras began to roll, there was a ghost-and-a half sitting in the front row. The crowds began to fill in the four rows of folding chairs behind them. The people that were too late gathered around the chairs, their bodies in too close. Sam felt something coming from the crowd, anger . . . and there was a scent of disgust that hit Sam as he was about to open his mouth. He smelled it; he felt it. The air smelled like the flu. He looked down at Simon, who for a moment looked as if he were listening to someone next to him as they whispered in his ear.

Whispers from an empty chair. The boy smiled halfheartedly. He looked at nothing, and then his gaze came back to Sam. His eyes were focused, albeit tired. The skin under his eyes looked thin and waxy. His mother sat next to him; she had a pack of Marlboro Lights in her hand, and she nervously tapped the pack into the palm of her hand. She was jittery, and Sam understood the look in her eyes when he finally was able to catch her attention for a fleeting second. She was bored, a woman who ached to be anywhere but there with all of them. He could see her, counting the fifty thousand dollars in her head. Sam took her for a junkie right away, not because his father had told him of the dayshifts she pulled at "Full Spread", a gentleman's club in a strip mall in Roxbury. No, he could see she was a junkie from the sores on her face, barely camouflaged under a thick coat of stage makeup. She continued to tap the pack of cigarettes against her palm and then she would reach up and scratch at her face. She winced every time she did it. Sam was about to start his speech, the one he had memorized, but he realized every time she scratched at her face, the boy, the too small for eleven-year-old Simon, would wince. Now, he may have been doing this out of embarrassment, but to Sam, up on that makeshift stage on the school steps, it looked more as if he was wincing in pain.

Sam could feel his skin as it began to burn hot under the navy fisherman's sweater he was wearing. He had been told to "dress relatable," and he didn't know what that meant. The sweater cost as much as a used car. Was that relatable? As he stood there now, he felt like he was dressed like a British Cop from a PBS mystery. He looked at the crowd and realized all the memorization of the index cards had been for naught. He cleared his throat and tried to speak from the heart, as he told Gretchen he would do, but there was nothing there. He closed his eyes and gripped the podium. He thought he heard a bell, it rang from the front row, but it couldn't be. He felt Gretchen's breath against his ear, cool like peppermint, as she hissed, "You need to fucking say something."

He knew the microphones would not pick up on it. All they would be able to hear was his unsteady breaths, his rapid heartbeat; all they could see was his hangover, and his sudden stage fright. The microphones heard his hands as they shook, his thumbs rattled against the podium, like offbeat percussion. He looked at Simon's face, and saw his eyes. He had no words.

He opened his mouth, prepared to start with, "I regret to inform you . . ." and then to speak from his heart, but all that was there, was Henry V, the Saint Crispin's Day Speech, but this time he didn't care about an audience, he just cared about Simon. He skipped the first few lines of the speech, and instead started with . . .

"If we are marked to die, we are enough . . ." Sam could see Simon's eyes

as they lit up. This may have not been the apology his father and Gretchen had scripted for him, but it was in some way the apology that Simon had wanted, had hoped for; the one he deserved. Sam did not realize that the boy had looked forward to the speech so much, and then had somehow missed it when it happened. Simon wanted to tell Sam this, when they were in line for *pizza day*, but he felt ashamed, and unworthy. Simon did not hear the crowd rustle around him, or the incessant chatter buzz of conversation . . . the hum of disapproval from the public. All Simon heard was Shakespeare, and in those words, he heard an apology from a man who was never taught to apologize. That class was not offered in his expensive private school.

Simon knew the script, he had been sent the notes that Gretchen had written on an index card for Sam. The boy knew to expect a speech, an admittance of a substance abuse problem, and then there would be a time that Simon was made to stand up and hug the man who had insulted him. He was not hearing that now, he only heard poetry, he only felt the connection that Sam, the tall man, was giving to him, and for the first time in Simon's life, he felt as if someone saw him, as opposed to just looking at him . . .

"We would not die in that man's company
That fears his fellowship die with us"

Sam finished the speech; he never took his eyes off Simon. Later, people would call this *spectacle* "too intense," the Twitter-Verse had already exploded with "the unraveling of a privileged psyche," "an audition for a repertory theatre company," and the very worst . . . tweeted by some conspiracy driven website, "A psycho-sexual threat and flirtation. THIS IS PIZZA-GATE."

When Sam had finished the speech, it ended and nothing happened. There was no applause, just silence followed by the ambient noise of distaste and held-in New England rage. Reporters hummed in snide whispers into their phones, all trying to get the scoop on the story. Simon, once the speech had ended, sat there perplexed, embarrassed, but most of all completely touched by all of this. He felt worse than he did yesterday, physically. Every part of his body screamed into an invisible pillow. He wanted that pillow now, but through all of that, he also felt understood. He had never felt that before.

He saw the tall man, Sam, who clutched the sides of the podium for strength, and for a moment, Simon felt that they were more similar than he thought they could have been. Simon knew somehow, that even though he received no apology, whatever had happened in this speech was more important than a simple *I'm sorry*; it was special. When Sam was speaking, it gave Simon the same feeling as when he was a boy and he would beg his mother when she came home from work exhausted, to *make him feel better*. For Simon this always meant the same thing, it was an elaborate game in which he pretended to come see her, a nurse, and he a patient with a broken arm. His mother would be half-asleep on their brown tweed sofa and he would approach her, with a box of generic Dollar Store tissues tucked under his arm. He would explain his injuries to her as she opened the tissue box and proceeded to tear the single ply tissues into long pieces. His mother's eyes were always sad and tired, but when he was young, she would take the time to tear the tissues into strips and delicately wrap and tie them around his 'wounded' arm.

Whatever this was, this game . . . it gave Simon chills that played up and down his spine like fingers on a piano. Simon could almost feel the tissues on his arm like a flexible cast . . . he felt the same chills when Sam looked at him and gave Shakespeare's words right to him. He felt those same chills, the ones that felt like a piano, except now they hurt. It was love and it was agony. He and this man, they were both a broken arm in a game. These chills made him feel special, but they also made his bones ache, and when he shifted in his chair, he could have sworn he felt the bottom part of his hip shift out of place and then break in two. He wanted to scream, but instead Simon placed his hand on the empty chair and pushed himself up to a standing position. As he did this, he would have sworn he felt a small hand next to him; it helped him up. He felt the little fingers that grasped under his arm and gave him the final push, a gentle shove.

Simon stood up, alone, and he began to clap. It was that slow clap of a 1980's teen movie where an over-privileged jock learns a lesson about life from a scrawny kid. His eyes were focused on Sam's head, which was facing down. Sam looked at the podium. Inside his mind he was looking at the index cards that he had forgotten at home, forgotten to memorize. He looked at the inside of a brass bell, so many divots, so many unanswered questions. He looked at the jar of moldy Luxardo cherries, and heard ice tinkling in a glass. When Sam lifted his head, he saw a shadow in the empty seat next to Simon. It was there for a split second and forgotten by her brother the next. Sam could have sworn he heard the bell ring, but he knew he left it at home, and the bell, it never followed him, no matter how much he wanted it to.

Sam the Eagle heard the lonely applause. He looked up and saw Simon. Sam did remember the part of the script— the apology, the handshake, the choreographed hug. Those three things played in his head like a dance that he couldn't quite master the movement. He wondered at which part it was exactly, that he had been meant to cry. Was it the handshake? The mention of Shannon?

Sam heard a sound, like a hand around someone's throat.

He saw the panic in Simon's eyes at the same time.

Sam did not get the handshake that was scripted. He felt the impact of the cement stairs fire up his legs as he ran, then he felt the cement under his knees as he knelt. It was like sandpaper on tender skin. He did not feel any of it now. The only thing he felt was the echo of his words as he whispered them into Simon's hair . . . "I'm sorry."

It was words unheard.

In the memory of this moment, Sam believed he saw recognition in Simon's eyes. He saw the boy, who was on the small side of eleven, forgive him. It was hope. It was a wish.

Sam the Eagle wrapped his arms around the boy and his arms were still there, as the echoes of the apology not picked up on a microphone still lingered against the boy skin and tangled in his hair. Sam could feel Simon's skin; it burned through his clothes. He held onto him even tighter and tried not to let the boy hit the ground. He felt two of Simon's ribs snap. It was the same sound as a wishbone broken in two. He saw himself and Shannon as they pulled with all their might, he saw Shannon win. What was the wish?

Somewhere in that hazy memory, Simon faded away, he was gone, but his body was still there . . . Shannon made it to the hospital before any of them. She knew the way.

Chapter/
eleven

OMELIA

The worms crawl in, the worms crawl out . . .

Omelia was being pulled towards wakefulness; she felt it as it approached, and she felt the other side of *this*. It stalked her like an angry goose. The first sign was that she started to hear the incessant *beep . . . beep . . . beep* of the machines. They came to her here where she slept in a world of low, low lying clouds. The stifled hospital room had turned into a milky fog-covered sky as she slept. The lights above her bed had transformed into the soft sun as it tried hard to burn its way through pain, time, and sickness to find her. The machines were all around her, one beeped irregularly, fast then slow, fast then slow . . . there were seconds that seemed to ache into tomorrow when it did not beep at all. It was in those blissful pauses that Omelia felt relief. It was then that she would open her eyes and see that milk-covered sun. She saw the fog and felt the way it made her skin turn cool and damp under the sheets. She could hear the beautiful silence, only to have it interrupted again.

Beep, beep, beep, silence, silence, beep.

There was something else in there with her as well, and it sounded like a stranger inside her body, one that breathed too loud. It was someone next to her, on top of her, inside her. Someone large enough to press their hand against her chest, they pushed it down, and then released, over and over. That heavy hand made her heart hurt. It made her feel like she never left that room with the two boys from the coffee house, it felt like she never made it to the payphone that morning, so long ago.

She was tired. She was too young to be this old.

She would linger like this, for what seemed like days, but she was sure it was just minutes, or maybe seconds of consciousness. The milky sky, the beautiful fog would burn away, and she felt it all, she felt the stiff cotton sheets against her skin, she felt her skin rubbed raw. She felt a long slender finger all the way down her throat. It stopped somewhere deep inside her. She felt the cool air of the room, the way it stung against her warm skin. She would try to look for Nurse Pugs, and then for Doctor Paul, but they were never there. She saw that she was alone, surrounded only with a plastic tent. It made everything look blurry and wet, if she could have touched it, her fingers would have come back sticky with morning dew; her world was bleary with condensation.

She felt like she was inside of a beach ball; everything was too bright, and too far away. She was able to turn her head back and forth a little, as if she were saying 'no' to a question not asked. As she moved her head, she felt something on her face. It seemed to have caught on something on the pillowcase, and she felt and heard a sound like Velcro being torn away. She could see the white pillowcase out of the corner of her eye; she saw a dark halo growing around. Her peripheral vision filled with a deep red with black tendrils. They floated on her blood like oil on water.

She must have made a sound, a muffled scream, a gasp muffled by a plastic tube and a ventilator. She heard the plastic beach ball she was in as it unzipped, and saw someone come into the cube, their eyes downturned, unable to look right at her. She felt the cool burn of something injected into her IV. She was almost back in the fog again, when she felt hands behind her head, her neck braced as she was lifted off the bloody pillow. There was a fresh one placed under her head. The other pillow, which was already beginning to darken to black, had become heavy, and stiff. It was placed in a bag that was sealed shut. She was being taken back into the fog when she saw the nurse write the words "Patient 474" on the label. Omelia tried to smile, but her face cracked and split around the tube in her mouth. She had always loved the numbers 4 and 7; they were her father's favorite.

She felt her chest relax, and she forgot about her skin, her face, her formerly beautiful face. She was back in the fog; her sweet buttermilk sky.

"What do you want to be? You know, when you're older." It was Meredith's voice; her husky, two packs of Pall Malls a day, low-cut blouse, wife number one voice. Omelia, who was still just Nicole then, had always thought that Meredith's voice sounded like the moment when the record changed in a jukebox—the way she talked just filled whoever was listening with static and anticipation.

"I don't know, I never really thought about being older. It was hard enough just to get to fifteen." Nicole had been living with Doctor Paul and Meredith for seven and a half months. She bounced around for almost a year in different foster homes, none of them a good fit, none of them a forever family. Meredith, who was a real bitch most of the time, could have been the most beautiful woman that Nicole had ever seen outside of a Vogue Magazine or a book cover, if only she had been happy.

"You know Paul may seem like a great guy most of the time, but you have to know he really is just like the rest of them, he just wants to look at something pretty," Meredith took a drag on her cigarette; she smoked 100's, and to Nicole they seemed long and glamourous. Meredith was the downtrodden Audrey Hepburn kind of 'wife number 1.' Too thin, too broken, and too hungry inside. Nicole, in the days before Omelia, never understood

Meredith's agenda, her games, and her deep sinking leach-field of a soul that would always collapse under too much pressure.

"This could be something we do together, just you and I kid, what do you say?" Meredith's smile felt like a trap with the juiciest of bait.

Nicole had not really listened; she just watched the ash of Meredith's cigarette as it burned away and still held its form. She watched it as it dangled over the carpet, danced on the ends of Meredith's acrylic nails. She taught Nicole things that she would understand when she was older. But for right now, Nicole only understood two things.

Smoking was cool, and being pretty was better than being . . .

"I don't know why we are bothering with this one; she was too far gone when they brought her in."

"I don't know, there are a few that have woken up now, the fever's gone and their sores . . . some of them are healed or at least starting to, I mean sure their faces are turned to shit, but . . . they're alive. That's something right?"

The room is silent as the Omelia body is shifted over, moved onto its side. The sharp cotton sheets jar her as they are pulled out from underneath her like a magician's trick. This would leave marks on her skin; she was sure of it, but no one will see them, they don't even look. Her sheets are covered in blood and are bagged and handed off to someone she didn't see, they might not even exist, not really. For a few seconds her body is on the plastic covering over her mattress.

Omelia liked the way the plastic felt on her skin, it was cool, detached; it doesn't feel like . . .

Nicole never had a grown woman pay any attention to her. Sure, she had her seventh-grade teacher who let her eat in the classroom after Nicole got a bad perm and the girls she normally ate lunch with threw peanuts and raisins at her. They were stuck in her new curly hair, and Nicole wished she had a peanut allergy so she could have gone to the hospital every time this happened. When Nicole tried to untangle them on the bus ride home, she realized what it would feel like to be ugly. Being ugly, she realized, might be the second worse thing she could have felt; the first would always be how it felt to have her mother's smile.

"You want to spend time with me?" Nicole said this and her voice went from fifteen years old to eight years old, just with the simple need in it.

"Of course, honey, we can spend time together, we just need to do something we both like, that's how we get to be girlfriends. Right? I mean it's not like I can be your mom, no matter how much he wants to be your dad." She laughed as she stubbed out her cigarette and then immediately lit two more cigarettes this time, she handed one to Nicole. When Meredith had said the word *mom*, Nicole saw her expression change. Meredith turned her face away from Nicole's and looked at herself in the reflection of the toaster. Meredith brought her hands to her face and with the palm and the side of her hands, she pulled her cheeks and eyes back. She pulled the skin so that it was taught towards her hairline. Her eyes squinted under the pressure.

"You look Oriental." Nicole giggled.

She felt Meredith's hand sting her cheek with a quick slap. The giggle had stopped when she felt Meredith's spittle land on her cheek and the corner of her mouth when Meredith said, "We don't say Oriental, we say Asian. An Oriental is a carpet." She took another long drag on her Pall Mall 100, the ash balanced on nothing, without a care in the world. "What you should have said is that when I did that it made me look younger." There was another drag on the cigarette, another aching pause as she exhaled, and let the smoke pool in front of her face before she inhaled again though her nose. Nicole hated how it looked but knew she should admire it anyway.

Meredith stared into the toaster again as she whispered, "This is why we have him, right?" Meredith giggled, and it was slow, quiet, and mean. She leaned across the kitchen table, like she was a waitress in a diner and gripped onto Nicole's chin as she looked into her eyes. "Did I ever tell you, I was crowned Miss Mill Yard when I was your age?" Meredith said this, but she didn't let go; she kept her fingers on Nicole's face, her eyes locked in hers. The fingers gripped tighter, and they tugged Nicole's mouth open a little, making Nicole's expression look both bewildered and scared. Meredith mocked the look on her face before she finally released her fingers. Nicole's chin had two red welts in the shape of Meredith's forefinger and thumb.

Nicole went to school the next day with purple bruises on her skin that looked like abuse. Her New Hampshire History teacher made her stay after class. He pleaded with Nicole to tell him if someone had hurt her . . . he asked if it was her father. Nicole had said nothing. She just shook her head no. Her eyes filled with tears as she left the room, her textbooks held tight against her chest like a shield.

There was no father.

There was hurt, but how was she supposed to say the words, form them, feel them? She didn't know. This was not one of the things Meredith had taught her.

During school hours, Nicole tried to be invisible through the early parts of ninth grade. By the second part of 10th grade, she spent a lot of her lunch hours on a rusted-out fire escape with the same teacher who asked her if she was being abused . . . they would both smoke cigarettes, Marlboro Reds. They burned Nicole's throat every time she inhaled. It felt terrible, but it felt real, the same way it did when she would dig her fingernails into the palm of her hands until she carved four half-moons in each palm. Her teacher never asked her questions again; they only sat silently on the fire escape. Every once in a while, one of them would scratch their finger along the metal ladders that led to nowhere, the rusted flakes building up under their fingernails before raining down onto the alley below.

It was beautiful. The rust flakes changed with the day.

It rained rose petals one moment.

It rained blood the next.

It was all in the mood, the emotion they brought to their silence, their nicotine lunch hour. Nicole learned something or thought she did . . . she knew she did not have much to give in this world; she could be smart, or she could be pretty. She wanted to be both, but she didn't know how.

There was nothing in her life that led to this rusted fire escape that told her she could be both. Most of the time, Nicole was a hole, too deep for anything to grow, and too shallow to find something special like gold.

Nicole and Meredith spent afterschool hours, before Dr. Paul got home, in preparation for the talent portion of her first pageant. ". . . and five, six, seven, eight . . . C'mon Nicole! Step, kick, step, kick, step, ball change." Meredith did the choreography herself, she spun, her arms reached up towards the sky and then, "Wrap, wrap, then right hand on the hip, then left hand on the hip…" Meredith did all the moves; her tits were out, chest pointed forward, so brave.

A girl fighting a bull.

Meredith's voice shook as she tried to mock the first notes of the songs . . . Nicole's song . . . a song too mature for her years . . .

"The minute you walked in the joint . . ." Meredith's hips bumped for the music that came after that. She reached over to the CD player and hit pause on the instrumental track of 'Hey Big Spender.' "Now you do it," She collapsed onto the red corduroy recliner. She lit another Pall Mall 100. The ashtray next to her had already started to overflow. Meredith had to aim just right to find somewhere to ash her cigarette. It was beautiful yellow and blue glass, the bottom was engraved with 'Murano, Italy.' Nicole thought that ashtray was one of the most sophisticated things she had ever seen. She had looked up Murano in the Encyclopedia and had to stifle a scream when she found out it was an island in the Venetian Canal. It made the ashtray, whether it was filled with cigarette butts or not, even more beautiful.

Meredith flicked some of her ash onto the coral-colored shag carpet.

It hugged the cigarette ember as if it were a beloved first born. When it burned into nothing, it left a little scar on the carpet, like Nicole's half-moon from the chipmunk bite. Nicole reached up and traced the scar. When she closed her eyes, she saw her father's face, when he looked at her school photo. She heard the rhythm of his body as it still swayed, fresh in death when she found him. He told her not to go upstairs, but she did. Now she remembered the way the peanuts and raisins felt when she untangled them from her hair as she gently let them fall onto the floor of the school bus before it dropped her off at the convenience store near her house. This was where the poor kids were picked up for school.

All of these things lived in that small scar, all the faded memories worked over her body. When her fingertips touched it, she could read her story like it was braille. It all played in her head like an old movie reel. All the moments flowed together at once. She dropped her hand and opened her eyes. She heard Meredith count her in . . . ". . . and five, six, seven, eight." Nicole opened her mouth, and she sang. She was not great, but in her heart, she knew, if she just tried a little harder, she could be more than just pretty.

It was hard to dance on the shag carpet, and the walls in their condo were too close for real reverb. The echo of song bounced back to her before she could get to the next line. The more she sang and danced, the echoes started to sound like a *beep . . . beep . . .* and she could hear her breath, moving even and mechanical, moving in time with the *beep, beep, beep.*

As she danced, the living room changed color in front of her eyes and started to be lit with fluorescent lights. The air around her smelled like disinfectant. It smelled like two different kinds of lemon.

Omelia had already started to claw her way to consciousness again. The fever burned the sedatives out of her system every time she got to the part in her memory when she sang, and maybe next time she would skip this part, and go right to when they put the crown on her head. Maybe she would be able to stay there in that moment forever; maybe she would never have to remember what came next.

Chapter/ twelve

SAM

I love this little bird.

Simon's heart had stopped by the time the ambulance had arrived at the school. Santo Anthony Alberti and Gretchen took turns doing chest compressions as the boy's mother chain smoked a few feet outside their small circle until she broke down. Sam held the woman while she sobbed and screamed; he felt that there was something off about her behavior. *Too theatrical*. He felt her press herself into his body in a way that was both seductive and animal. He was reminded of the character of Blanche Dubois, who was always portrayed with a visceral emotional hunger. He felt that in this woman's borderline hysterical embrace. She felt dangerous and smelled like sour secondhand smoke and barbeque chips.

He didn't know why the thought came into his head, but all he could think was that she smelled like old wallpaper.

The second time that the woman, that he found out was named Melody, pressed herself into him, he felt her fingers play against his back. It reminded him of a cat *making biscuits*. He looked down at her and saw that even though she was making loud crying noises, her face was dry; her glittery blue eyeshadow and thick mascara that was clumped like tarantula legs still lay thick on her eyes. Her foundation had started to cake and had turned orange since morning, but there were no tear marks, no streaks of sadness.

Though, who was he to judge grief? He had been grieving his whole life and he was still terrible at it.

The mother, Melody, didn't ask to ride in the ambulance with her son; instead, she let it leave without her. She held onto Sam's hand as she watched it speed down the road, ignoring the 20MPH School Zone signs. The lights were on and the sirens blared as the vehicle turned the corner and faded away. Sam closed his eyes and listened to the siren, and he could swear that somewhere in that cacophony he could hear Shannon's bell; it cried out for attention.

Once the ambulance was out of site, Melody looked at Sam; her bony hand squeezed his as she looked up at him and said, "I'll see you at the hospital." Her voice sounded bored, and tired; she was the type of woman that woke up tired every day, and always would.

Sam had not thought that he would accompany anyone anywhere that day, but as she said it, it was as if it had already been decided; he nodded yes and knew there was nowhere else he could be. The media circled his father and Gretchen; they both beamed with humble smiles and shook their heads no when the crowd called them both heroes. They brushed off the words that they heard, the words that said, "If that boy does live, it will be because of both of you." In this moment Sam realized he got what he had wanted all along: he got a story bigger than himself. The sleazy words that went out on the news station Twitter feeds were eclipsed the moment that Simon had made that startled choking. By the time the boy collapsed a few seconds later, Sam was now the ghost. The cameras didn't pan over to him as he walked away from the crowd and made his way towards the black Mercedes. Sam half-expected to find George asleep again, but instead saw that the man had waited outside the car. The old man had kept an eye on Sam the entire morning.

Sam didn't notice that when George stepped away from the car, he left two nearly perfect handprints on the driver's side door; he also didn't hear the man as a violent coughing jag took over his body. Sam was in the backseat, already putting his earbuds in before his door closed. Sam didn't see the dark blue-black tendril that George had to spit out onto the sidewalk. Instead, he saw George wipe his mouth on the hanky he kept in his pocket, and then get into the front seat of the car, nothing unusual there. George reached for a bottle of water in the passenger seat, his hands shaking. He took a large sip of the water that had grown warm under the morning sun and swished it around in his mouth before he swallowed it.

There was a disgusted and pained expression on George's face, and not just because his throat was rough like dried hay, but the water that he cleaned his mouth with tasted bitter, like a dirty penny and mushrooms from the darkest part of the woods. George turned around, reached over the seat, and rested his hand on Sam's leg to get his attention. He was out of breath as he said, "You okay Eagle?" His voice that sounded ephemeral. As if his words had already become a memory. Sam could almost hear every moment that he had spent with this man turn to brittle paper and then to dust.

Sam took his earbuds out and said, "I'm fine, this isn't about me, it's about him." He paused. "I need to get to Boston Children's Hospital."

"Okay Eagle." George turned around but still eyed Sam in the rearview mirror. He saw the boy in him. The same hooked nose and angular face. The same fierce determination to not feel anything that he would go to any length to run from. But today, here he was, his Sam the Eagle, he ran right towards it, headed right for heartbreak. George knew that if Sam had to watch another eleven-year-old die that he may never recover. He saw it in his eyes as they stared out the window. He could tell Sam didn't see the school and the crowd of reporters as they faded like a dream. He could sense that Sam saw past all of that: he saw all the way to a night almost 24 years ago. Sam's bottom lip started to tremble; he bit his lip then, so hard that it bled. Sam wiped the lonely trickle of blood onto the backseat of the car.

Sam stared out the window, as the neighborhood around him blurred away. He said, "George, I don't know how many times I can watch an eleven-year-old die . . ."

Yes, it was as if George had been able to read his mind. He knew Eagle better than anyone left alive. "You'll do the best you can." George tried to catch Sam's eyes in the mirror, but he couldn't make his eyes focus. The car rolled past a church, with its bells chiming that it was now eleven am.

The paramedics had not known when they put the boy's body into the back of the vehicle, if there was anything else that they would be able to do for him. The two men were in Hazmat gear, they knew when they got the call that it sounded like one of the infected. The paramedics had already started to refer to it as *Interitus*, which was Latin, and it meant ruin, rot, and an untimely death.

No one was sure exactly what it was, but people all up and down the East and West Coast had it, and all anyone in the past twenty-four hours could do was watch the numbers rise as this dark creature crept towards the flyover states, through the cornfields and into Middle America. Over half of Boston's Emergency Medical Units didn't show up for work today. Anyone who could was headed as far inland as possible, as if it would help . . .

Because of a lot of the call-offs, the ambulance wait time sometimes stretched for close to a half hour. They heard rumors of smaller cities and up into the other states of New England that had emergency wait times for hours. Many of the patients were dead by the time ambulances arrived, but they had heard rumors of some patients that snapped out of it after eight or twelve hours. But seeing as they were all only seventy-two hours into this nightmare, where the sleep paralysis nightmares were real . . . it was too early to say anything.

All they could say was, Interitus.

Rot.

Ruin.

Untimely death.

It was a masculine noun if that mattered at all.

The Emergency Room RN's who had seen it all said it was new *leprosy*, which was bullshit, as this was obviously a virus of some kind; it wasn't bacterial, people were catching it . . . some of the paramedics that came in from the night shift said it looked like the patients had been in a war, their faces half blown off. "Naw, it's not Leprosy, it's more like Herpes, or Ebola . . . Some germ warfare shit," while others whispered that they heard the ER doctors at Brigham and Women's say that it was some kind of new Meningitis, that it had attached itself to the Herpes Simplex, and that, "anyone who had any kind of autoimmune disease or allergy was fucked."

Simon has eczema, asthma, and Celiac disease. None of these should kill you, until it does.

The paramedics that rode in back with Simon had hammered his chest the entire way to Boston Children's Hospital; they felt his broken ribs as they performed chest compressions until they finally got a heart rhythm back. It was still unsteady and fluttered like a bird with a broken wing, but after defib shocks every two minutes it was there, like the echo of a pebble on a long dried out well.

The BVM mask seemed to be holding the blood in around the boy's mouth, and every few minutes it would slip off as it lost suction and slid over the lower part of his face that had started to peel away. By the time they pulled into the ER bay, everyone that was in the back of that ambulance was covered in a dark black blood that thickened to tar when the ambulance doors opened, and they were all met with the cool October air.

Ken, the paramedic that had worked on the drive to get the heart rhythm back, was shocked to see that it was still day, it was not even noon. Somewhere in the back of his mind, he thought that if an eleven-year-old is in heart failure, it should be something that happened at night, when no one was looking, not something that happened in the middle of a late Saturday morning, in front of CNN and all the local media. Paramedic Ken wondered if they would replay this on the nightly news, and he felt sick inside at the idea of this boy's death going viral on YouTube. As they wheeled the boy into the ER, he took his face shield off and without a thought, went back into the ambulance to start to clean up.

Hospital time is different from real time; Sam remembered this from his childhood, the afternoons that whiled away like a drowsy bored summer vacation, clocks that always seemed to click back and forth in the same spot. They were always yesterday, and today. In the years that his milk teeth fell out and were replaced with his grown-up teeth, and his face was awkward and looked like it had been painted in all the wrong directions, like a Picasso painting, he sat at Shannon's bedside. They played games they never had at home: Othello, which she always won, Chess, which she always won, Crazy Eights, which was hit or miss, Mah Jong, which he never understood . . . eventually their game became Cribbage. It was the only one where he stood a fighting chance against her. Sam had somehow soaked the game in while sitting silently in the room. His grandmother on his mother's side, and his mother, they never looked at the children, only at their cards. They clinked the ice in their empty glasses.

Shannon was always up first, eager to please, eager to get to those cherries. Sam had always been too busy watching the game; he tried to understand the doubles, and all the ways to get to fifteen.

Numbers were easier than words for him, even though it was words he loved more.

Now, at eleven-forty-eight in the morning, he didn't have games as he paced though the labyrinthine set of blue, too-small-for-his-body chairs that clogged up the ER waiting room. The walls were painted in soothing tones of English Water Garden, and every time he looked at them, he heard the ocean, and smelled cherries, two kinds of lemon, and Baby Soft Perfume. Melody had gotten there before him, and when he got here, she was still in the waiting room. She immediately asked him for five dollars so she could get a Diet Cherry Coke and a Milky Way Dark from the vending machine in the corner by the bathroom. Sam didn't usually carry cash, but he did have an emergency fifty tucked behind the condom in his wallet. She promised she would go get some change and come right back.

He knew she saw the condom when he handed her the cash, and her eyes reminded him of a stray cat that is willing to eat a slice of cheese right out of someone's hand. She headed down the hall and towards the elevator; it was the opposite direction of the vending machines, which were tucked near the bathroom. He wasn't sure if she would come back. She had a wild look to her, and the scabs near her mouth made her look like she spent a fair share of her time on one end of a glass pipe.

When he thought about those sores on her face, he started to feel it—the hum in the air that seemed to pulse a beat off time with his heart. It overwhelmed him. He felt the heat rise from the small of his back and walk like a spider up his spine. When it got to the back of his neck, it held on tight, each of the little eight legs was a pinprick of fear. That was when the flop sweat started, less than a minute into a panic attack. He walked back towards the front desk, somehow while he paced, he had cornered himself in the middle of the kids' play section. He kicked the table with the little Amish style wooden trainset, and the blocks fell to the floor like a building collapsing in a fire. He used the hand sanitizer at the desk; he rubbed the watered-down disinfectant all the way up to his elbows as if he were prepared to perform a back-alley abortion. He took a couple more pumps and rubbed it on the back of his neck. The alcohol made his skin sing, and for a second he felt the temperature in the room drop. The air felt cool around him and there was hope that he could get through this endless day.

Shannon spent months here, in this hospital. It was just 12 minutes with no traffic from the brownstone in Back Bay. Her room had a spaceship theme. Shannon always hated science fiction.

No. He couldn't go there.

She died at home though, yes, so that was better right?

That was better for all of them.

He thought he heard a brass bell somewhere, but it wasn't that. It was a siren, and then a few seconds after that there was another, and then another. Many of the ambulances waited in the lot, bodies fumbling around inside as they tried to bring dead children back to life.

Simon was in one of those ambulances that waited, that tried.

Sam breathed deep and the corners of the English Water Garden painted walls started to get dark, and mossy. Black vines crept in from the edges. He needed to sit. He decided on the closest seat to the door and the desk. The place where the automatic doors would rush open and closed anytime someone walked near them. The little blue chair was narrow, and it hugged his hips as he sat there. It was too close to the ground.. His knees seemed to come up and almost cover his face. If he let his arms and hands relax, they would graze the floor. It would happen if he could just relax and breathe into it; breathe into the slouch that was his life.

He was too big for this . . . He had been here so many times before, and he had felt the opposite way, that this place, this hospital had been too big for him, and too big for Shannon. Shannon had grown smaller and smaller every day. She would have been lost in these blue chairs. These chairs were made to hold a sick child. The parents were never meant to sit in these chairs, they were only ever made to pace between them, get lost in their labyrinth of uncomfortable blue worry. That's when he remembered, Shannon never sat in these chairs, she was always rushed here, with a "direct to bed." Shannon never had to wait, she never had to drown in these chairs, the same ones that strangled Sam now.

"Trauma Three, Code Blue, incoming, 90 seconds," the speakers crackled like an old radio announcement about World War II. Sam stood up, and even though he knew he had no real place there, he understood this is where he had to be. He thought he felt a small hand in his, a hand that gave a squeeze and then was gone. He was facing the doors to the parking lot, and he saw an ambulance scream into the lot. What was going to be expected of him?

He's never known.

He could smell Melody before he heard her; it was as if a CVS perfume display rack had become sentient. He's no expert at CVS, he only goes there for condoms, and sometimes deodorant when he runs out of the $28 kind that he buys so it doesn't clog his pineal gland. The fanciest of the cheap perfume is always kept close to the counter though, and he knows the smell.

Melody. He hated the smell, but it also reminded him of condoms, sex, and the ways he knew how to run from feelings.

Melody doesn't bother to give him back the change from his fifty, and if she had heard the alert as it crackled from the sound system, she hasn't shown it. When he turned to her, he saw that her arms were full. She had a huge cup from Starbucks with a Milky Way Dark balanced on top. He could see the Cherry Coke, not diet, sticking out of her purse. "Did you know they already started making peppermint eggnog lattes? I thought they waited until after Turkey Day. I thought I would be stuck with pumpkin spice." She holds the cup in one hand; the candy bar balanced like a seesaw on top of her to-go lid. "Oh and look what I found." She awkwardly pulled a Tweety Bird stuffed animal out of her purse, the Cherry Coke almost fell to the floor, but she caught it on her thigh and nudged it back into her bag. "I'm gonna hang this little guy from my car mirror, he's perfect." She smiled at Sam, and for a few seconds he knew that at one time, she was beautiful, and now she was this, now she is a tired version of herself, she was nachos cooked in the microwave. "I love this little bird . . ." The light in her eyes dimmed a little. The smile over the stuffed animal stayed the same, but the feeling never made it past her teeth. She looked like a haunted puppet in a tunnel ride at the second-rate amusement park he went on during that summer his family spent in New Hampshire after Shannon and his Nonna died. His non-Italian summer.

"Code Blue, I repeat Code Blue" This comes through the speakers; it's static and it's inevitable movement at the same time.

A young woman from the check-in counter leaned towards them, masks, and medical gloves in her hands. She gestured to them, like a tourist with a map in a foreign country. "Sir, Ma'am, your son is being brought in."

Chapter/
thirteen

"**Y**ou're a fucking asshole!" Meredith shouted as she followed Paul up the stairs of their condo. Her steps were heavy with the weight of a thousand little disappointments. Her movements could be heard even through the thick carpet. Paul, who was at least 60lbs heavier than she was, barely made a sound as he moved. He gave off an air of quiet disgust. He had not tried to engage with her as he could tell when he walked in that she had been drinking most of the afternoon. He saw Nicole's eyes when he got home from work, and they looked bleary and out of focus. She and Meredith had been sitting on the floor, their shoulders were close as they leaned towards each other and looked through fashion magazines. Next to Nicole, there were stacks of pages she ripped out of them. Models, makeup, and headlines about sex . . . Nicole kept all of these ripped out pages in a box that a dress shirt had been wrapped in last Christmas.

Nicole had become a stranger to him over the past four months. When he caught her out of the corner of his eye, he would always think she was someone else at first, and though they were not related, Nicole was starting to look, and act, like Meredith. He never saw her without makeup these days, even first thing in the morning when she would come down for breakfast; well, breakfast was an exaggeration, when she came down for a cup of black coffee. Meredith had allowed Nicole to smoke as well, though she was not allowed to do it in the house. Nicole had skirted this rule every morning. She would crack the sliding glass door that led to their small deck and stuck the hand that held the cigarette outside into the cool morning air. She smoked with her right hand and held the coffee against her chest to keep warm with her left. The steam from the cup would fog up the windows, and when she was done with her before school smoke, she would close the door, doodle a sad face in the fog, and then be on her way to school.

She glared at him a lot these days; actually, both women did, and he didn't understand why. He knew he should ask, but he could never do it, never build up the courage to form the words. Nicole had lost about 15lbs in the past couple of months. At first, he thought it was because of the hours she spent rehearsing for her pageants, but then there were the few times during their rare family meals that she excused herself in the middle of dinner. Their condo was small, and both he and Meredith could hear Nicole as she threw up in the bathroom in the downstairs hallway. He never mentioned that to her either. He had tried to bring it up to Meredith, but she brushed it off, said it was a phase, that "All girls go through it. They're bulimic for a few months, they're druggies for a few months, they're cutters for a few months, they're sluts for a few months . . ." She had likened it to trying on different outfits to see which one fit.

Paul didn't want any of those outfits to fit Nicole. He just didn't know how to say that.

Paul tuned to Meredith, right before they headed into their bedroom upstairs. "Did she go to school today Mere?"

"We were busy today; she has the Miss Maple Pageant on Saturday. She needed to focus on that. YOU know how important it is to her, this is her future."

"No, Meredith I know how important this is to *you*, I don't know anything about Nicole anymore." Paul glanced at the framed school portrait they had of Nicole that hung in their upstairs hallway. It was the last one she had done before her father had died. The social worker had found it in her home and had given it to Paul; he had it framed and gave it to Nicole for Christmas. He loved this photo of her; the only picture he had seen with her real smile. She looked happy, her smile was crooked, and her eyes squinted a little, especially her left one. Any time he had tried to take a photo of her in the months that she had been living with them she had simply stared deadpan into the camera. Her eyes were alive but wounded. She reminded him of a Victorian photo, a girl with haunted eyes who didn't have the energy to smile.

"The school calls me every time she doesn't show up, they let it go a lot, they know her history, but she's missed two days a week in the past month, sometimes three. We can't keep doing this."

"What do you mean *we*? Where is *we* here? You are at work, and I am the one here with her, I take care of her. *You* get to leave." Meredith's voice was raised, and her breath smelled sour and wintery like juniper. Meredith was always the type of woman who talked loudly; she always wanted an audience. This argument, this wasn't for Paul, this was for Nicole, downstairs. This argument was just another reason for Nicole not to smile, another thing to put in her cardboard box with all the torn-out magazine pages. It was just another ripped out dream. "You should be lucky I found something she and I can do together, you're never here, and you were the one that wanted her. I didn't want her." She said that last part in a whisper.

"We are not going to have this conversation again Meredith. We made the decision together; you can't take that back now. You can't go back and make another choice, it's our life. It's not a, Choose Your Own Adventure novel."

Meredith swayed a little on her feet and braced herself against the doorjamb. "You're such a jealous, petty little man. You think I don't see what this is? You wanted to be some big hero, but the truth is, you're like your dad, you're a shitty father who only ever liked the idea of being one. When you couldn't be Nicole's hero, you just gave up. You got bored. Now, you can't stand it that she and I are close, you wanted to be the good one here, but you're not, I am, and you hate me for it." She paused and waited for him to respond, but he didn't, he soaked it in. "*She* doesn't need you." With that, Meredith turned around to leave the room, and her shoulder slammed into the doorframe and she ricocheted like a pinball to the other side of the hallway. Right before she was about to stumble, her hand shot up and clipped the corner of the picture frame, which sent the photo of Nicole's smile crashing to the floor.

The glass broke, like a spider web growing from the corner of the frame. Paul heard Meredith chuckle a little when it happened and she said, "It's a good thing it broke, she hates that photo you know? Besides, we have better ones now; she looks like a completely different person." Meredith held onto the railing as she walked down the stairs, being extra careful as people do when they have realized too late that they are drunk.

Paul hated to raise his voice, hated to be the shouting angry man his father had always been, but he realized he had yelled, and it was already too late. "You're a mean drunk, Meredith."

Meredith yelled up at him from the bottom of the stairs through aching bitter laughter that sounded like licorice. "You're the one who made me mean, asshole."

Nicole just sat on the floor, listened, and soaked it all in. Her face was solemn; scattered around her were stacks of her favorite models, and her favorite magazines. Issues of Vogue from Italy were her favorite. The models looked like live versions of the book covers she loved so much; the Gothic horror novels her father let her buy at the flea market near their house. The man that sold them to her had a bright green parakeet on his shoulder, and he let her have the books 10 for a dollar. He knew her father, and every time he saw Nicole, he would tell her how much she reminded him of her mother, and "what a shame it was," that she was gone.

Those books, they filled her with grief and horror when she looked at them, but even more than that, they filled her with a longing. A beautiful woman as she ran from a house . . . that was what Nicole had always wanted to be.

She opened her mouth to say something as Meredith made her way through their living room, but Meredith lifted a finger, pointed at Nicole, and whispered, "Not a fucking word from you, not now." She grabbed the gin and the pack of cigarettes that were on the coffee table, along with an afghan that was tossed over the back of the couch. Meredith draped that around her shoulders like a cape and headed outside to sit alone on the deck.

Nicole thought that Paul would come down, as he had just come home from work, and none of them had eaten; neither she nor Meredith had made anything. She got up from the floor and walked halfway up the stairs before she saw it, her school photo, the one with her mother's smile had been knocked from the wall. The door to Paul and Meredith's room was closed. She walked backwards down the stairs, keeping her eye on his closed door; and it reminded her of walking up the stairs to another closed door, almost two full years ago now. Every time Nicole saw a closed door, she saw him, her father, and the gentle comforting way his body still swayed when she walked in the room. She remembered the beautiful musicality of the beam that creaked overhead. She remembered the way his urine had dripped down his pant leg, caught on the rim of his work boot, and then hit the floor with a permanence.

Drip.

Creak.

Drip.

Creak.

Closed doors were why she was afraid to go to school some mornings, too many stairways, long hallways, and closed doors.

His body had still been warm. She had touched his hand with just the tips of her fingers. She left the room, closed the door, and crossed the little hallway to her room and did her makeup. Her hands shook the entire time, and she went through half a container of baby wipes as she wiped off each failed attempt at lipstick and eyeliner before she finally got it right. By the time she looked at her reflection and saw someone else, she knew she was ready to make the call. She went back into his room, the swaying had long ceased, and the urine no longer hit the floor with a loud drip. It had all stopped . . . she reached up and touched his body. This time it was cold.

Nicole stepped over the piles of Vogue Magazine scraps that were piled in a semi-circle around her. Meredith was always after her to hang up the important ones on her inspiration board, but Nicole couldn't do that, she couldn't look at a corkboard on a shitty condo wall and see her future, what she wanted, what she needed was it to be in a book that she could page through at night. She needed something to do in the slowed-down minutes after midnight before the booze and the Benadryl finally took over for the caffeine pills and Diet Coke that sustained her during the day.

She knew that Paul, for some reason, was always given bottles of low-end Scotch and Crown Royal every year for Christmas from his patients. She knew he kept all of these in the bottom drawer of the old metal filing cabinet that was tucked next to the desk in the corner. Paul, who didn't drink, for reasons he had always been too polite to mention, would accept these gifts with a smile and he would place them in the drawer as soon as he got home. Sometimes they were still in their gift bags, adorned with shiny premade bows. The one that was attached to the small bottle of Dewar's that she took out looked as if a cat had played with it. The ends of the ribbons were frayed and appeared chewed.

Nicole hated Scotch. To her, it tasted like the time she was at a party, and someone had ditched their cigarette in her whiskey and coke. She took a huge sip before she saw the cigarette butt; she reached in and tossed it away.

She realized she was too embarrassed to ask for a new drink or even to cross the crowded living room to make herself another one. So, she drank it as it was, and grimaced in between forced laughter.

Nicole, like the cheap Scotch, was smoky, bitter, sad, and trying way too hard to be better than what it was. It was the story of her now 15-year-old, two beauty pageants' winning life. She took another sip, and her eyes watered from the taste. That was when she saw it, tucked at the back of the file cabinet drawer, sandwiched between bottles of booze and empty file folders. It was an old photo album. The cover was a plastic pleather that had started to crack along the edges like scorched earth. It had gold ornate scrolls that were all but worn away. The album looked old, and she wondered if it was filled with dorky photos of Paul when he was a kid. At any rate, this old album would be the perfect place for her magazine pages.

She walked back to the coffee table, with the Scotch and the photo album tucked under her arm. She didn't know why, but she walked quietly, as if her bare feet on the shag carpet would disturb Meredith, who was still outside, drinking gin straight from the bottle, chain smoking, and shivering from rage and the cold. That old afghan did not seem to help her at all. Paul did not seem like he was coming down at all tonight. Nicole took a swig of the Scotch, her cheeks puffed out and the smoky brown liquid stayed in her mouth. She tried to swallow but just couldn't do it; this happened sometimes. Her social worker had told her it was panic. Just at the moment she thought she would have to open her mouth and spit out the booze, she relaxed enough to let a little of it down her throat, and it was disgusting. She fought the rest of it down a few seconds later. There was a moment when she thought that she would throw up, as she felt the fire burn back up her throat, and her mouth filled with saliva.

Nicole had amazing self-control over when she chose to vomit. Over the past few months, it had become a sacred ritual to her. The best thing that Meredith had taught her was to purge herself after she ate. She had said that it was the only way that Nicole wouldn't get fat, and if Nicole wanted to waste calories, then she should save it for the cocktails . . . it was more fun. She took another small sip from the bottle, and she thought she heard Paul as he moved around upstairs, but when she listened closer, she realized it wasn't Paul, it sounded instead like a creak, and then underneath that, there was a drip. It sounded like a closed door . . .

The more Dewar's she had, the easier it was to go down. Her sips got bigger; this time her mouth filled, and her cheeks puffed out, but she was able to get it down. The panic started to blur. Her arms and legs hurt when she drank too much, but it was a small price to pay, and her heart hurt worse than that when she didn't. She leaned back against the couch; her legs folded under herself. If she closed her eyes, she could almost sleep.

Creak.

Drip.

Creak.

She took another sip from the bottle.

She remembered the cigarette butt.

In the back of her mind, she heard her father whisper that when she smiled, she looked "just like her mother."

Creak.

Drip.

She opened the green photo album . . .

Interlude/

If a Book Could Talk
Pictures of You

For most of the time, before the girl got curious about the booze, I lived, mostly forgotten, in the bottom of the filing cabinet. My green pleather cover with gilded gold designs sat sleepy and dusty tucked behind and underneath several years of bad gifts. From where I sat, long ignored, I could hear her, the young stranger that came to live in this house. The girl that turned the two, into three. She was brought here to make up for something that was already starting to fade . . .

She ignored me at first, the first few times she snuck into the drawer, hungry for something that she didn't understand.

She knew, of course, that I was filled with photos, but as a teenager, and as an only child she was not curious about me. I was the book that held relics of the time before her. The time when they were not a man, a woman, and a foster kid; it was a time before three, a time of two. A time of before, when she belonged to someone else, and she was part of a two, not a three.

I can't be sure what made her finally see me today. I am not much to look at, my façade coated with thick dust that is sticky with time and stale metallic air. She rubbed my cover against her little plaid skirt. The dark navy tartan, it is her school uniform. She didn't go to school today, but she wore it anyway, like a costume. She flips through my plastic pages, my cellophane-like sheets, which are barely sticky now; they hardly seem to cling to the yellowed cardboard. Some of them shake loose as she flips through my pages, and photos fall to the floor and the cellophane makes a sound like a bird as it learns to fly.

There are years inside this book, and flashes of things she cannot believe are real. She sees Paul who smiles and was painfully sunburned. His skin was vibrant red with raw pale patches where the skin had already started to peel away. He wore shorts and his bare feet were covered in white sand. She saw Meredith in a bikini, her hand perched on her hip and she held a cigarette; the ocean behind her looked like an ad for a resort. Meredith's smile showed too many teeth. The water is a brilliant turquoise, and not the dark gray of the beaches in New Hampshire. This beach exists in a dream, a memory that doesn't belong to her.

It's not her life; it's not her photo.

The girl remembered that Paul had whispered to her once that he married Meredith because she looked "just like a young Elizabeth Taylor." The girl never understood that. It was such a strange old-fashioned reference, she never saw Liz Taylor in Meredith, until now.

The photos make the underside of her heart flutter and then ache, the same way it does when she thought of her school photo, the one with the smile. The two people in this book are already strangers to her. She doesn't ask permission. Instead, she takes the photos out, places them in a pile on the floor, and for a reason that she is years away from beginning to understand, she is angry at them, and she is angry at herself for coming along, for ruining their smiles, their day drinking on the beach, and their long road trips to Florida.

She has never seen Paul have a sunburn; they had gone to the beach once after she first came here, but since then she has never been anywhere with him further than the grocery store. Meredith wears a bikini now, but only on the deck, where she falls asleep on a lawn chair reading sex articles in old issues of Cosmopolitan.

Summer sun, Valium, and gin.

Now, Meredith must be shaken awake "before Paul comes home."

The girl shook the photos from my pages. The ones that are not easily freed she pries from the cardboard pages; their backs are sticky. They cling to me, these photos that don't want to let go of where they belong, these memories; they are only treasured here. Nicole puts the pictures of their past in a box that still has tape residue and fingerprints of Christmas wrapping paper that cling to the sides. This is the box her magazine clippings have been in, and now they in turn fill me up. She is angry that my cellophane pages do not cradle her prized possessions and hold them tight to my chest with love. My pages were never meant for her. She is angry that the yellowed cardboard pages still hold the scars of the time when Paul and Meredith were happy. Scars that she didn't even know should exist.

Their happiness is a betrayal and a whispered confession.

She looks at the models from the magazines now inside of me, and I don't know why, but she cries.

I wish she had never found me.

Chapter/ fourteen

SAM
It's Flannel Season

She had wrapped her hand around his wrist, and he realized he was being pulled along with her, the current of this day had pulled him under, and swept him further and further out and away. That had to be why he was here, wasn't it, why he had ended up in the hospital with them to begin with. Right?

There was nowhere for him to stand, or to be. He didn't belong in this cramped hospital room with Simon and his mother; it was already too crowded with doctors, with machines. The walls were painted with an underwater scene; there were large fish with strange leering eyes. Sam found them unsettling.

The boy seemed even smaller now. His face seemed to shrink under the plastic mask, his body dwarfed by the nurses and doctors that cut his clothes away. They attached little electrodes on his chest and on parts of his legs. One of the nurses tossed his bloody clothes towards the corner of the room; the jacket and shirt landed close to Sam, who stood half in and half out of the room. A voice that doesn't belong to anyone with a face says, "Someone bag that, we need to send it to the CDC." No one does it; no one *bags it*. The sleeve to the boy's Boston Red Sox jacket had filthy cuffs, a mixture of general eleven-year-old-boy grubbiness, and blood that had been coughed into his sleeve over the past couple days. That was a secret little Simon had not told anyone. The jacket reached out into the hallway, towards Sam's half-hidden vantage point in the doorway. He stepped away and leaned on the frame outside of the room. The sleeve still reached for him, but now thankfully it was out of eyeshot.

He hated hospitals. He leaned his head against the wall and breathed in, and out, the hallway leaned in around him, this hallway and this entire day felt like falling downstairs. Everything around the edges of the hallway grew darker. He felt a nurse walk by him and her gloved hand slapped a sticker on his chest. He knows what it is without having to open his eyes; it's a visitor sticker. It says he belongs here; he belongs to room number . . . he opens his eyes and peels the sticker off his sweater. He belongs to room number 7.

It was Shannon's favorite number. Her brass bell can be heard underneath Simon's heart monitor. A nurse started to cry at the nurse's station. He heard her say, "We just lost another one, he was only four." She wiped the tears away from her eyes and then turned around because she felt like she was being watched. Sam closed his eyes as fast as he could, he felt guilty like he was caught reading someone's journal or a stack of letters found in his mother's bureau. He placed the sicker back on his sweater, he pressed down hard on it. He realized that he doesn't want it to fall off, he doesn't want to be the man in the hospital hallway that doesn't belong to anyone, and he wants to belong to room number 7.

He had not belonged anywhere for a long time.

He could hear Melody crying; it is high-pitched and seems to be caught in her throat, a keening wail. She shrieked instead of talked, sounding like two sheets of sandpaper that have rubbed themselves raw against each other. He peeked in the room. The doctors and nurses have all surrounded Simon, and it reminds Sam of the Wise Men in the antique Nativity scene his parents would put out every Christmas. They all pretended to be Catholics during the major holidays. Melody has been pushed aside, she is outside of them now, in the manger she would be the donkey. Sam realizes this made him the camel; the strange-shaped figure that was too big for the manger, it was always placed on the outside. He remembered his mother putting her cocktail down on the mantel right next to the camel. The brown liquid was the same color as that unruly beast.

Sam reached in and tugged at Melody's sleeve; he started to whisper to her even before she turned around, "I'll be right back, I need to tell my driver to head home, that I'll be here a while." There is a pause, and an anxiousness like someone fearful of a birthday balloon popping. He pulled at his sweater and showed Melody the room sticker; he said "I'll be back. I belong to room 7 now." He chuckled a little and hated himself.

"You have a fucking driver?" She turned around, her focus now on the backs of the Wise Men, the holy men, the ones that will try to save her son.

Sam had been dropped off at the door of the emergency room when he got here, he told George to go park, but now as he was on his way out the door, he realized he didn't know where that was, or how to get there. He tried to call George on his cell phone, but there was no answer. He made his way through the too-wide corridors that now seemed to curl in on themselves. The corridors were lined on each side with gurneys. Little children who had breathing treatments or were hooked up to IV's. The ones that were able to breathe on their own wore masks . . . there were no healthcare workers here in the hallway.

The children were alone.

He wondered if they could hear Shannon's bell, the same way he could right now. It was odd, he had never been able to hear it before, except when he was home, but he heard it now. It echoed off the sterile walls and pinged like a terrible song off the shiny metal IV stands, and off the elevator doors that were wide enough to fit a bed with a dying child flanked by a parent and a nurse. He followed the red line painted on the floor that led away from the Emergency Department and followed it trusting it to lead his way as if he were in an airport.

At the junctions of hallways, the lines crisscrossed and overlapped, some disappeared completely, and he understood that.

Sometimes there was nowhere left to go. He remembered seeing billboards on the highway on his way home from NYC. They said, "If you Lived Here You Would be Home Now," yet they were always in the middle of nowhere . . . *miles to go before I sleep* . . .

The red line he followed turned into red dashes, and then led him down a hallway that looked like the hallways that ran along the backs of stores in a mall. Garbage cans replaced gurneys, and things that he thought should be covered, were not.

There was just so much blood, and little clothes, cut down the center and discarded. When Sam pushed himself against the door at the end of the hall, he half-expected an emergency siren to go off, but there was nothing. Instead, he was met with the smell of car exhaust, burning oil, and gasoline. He had always found comfort in the smells of a parking garage, the sense of having 'fresh air' without having to face reality. He checked his sticker for room 7 one more time. He saw that it was already beginning to peel away at the edges, as if room 7 did not want him to belong to them.

Room 7 was a room for two. A mom and a boy. Not a mom, a boy, and the adult male who ruined what could be the last day they had together as a family. He ruined it just by being a dick.

He spotted the black Mercedes; it was in one of the last spots in the "Emergency Room Only" parking area. It was a spot right on the edge of the garage; the driver's side was cut in half with the sun. Sam couldn't see George and assumed the man had moved to either the back seat to stretch out or scooched over to the passenger side to relax with his head against the window, his old, pay-as-you-go Walmart iPhone in his hands, passing the time by playing a slot game.

George had liked it when he got three cherries in a row. He had once told Sam that that always reminded him of Shannon and Sam, and how they sat in the back of the car and ate expensive cherries out of a jar. He would look at them through the rearview mirror and see their little fingers as they warred with each other over the biggest ones. Their hands, with their dirty fingernails, poked into the jar . . . Shannon would try to put a cherry onto each finger. He could still hear her laughter, as she would poke at Sam, a cherry on each finger. Her laughter interspersed with asthmatic coughs, "they're not cherries Sam, they're eyes . . . look at them . . ." In George's mind, Shannon's laughter has always sounded like a cough.

Sam was petrified of eyes, due to a second-grade incident with a pencil that is best left unsaid; Shannon knew this, and she teased him, not out of spite, she did it just because . . . just because part of her always knew he would need that.

Sam needed fear, he needed to feel it brush up against his cheek; he wanted it to leave a sweet-smelling mark that would always remind him of . . .

George is asleep again, and Sam really did hate to knock on the window to wake him up, just to tell him to leave again, to go home and wait to be called. Maybe he could sleep for a few hours and then come back, for Sam, come back for The Eagle who would belong to room 7 until he could not.

Sam knocked on the window.

Sometimes cars look like boxes of shadows. When you see them, they look like nothing more than a canister of lost dreams and horsepower. There are times, Sam told himself, that you could see a car, half-draped in and out of sun and shadow and it would seem like a regular day. Yes, it is a day gone horribly wrong, but it is just a day . . . he knocked on the glass, again, and this time it was a little louder, more forceful. He stepped away from the car and into the sun; this bruised version of daylight on a busy street in Boston . . .

the door didn't open.

George didn't pop out to see him, to call him Eagle . . . and before he knew it, he *knew it*. Sam had a key to this car that he had never used . . . his head looked over his left shoulder, and he saw him, this shrouded figure. A little black cloud, lit up now from the sun as it crept its way in. Sam could see George, crumpled over. His silhouette made an awkward maze that led his body from the driver's seat, and up and over the gear shift, to where his head, dangled down from the passenger seat like a Chinese lantern, days after celebration.

As Sam walked back towards the car, he had the same sinking feeling he had on a morning so many years ago, when he knew Shannon was dead before he even touched the doorknob. As he turned the key into the driver's side door, he heard the brass bell, the door opened and there was a familiar smell of copper and rotted leaves. George's lifeless left foot snuck out and bumped against Sam's shin.

This bump, this involuntary thing . . . it felt like love somehow. But also, it felt like goodbye. He understood now that there is no one left that will ever call him Eagle . . . and that realization felt like a hand inside his chest, pulling his rib cage down into his stomach. The realization pulled Sam's body towards George. "No, no, no, no, no." He whispered this as he reached out to touch the man's skin. It looked ashy and felt clammy, but cool. He leaned in close and crouched half in and half out of the car; he waited to hear a breath, a moan, an anything . . . but all there was, was the bell, and a little shadow that stood behind him. He closed his eyes and rested his head against George's chest, near his heart that had stopped its skittering mere minutes after he had parked the car.

Sam should have known, he should have felt it, he should have heard it in the silence between Shannon's bell last night. He hadn't heard it then, the warning, but he heard it now. George wore a red flannel shirt with a white V-Neck T Shirt underneath it. It felt soft against Sam's cheek. Sam thought that the shirt smelled like time he will never get back. He can't be positive, but he thought that this was the same shirt that he had tossed in the backseat one day when they were kids. Shannon took the shirt, claimed it for her own, and she wore it like a young baby grunge girl, during her almost yearlong mourning of Kurt Cobain. She wore George's red flannel over her hospital gown when she was away from home, and she wore it constantly in the house. A month before she died, she had gotten sick all over it. She hand-washed it in the sink between their rooms and dried it near the fireplace in the study. When she gave it back to George, he had tried to refuse it, but in the end, no one could say no to Shannon.

He wore it now. What were the odds? It was like three cherries on a slot game.

The red fabric had grown thin over the years, especially at the elbows. Sam could see George, a man who seemed to have spent half his life waiting for something . . . Sam's silent tears easily soaked through the fabric and onto the white T-shirt beneath it. Still crouched over him, Sam began to unbutton the red shirt and because the body had not yet grown stiff, it was cumbersome, but not an impossible task to reclaim the shirt. Sam wanted to have it, wanted to hold the fabric in his hands. He wanted to bring it back to Shannon. He was able to get the shirt but had a harder time as he fumbled with George's leg that had popped out of the driver's side door. Sam had to force his leg into an unnatural position. He was able to close the door and when he did, the bell stopped, and the ambient hum of echoes from the parking garage and the traffic just seemed to disappear.

Silence.

With the red flannel shirt clutched in his in his right hand, he made his way back to the emergency room entrance. This time he trailed along the outside of the hospital, he stuck close to the building. His left hand traced his path like a child in a corn maze. He did not even realize he was back at the Emergency Room entrance until the doors opened automatically. He was met with the rush of sterile air, and two kinds of lemons. He saw them open, but he did not hear them. The only thing he heard was his own voice as he said, "I belong to Room 7."

Chapter/
fifteen

Things You Do When You Hate Yourself – Part I
Nicole

"He looks at me weird." Nicole had practiced how she would say these words. She wanted them to sound truthful; she wanted to be able to believe them when she said it. She wanted them to land on her social workers' ears with a slap and not a punch. She did not want Doctor Paul damned, or jailed, she just wanted to be out of the house.

Sure, it was a lie, he never looked at her weird, but he looked at her with love, and for a reason she didn't really understand, that made anger and hate form in her stomach; it made her start to hate her father . . . and she didn't want to do that. She couldn't do that.

Loving the dead was like asking questions in a letter: it is futile and necessary, and at fifteen, being loved by Doctor Paul felt like a betrayal to the man who raised her; the one who smelled like old-fashioned country music that played on a crackling radio. He smelled like the morning before school, and the little garden he planted in their backyard. He smelled like wet dirt and carrots; he smelled like sawdust, and rust.

"Has he ever touched you, or said anything to you in a sexual nature?" Andy, her social worker asked her. Andy, which was short for Andrea, had a voice that rarely reached much above a whisper, and a cadence in her language that soothed anyone who heard it and made everyone in the room feel as if there was a sleeping baby tucked in the corner.

Nicole breathed in and held it. Her hands were in fists. Her fingernails were sharp acrylic. They were painted a deep bruised raisin color to match her favorite lipstick. She dug them into her palms; they made little half-moons in her skin. She knew if she opened her hands and looked at herself, she would see four little smiles in each hand. *"You look just like your mother when you smile."* Her father's voice is always there. She closed her eyes and tried to steady her heartbeat. Behind her eyelids, she can still see the flash of the camera of her last school photo. She could see the photos of Meredith and Paul on a beach somewhere, their smiles looked the way summer vacations were supposed to feel. They fight all the time now, their arguments are tied to her, she knew that much. Right before she opened her eyes, she knew she heard it, the creak of her father's body as it swayed; she heard the drip underneath it all.

"No, no, he never touched me, or said anything, it's just ... I don't know. The way he looks at me. There's just something that feels wrong in there." She paused and wondered if it were too late; could she take it all back? She thought about telling Andy she was lying, but she just couldn't. "It's different than when I first came to live with them, everything feels different, in the house, and . . . with him." She unclenched her hands and her fingers ached. She noticed that on her right hand she had managed to draw blood. Nicole wiped some of her hair off her face and as she did this, she realized that the blood smelled like Flintstone Vitamins and all it did was make her think of a time when she would never have made up a lie like this. Was there a way, she wondered, years from now to make Paul and Meredith understand she was doing this for them, not for her? She was doing this to give them a chance at happiness.

"What about with Meredith? What is your relationship like with her?"

"She's fine. It's fine." Her words sound like paper being ripped. Nicole clenched her fists again; her fingernails dug a little further into the rivets that already formed. "She drinks too much, but she's fine. She's nice to me, and she's helped me a lot." Nicole thought she was done, but then the words tumbled from her mouth, "They fight a lot. All the time."

"Does Paul ever get violent?"

Nicole couldn't help but laugh, the thought of it was ridiculous, but the question was not, not with the story that Nicole was telling. She swallowed her laughter, and it made a sound like someone who woke from a dream, one where there was a snake down his or her throat. "They were fighting the other night, upstairs, so I didn't see them." The fingernails dug in a little deeper. "A picture frame broke, and there was glass everywhere. I don't know how it broke but it broke when they were fighting." She relaxed her hands again, and as the pain from her nails started to lessen, she said, "It was a photo of me. It was my school photo from right before, from before I came to live with them, before my dad . . ."

Andy pushed a box of tissues towards Nicole. Nicole wasn't crying, but she realized she probably should. She grabbed one of the tissues and it already felt wet, it was one of the kinds that had lotion already built in. Gross. She held one in her right hand, and the little cuts bled a Rorschach image onto the thin paper; when she spread it open on her lap, she thought it looked like a butterfly in a mirror. On one side, it was a butterfly, and the other was a moth with dusty wings. It was Nicole, trying too hard to be the butterfly. "I don't want anything to happen to them, I don't want him, I mean them, to get in trouble, I think maybe, maybe I should just go live with another foster family now." She paused again, and this time the tears did come. "I just don't want anything to get worse, for any of us."

"Sweetheart, I understand. If you don't feel safe, we will make sure we can find somewhere better for you. But just so you know it will probably be in a group home for a while; it's harder to place older kids in families."

"That's fine."

"And then there's your school." Andy stopped looking at Nicole, and instead busied herself with the girl's file that was open in front of her. "Now, you have been going to a private Catholic school your whole life, and you go to a private high school now. That was made possible because Paul and Meredith have paid your tuition since your father died. His life insurance didn't cover his death, it was still a new plan, and in the first two years, there's no payout for suicide. The sale of the house covered your tuition last year . . . the house wasn't in great shape, so there's no money for you." When Andy closed the folder, the pages sounded like wings turning to dust. "That means after this semester you will have to go to a public school. That will be a big adjustment for you."

The air in Andy's office was hot and dry, and Nicole's hands had already started to scab over. All the little cuts were already old wounds.

"Yes, that's fine. When can I move out?"

"In situations like this we usually make sure the children are removed right away, so I can make some calls and then go with you and help you pack up your things, and we will get you settled in a group home tonight okay?"

"Okay. Just, please don't tell Paul what I told you."

In the end, Nicole had been able to go to the condo and have everything packed up just as Paul had returned home from work. Meredith was out, so all the tears and drama that Nicole had been scared of never happened. She packed her school uniforms, her makeup, and her two crowns from the pageants she had managed to win. She took the green and gold photo album, now filled with her magazine clippings. She took the box of the vintage Gothic Horror novels that she had carted around with her since a flea market when she was ten. She looked at each of the covers and saw a little of herself in each of them, a beautiful girl, running from a house. She took one last look at Paul before she left; his eyes were like the vacant windows in an abandoned house.

It would be years before they spoke again.

By seven that night she was at a table with strangers; she didn't make eye contact with the other girls, she just stared at her plate as she pushed the mashed potatoes around and around. When she got up three times during the meal to vomit, no one said anything; they barely even glanced up. That night when she was trying to sleep on a lumpy twin mattress on the bottom bunk of a mint green room, all she could think about was that each room in the house was painted a different shade of green, and in the dark, she swore she could hear the different shades all warring with each other. Then she heard it, the creak . . . and the drip . . . the madness green of the walls as she tried to think of a new name.

Chapter/
sixteen

SAM

"They've been moved to a different unit, a special ICU ward that's been set up." The nurse looked exhausted; her face had deep red marks from hours with goggles on over her glasses, a limp medical mask dangled from one of her ears. When she looked at Sam, her eyes barely seemed to focus, and if she recognized him, she didn't say. She saw the half-peeled "Room number 7" sticker and he was good to go. She didn't ask if he was family, she just took his temperature, wrote it down on the corner of a new badge with a different room number, and slid it across the counter of the nurse's station, past the bowl of community Halloween mini chocolate bars, towards him. "They will suit you up before you can enter the ward; once you go in, you're in. There's a family waiting room outside the ward, make any calls or anything you need to before you enter the ward. There's not a lot of coming and going after that."

Sam looked at the badge; this one lived in plastic and needed to be attached to his sweater with a little silver pincher. It reminded him of a nametag at a school reunion. He had never attended one of those; he always felt as if he wouldn't belong. Now he belonged to room 319. He looked at the room number for what seemed like too long. He tried to find Shannon's favorite number hidden somewhere in there, like a math equation. He couldn't find it.

"We're asking visitors to take the stairs if they can, we are limiting elevators to one passenger each trip unless it's medical personnel." The nurse's face lifted to his, and for a flicker he saw something in her eyes. A vague recognition, as if he reminded her of an ex-boyfriend who had date raped her in college. A moment of warmth in her eyes was quickly overshadowed with something else. This time when she spoke the tone was more than exhaustion, there was a thin layer of veiled disgust. "If you follow the blue line on the floor it will lead you to the stairs and elevator. Once you get to three you will see a new line, it's freshly painted so don't step on it. Follow orange until it ends. Try not to touch the railings or any of the door handles."

"Yeah, thanks." He looked away from her and clipped his 319 to his sweater. His fingers were awkward, and then he realized he was using his left hand. In his right hand was the red flannel shirt. It was soft and felt fragile like cobwebs and time. He started to cry as he walked away. "In the Emergency Room parking garage, there's a car on the first level, near the exit, it's a black Mercedes. There's someone in there, I think he's dead." He didn't turn around to say this; he just stopped for a few moments and then kept moving.

Sam was not sure if she heard him, but he thought he heard her call after him. "I'm sorry about your son, I'm sorry about . . ." even from down the hall he could hear the papers flutter. He could hear the determined need in her voice to find the paper that held— "I'm sorry about Simon." The papers still rustled; their sound amplified in the hallway as if they were being picked up on a microphone.

He followed the blue line until he saw the orange one. He went up the sterile stairs to the third floor. He remembered during Shannon's first stay here that he had been in her room right after she was admitted. It was the first time he had seen a machine that made another person breathe. He remembered the fear that felt like a cold fire inside of him, it slithered like a snake out from under his lungs, this fire swam in his blood the way the cancer swam in Shannon's. It burned him in a way that just left him colder, in every way. He ran from Shannon's room, with its starry sky, and pressed the button for the elevator and when it didn't come, he headed for the stairs. When he got to the stairwell, he made it just a few feet into the flickering greenish light that bounced off the concrete walls before he got sick.

Sour cherries. Not yet dusty on a shelf.

Hospitals still made him feel like that, the fire, the desire to run. He had thought one of his parents would follow him that day, check up on him, but no, they were busy of course. He wandered down the stairs and found George waiting in the lobby of the hospital; an extra-large French vanilla coffee in his hand, and next to him, folded nicely . . . was a red flannel shirt, while he wore only a white t-shirt. "You alright Eagle?"

It was over twenty-five years ago, and it was right now.

Sam opened the door to the third floor; he saw the new orange line, saw the scattered drops of paint every few feet; they were still fresh. Its trail wound through the halls like breadcrumbs in a forest. He was Hansel without a Gretel. There were doors to the other wings, but they were all closed, orange spray-painted X marks crossed them.

Through the narrow windows on the doors, he saw armed guards. He should have understood then how serious this all was, but he didn't.

Melody's voice was like fists hitting drywall, and he heard her before he saw her. She paced in the hallway. She walked in tight circles like a cat before an electrical storm; she was one of those people that held her cellphone in front of her when she talked. Her voice was too loud for this echoing space; it reminded him of when his family was in Italy and his mother had tried to communicate to the servant at his Nonna's house that she didn't want prawns in her breakfast omelet.

"I don't know what happened. He's sick." The words from the other end of the line sounded like the schoolteacher in a Peanuts cartoon. "I don't know, really sick." She saw him then and held her finger up; it was less as if she was telling him to wait, but more like she was telling him to keep quiet. "They are saying if I go in, I can't come out, okay— So I am just trying to figure shit out right now . . . okay, okay . . . I will be there when I can—hello, Jesus Fucking Christ . . . Hello?" She stomped her foot and held the cellphone to her forehead. She breathed in, and if there were tears, she swallowed them. She made a sound like a grunting hog. It was visceral, and it was honest. She looked up at Sam, "These fuckers, my job is so competitive, and I'm already late."

Sam remembered then that his father had told him that Melody worked the day shift at Full Spread. "Fuck, FUCK!"

There was a desperate desperateness that ached off her. He could see her ripped off fingernails, and they were raw and bled at the quick, and they were shameful reminders that lived at the edges of her once beautiful hands. She had piano hands too. Her fingers were long and slender, and every time she moved them, even without knowing, they looked like a ballet, like a symphony.

Sam loved Claire De Lune; Shannon hated it, said it made him a "basic bitch." She told him if he had to listen to classical music it should be contemporary, it should be Phillip Glass . . . he should feel the ruin in each second of silence between the notes. He did not know what that meant then, but he knew he felt it now, looking at Melody's hands.

Sam tried to fight back the memory of when George wrapped his arms around him, and whispered into the boy's hair, "Oh, Eagle;" he had let him cry against him until Sam was spent. "Eagle . . . there's gonna be a time, probably soon that you are gonna need to spread those wings and fly away from here. From all of it." George's arms squeezed him tighter. Sam had felt George kiss the top of his head; it was a strange and awkward feeling, like a door that was being opened and Sam did not understand the other side.

"Your sister's strong; hell, she's probably the strongest one in your family. Try not to worry. You're too young to be this old . . ." Were those George's words? Did he tell him to fly away?

Why hadn't he?

Sam's not there yet, soon he will be, right now he can't think of flight, of being away from this. Today, there's no flying. He is slouched against the wall near the doorway to the new ICU, he wants to be buried alive, and maybe that's what this is. There are guards on the other side of this door too, but they try not to look at what is happening on the other side of their door. Once you're in, you're in . . . there is still time; he could leave.

Sam could hear the brass bell as it rang; maybe it had never stopped, maybe all the silence he had thought of over these years wasn't there, and maybe he had forgotten to listen.

His footsteps echoed on the floor. He walked in a large circle. There was a room on the left, the empty family waiting room before the "once you're in you're in," section of the hospital. : He stepped through the orange drops of paint, leaving a confusing set of tracks which went in the opposite direction before they looped back. To this. To now.

"I think they're going to try and fire me if I—"

Sam's hand was around her wrist. The fluorescent lights in the hallway seemed to get darker as he touched her. The shadows on the wall were filled with black vines. He pulled her into the small family waiting room. On the wall there was a television that felt too big for the room and the air smelled like a new sofa. There was a gray clock on the wall, right above the couch. He saw that the time clicked in place, it had probably stopped sometime yesterday. Sam thought that there would never be a clock that scared him more than the Grandfather Clock in his family study, but he was wrong, this one was worse.

He will never be able to forget it.

He knew this because that was what he was looking at as he put her on the couch; she was kneeling away from him, her face pressed against the wall. Sam faced the clock and watched as the minute hand clicked in place at 11:48, and then jumped to 12:00, and then back again. He dropped the red flannel that was in his right hand and managed to open his pants and rub his dick until it was hard enough to forget the flannel shirt completely. Melody was many things, and one of them was good at the side aspects of her job. She had already taken her jeans and panties down and was touching herself before he had the condom rolled all the way down. He spat in his palm and rubbed it against her. He tried to enter her. She was almost dry. None of that mattered.

It wasn't all the way at first; it took a couple thrusts to get all the way in. All the way to rock bottom. He was inside of her. The left side of her face hit the wall a little too hard. He liked that even though he knew he shouldn't. He was about to apologize but he saw her smile. He tried not to think of the fact that this was the only moment of pleasure he thought was genuine in all of this.

Her skin rubbed against the wallpaper, which had the texture of gray corduroy pants. Her cheek made a zip, zip, zip, noise with each thrust. It started to bleed a little and neither of them cared. He came. It took less than two minutes. The anger inside of him came out of his mouth like claws and it scraped away any version of him that wanted to be more than this.

When it was done, Sam looked into the clock; it stagnated between yesterday, and today. Click, click, clack . . . like the tango he learned for Cotillion the year after Shannon died. Today—he saw that inside the clock was a dead moon moth, still so perfectly preserved; its wings had a pattern that looked like planets. Wings that looked like yesterday and tomorrow. There was nothing that looked like today, and he thanked God for that.

One-half of the moth was a delicate lace, and the other turned to dust on the edges.

It was the most beautiful thing he had ever seen.

When he came, it was not out of lust or connection, but in part because he needed to belong to room 319. He needed to make that real, and because he knew, or thought he knew, that they would all be dead in a few days.

Melody didn't care that she felt filthy and wet as she pulled up her panties and jeans; her face, which was already bored, never let on. "I need you to stay with him, for a few hours, I need to do a shift and then I'll be back. He's asleep; he'll be asleep the whole time." When she looked at him, he saw the lies that stacked up, one on top of each other, each one a vertebra keeping her standing up.

"Yeah, yeah, I'll stay."

There was a thing that happened here, something that he would never be able to describe, other than it felt like there was a room, covered in fireplace soot. She needed him and it made him feel real, but it also felt like a noose around his neck, or rocks in his pockets.

"If he wakes up, you can … just tell him that I did the best; I did the best I could." Melody peeled off two of her acrylic nails then, the ring finger on each hand. She grimaced as she did it. "Tell him, if you can … that when he smiled, it reminded me of his father." She dropped the fingernails on the floor of the family waiting room; they left a short trail on each side of the doorway. One nail still in his life and one nail out of it. She pulled the Tweety Bird stuffed animal out of her purse and waved at him with that little bird clutched in her hand.

He would never see her again.

Chapter/ seventeen

Waking Up is Hard to Do

OMELIA

"**W**hat's your love language?"

Omelia could barely hear her; the music was too loud, the bass pumped, and it made her heart vibrate and her eardrums made noises like she was underwater. The girl in front of her pressed against her legs and smelled like a summer day, like coconut, and afternoons you never wanted to end. Her skin had a golden shimmer as if she were the type of woman to add a pinch of fine gold craft glitter to her moisturizer. Omelia knew that her name was Kim, and that they had gone to high school together. Public high school. Kim had been a junior when Nicole was a sophomore. She could tell that Kim, who smelled like sunshine, didn't recognize her. Even though Nicole had spent long hours staring at her in the cafeteria, and they had shared the same German class for two years.

After everything with Doctor Paul, Nicole went through her phase of just trying to blend in; her main goal was to try not to be seen. She knew that when they passed each other in the hallways of the overcrowded school that Nicole was nothing more than a blur, a noiseless hum of a girl. Nicole would wear long flowy dresses and sweaters that looked like badly knit doilies. In the years after she left Doctor Paul's, she faded from the version of her that she was then . . . the beauty queen in a sparking crown, into a little black cloud in a dress.

Nicole had heard Kim's words, but just wanted her to say them again, she wanted to see the way her mouth moved over the word *love*. "What did you say?"

Kim leaned in towards Omelia, and she felt a warm breeze that kissed just below her ear. She felt Kim's lip graze her there, and it reminded her of the white floaties from a dandelion. "I said, 'What's your love language'?"

Omelia straightened up a little more. The corset top that she was wearing, the one that one of her most loyal fans had sent her, was stitched together with pieces of vintage book covers and bindings. It had begun to dig into her skin. She wore vegan leather pants, and she wore her hair long and loose. It gave her a look that was reminiscent of a Gothic horror novel from the seventies. Like the tattered ones in her collection, the ones she based her makeup tutorials on, the ones that still smelled faintly of secondhand smoke and bright green parakeet. "I don't think I have a love language." No one had ever asked her that before. "What's yours?" Omelia was thinking that Kim seemed like the type of person to ask a question just so someone would ask it of her. Also, Omelia was hoping that she would need to know Kim who smelled like sunshine's love language before the end of the night.

"Um, I guess I would say . . ." Kim paused, but it seemed staged; it lacked the panicked authenticity of truth telling. "I would say Words of Affirmation for sure . . . but also . . ." she paused again before she continued, and bit her lower lip, which was coated with a bruised peach lip-gloss; a color that only a woman who smells like the summer can get away with. ". . . also, gifts."

Of course.

"So come on, you have to know one of your love languages. It doesn't have to be one from the book."

There's a book?

"Okay, then I will have to say . . ." This time when Omelia paused there was a moment of panic. She was panicked because she didn't know; she didn't know what would make her feel loved. "I guess Metaphor, Metaphor is my love language."

Kim laughed and it sounded like an ocean wave hitting a rock, it sounded like the way a frenzied seagull cried as you fed them the dried-out french fries from the bottom of your McDonald's bag. Her laughter sounded like summer, like photos in an album. As Omelia gestured to the bartender that she needed another drink for them both, she closed her eyes for a moment, and all she could see was the faded photos of a sunburned Doctor Paul, and Meredith in her bikini. She saw their happiness in her memory, and she knew that once they had smelled as Kim did now.

"Metaphor's not a love language." She laughed again. Seagulls. The bartender came back with two more Cosmopolitans. Omelia wished she were drinking scotch, anything that would be bitter in her mouth would be better than these pink drinks, in their delicate glasses, but these drinks looked better in photos. Scotch always ended in heartbreak. With that thought, she took out her phone and snapped a couple shots of the drinks, then a quick selfie, and then she pressed in close to Kim, and took another photo of them. Their faces smushed together; one smiled, the other was a haunted doll. She could feel Kim's smile, she could feel her cheek tense up and then relax. Omelia's face did not do anything; she didn't smile.

"You look just like your mother when you smile." Creak . . . Drip . . .

Kim finished off half her Cosmo in one thirsty gulp. "Okay then besides metaphor . . . tell me something that makes you feel loved." Her face looked like a child who was about to open a present. "Just say the first thing that pops into your head."

"Being almost crushed to death by a building collapsing on me."

Omelia nervous-laughed. Honesty. There were no seagulls when Omelia laughed. Hers was that of the empty McDonald's bag being thrown into an already full trashcan at the beach. Her laugh was the splotchy sunburn and the water too cold to swim in, the cotton sheets that hurt her skin.

Kim leaned in closer now; where their knees were touching before, it was their thighs now, and Kim's right leg went between Omelia's legs. Kim's knee was just barely touching between Nicole's legs. Kim was able to slouch down a little and peer up at Omelia from a few inches below. And even though the music was still too loud, and it should have been impossible for Omelia to hear her, she heard Kim whisper, "Describe the building." Kim reached up and scratched a little at a red patch by the side of her eye. Her face had winced, but just a little. Omelia never saw that, all she saw was the building.

"It's the school I went to when I was a kid, before high school. It's not far from here actually; it's just across the river. A weird old brick box of a place. A cross between Mid-Century Modern and Brutalist. This school, it's used for storage now I think, but back then, it was just us Catholic kids in a big square building. It stood in the shadow of a beautiful church, and the Catholic hospital. Have you been in there? The church, I mean the church . . . Do you know it? It's called Saint Marie's." Kim shook her head no, though she had to have seen the church. "It's the most beautiful church in this city, it has seven altars inside, and I can see it from my apartment. I can see the steeple stretching up into the sky right between the mountains, the Uncanoonuc's." The way she said that sounded like an invitation; it was not. Omelia drank the rest of her Cosmo, and then waved to the bartender and mouthed the word "whiskey" and then gave him a thumbs up. "Did you know that is the Indian word for breast? Sorry I mean Native American . . ." She laughed a little again and she sounded like a brown paper bag being crumpled and tossed away; Kim did not seem to mind. When Omelia had said *breast*, Kim leaned in a little more, and suddenly this October night smelled like late July . . .

Kim's hand started to trace inside Omelia's thigh. It was saltwater and fried dough on a boardwalk. "The building, I want to hear more about the building on top of you."

There is innuendo there that Omelia can't think about, not now. All there is, is the building, the being crushed. "When I was six, my father thought he was having a heart attack, but it turned out it was a blood clot; he had to go to the hospital. He was there for almost a week. I stayed with the neighbors, but sometimes during the day, I would walk to the window of my classroom and I would look out to the hospital and I swear I could hear him whisper to me, his words would bounce off the church and into my classroom. I was six, but I was forty at the same time." The bartender came back with a rocks glass filled three fingers deep of whiskey, probably hobo brand, but Omelia didn't care.

"You're not driving, are you?" the bartender said in a whisper that sounded like non-vegan leather. Omelia shook her head no. She kicked back two fingers of the bitter brown liquid. Yeah it was definitely hobo brand, smoky, like newspaper from under a birdcage.

"My school, this building, it stood between the two things I feared and loved the most: the church, and the hospital. It was the cheese in between two slices of confusing white bread. I had to stay in that hospital once, when I was seventeen. I bought a bottle of children's chewable vitamins and I ate the whole bottle while drinking some wine coolers. It wasn't a big deal. Not like a suicide attempt or anything . . . It was just iron poisoning really . . ." *This is what happens when you kiss boys.* "Anyway, in this school, the cafeteria, the library, and the theatre were all in the same place—the basement. So, I could always feel it, four floors of Catholicism were on top of me all the time. Every time I filled myself with love, food, words, characters on a stage . . . it was always on top." She reached for that last finger of birdcage whiskey but saw how little there was left and thought better of it. "We had Book Fairs, Bible Study, and the Halloween Haunted House all in the same place. That basement, it always smelled like mold and pizza day, but it was also everything

I always wanted, and everything I knew I was, everything I wanted to be." Omelia kicked back the last finger of whiskey. She felt Kim's knee press a little further into her; there was just a slight pressure of her against Omelia's crotch, and she wondered if Kim could feel her heartbeat, all the way down there. "So yeah, like I said before . . . Metaphor."

Kim stood up, her purse fell to the floor, and it made a sound that was heavier than the bass that pumped from the speakers, the sound that made them both delirious for the past hour. With her right hand, Kim grabbed her bag off the floor and with her left, she grabbed Omelia by the wrist and pulled her off her barstool. Together they slinked between the tightly packed tables towards the door that led down a steep and very narrow staircase into the basement. In between the restrooms, there was a small loveseat couch, and then around the bend there was a dark corner that pressed up against an *Employees Only* padlocked door. That was the destination. Omelia felt Kim's mouth on her, like the velvet lining of an antique purse. She fell into summer, and Nicole felt what could have been close to happiness, at least for a little while.

What Omelia didn't know was that every time their mouths touched, there was a new little red spot in the crook of Kim's mouth, and it would scream, it would send fire and angry fingers that pulled at her veins, through her body. But for Kim, who was sunshine and light, it was worth it. Kim had never met anyone like Omelia before, except of course, she had.

And for what it was worth, it was Omelia that Kim was thinking of the next night as she died in the waiting room of the local Urgent Care.

Omelia had felt Kim's fingers and the way her manicured acrylic nails dragged lightly across her skin. Her nails were painted a Caribbean Ocean shade that was such an unearthly blue that it tumbled over into green. When Omelia felt her nails clawing against her corset, she was reminded of a stray cat that clawed at a door for warmth, for love. She wanted to give in, but in Omelia's mind, the color that tumbled over into green reminded her of the group home, it reminded her of the different shades in every room all fighting with each other. It reminded her of madness green, and how if you listened to the color of those walls long enough, you start to hear why they were painted that way . . .

You start to hear them all say, "Omelia."

She felt Kim's fingernails against her corset; they made a sound like a possum trapped under a sink. They started to ride up Omelia's body; these feral claws seemed to scratch at the top of Omelia's breasts and then reached for her throat. When she felt Kim's fingers against the skin of her neck, it felt like all at once she swallowed a gristly piece of chicken . . . but it was even more real than that . . . it felt like fingernails on her throat, which dug in, dug down.

The light in her memory had already changed. The madness green changed into the greenish hue of fluorescent lights; the kind that looked too bright with her eyes but then looking back she saw it was too dark. There were shadows in every corner. Shadows that had fingers like a spindly birch tree that bent over with time and last year's mud season snow. Those shadow fingers are on her neck, they are down her throat. They don't push down; they pull out . . .

"NICOLE . . ." He shouted from far away: she could not hear much besides Kim's fingernails scratching against . . .

She heard a beep; it repeated in an even rhythm, it was just a repeated sound, no longer a dramatic tango, off rhythm and exciting, instead it was steady. Instead, it was walking down a high school hallway on the way to German class. Invisible. Unseen.

"She's waking up . . ." His words were underwater, garbled, but loud. He could have been a father, or a stranger. His words are waves and pressure and she felt them more than heard them.

She felt plastic gloves reaching through a hole in her world. They reached for her hands that had somehow woken before the rest of her. She felt her fingernails; the French manicure that over the past few days had felt in her unconscious as if they had been pried off her body and underneath her nails had begun to disintegrate into the past. Little memories and flashes of hope were stuffed under her nails with a file. Underneath each nail was a layer of dried skin, scabs, and human hair. If it were the Victorian era, her fingernails would be wrapped in silk thread and worn on a chain around someone's neck, it would have been beautiful then . . .

She felt his hand now; it pulled at her from far away. It pulled her away from herself. She understood it now, that moment wasn't Kim, it wasn't the late July sun and coconut-scented happiness; it was her fingernails that scratched against her throat. She tried to claw the snake out, the one that wound its way down her gullet. The one that felt like hard plastic as it started finally to melt.

She closed her eyes, and she could see a boy jerking off on her while another held a phone.

When she opened her eyes, she saw the light as it flickered. Darkness. Madness Green. She did not want to live in either of those places.

She closed her eyes again, and was happy to see nothing, but then she heard a creak, a drip and creak . . .

Dr. Paul wore a plastic skullcap over his hair. There were little salt and pepper curls that peeked out around his face. They were heavier on the salt. He looked like an elderly French lady getting a perm. She saw his gloved hand as it reached into the bubble she had been sleeping in. Her eyes had opened, and this time they stayed like that. She felt his gloves against her skin; he pulled her hands away from her throat, away from her clawing into the sunshine and summer that Kim had kissed into the bottom of her ear.

The snake inside of her throat, the one that is inside of her lungs felt different now, like it has been warmed in the sun. The snake inside of her relaxed for a moment as she coughed, and then Omelia felt it move a little bit. Maybe it's not there at all, maybe it is a memory, and it's just something that was . . .

Her body moved now with an involuntary reflex. She clawed at her throat again; she coughed and forced herself to gag like when she was a teenager eating meat that tasted like animal's tears. Paul tried to hold onto her hand, his latex gloved one to hers. It was slippery and their hands made a strange sound like a squeak as he rubbed the top of her hand. His glove kept sticking to her hand, and it caught on the rubber tubes. After the first few times, she couldn't hear it over the beeping, and she can't feel it over the struggle in her chest.

The *beep, beep, beep* stayed steady. She was alive. She heard a shadow, the one that had replaced Nurse Pugs. The shadow said that Omelia's temperature had dropped a couple degrees and was closer to the "normal kind of high fever." There was a pause; Omelia could see the nurse as she put something into her IV. Omelia's hands no longer wanted to claw at her throat, no longer wanted to dig the snake out of her, the one that invaded her lungs. She tilted her head a little towards Paul, and she felt herself try to smile, but she couldn't. All she could feel before she fell back into the milky fog was something cracking, like pavement with a fire underneath. She thought she felt her face crack, she felt spindly branches going up towards her eye.

The *beep, beep, beep* started to fade away, like a long shadow, as afternoon became evening. She could no longer hear it, but knew it was still there, this shadow of her heart. "What will happen when she wakes up?" His voice had hope underneath the exhaustion. She had no idea how long they had been there. Had he left, had he slept, had he eaten?

She wanted to tell him that before all of this, she had kissed a girl who tasted like the same kind of happiness in his green photo album. She wanted him to know what he had given her, in his way.

"I don't know, we haven't had too many of our patients wake up yet." The voices were getting further away, their shadows blending in with the night.

Omelia had been asleep for thirteen days.

Chapter/
eighteen

There's nothing like waiting for an eleven-year-old to die...

SAM

He did not correct anyone when they referred to him as Simon's father. With his medical mask on, and his jet-black hair tucked underneath a cap, he was not recognizable. The hospital didn't know that just yesterday, Simon had been most famous eleven-year-old in the United States. He was the *broken-hearted boy*.

Sam thought of the fifty thousand dollars that Santo Alberti had promised Melody, and he knew he would not see her again. In a way, he hoped that she could find happiness, or at least maybe relaxation. He wanted that for her. What he wanted for himself was a night that he would not scream into a pillow, a night without hating himself. A night without . . .

The bell.

He hated himself for it, but he wanted a night that Shannon didn't exist, not in the room next door to his, and not in his memory, nowhere. He wanted a life lived, not what he had now, a life as someone missing the most crucial part of himself. Sam, the Eagle, wanted his heart back. It died with Shannon, and he was tired. The energy it has taken him to live without a heart . . . he was tired. He was more tired than he thought he was. It was harder every day to live without, without that thing that would make him human, that thing that would make him humane . . .

The drugs, the booze, every time he fucked a stranger he met online, the expensive shoes and the burned-out dreams. Those were just the things he used, the things he balled up in his hands and shaped into a thing that took up space in his chest. In place of his heart, there was a box; in it was a dusty jar of cherries, George's thin red flannel shirt, a brass bell, and Shannon's laugh. If there were pieces of his mother and father in there as well, he didn't know what they were; maybe their piece was Shannon.

Their table for four, now a table for three.

The nurse had him put his arms out and she dressed him in a pale blue gown and tied the back of it for him; this was all done in the hallway, which flickered in green light that sounded like parents crying. He thought he saw blood speckled on the wall, near the murals of a mermaid on a rocky shore. There was no music playing over the sound system, and besides the crying, the place was silent. Occasionally, the armed guards by the door would shuffle in place. The way their shoes scuffed the floor sounded like the end of the world. If he strained his ears, which he was used to doing, he knew he waited for Shannon's bell . . . he could hear the unsteady rhythm of machines, the beeps, the drips, the mechanical inhaling, and exhaling. He was nervous, he felt unsteady on his feet, and as he walked into the hospital room, it felt as if he had just gotten off a boat. It was the same feeling as walking along a wooden dock; there was a gentle but different rhythm, and the things around him did not match up with what was inside of him. He glanced over his shoulder to look again at the starry sky, but saw he was mistaken. It was dragons and elves.

The starry sky, yes, that had been Shannon's hallway.

He rested his gloved hand against the doorjamb to Simon's room, and he closed his eyes as he steadied himself. Sam remembered sitting in a hospital bed with Shannon, as they flipped through an illustrated copy of Hans Christian Anderson's *The Little Mermaid*. It was Shannon's favorite, even when she was 'too old' for fairy tales. She always said, "This one's different, this one shows you that pain and death can be beautiful." They would flip through the book, neither of them talked or read the words, they just mindlessly flipping through the pages for hours. They did this without thinking, when she was too weak, and Sam, too tired, both too old for their years to do anything else. The night before the family had decided to bring her home *for good*, they had flipped through the book, Sam's long legs, already gangly for his age, were tangled on the small hospital bed with Shannon's shorter, bruised legs. She had not grown much in the past year and a half, and there was something about that, that made Sam feel important but also sad. It was a thing he couldn't understand, the differences between them now. In his heart, it felt like being happy for the end of summer.

They were on their third or fourth slow motion flip through of the book when Shannon coughed, and a red mist came out of her. It speckled the pages at the end of the book right at the mermaid's tragic end. They had looked at each other, and Sam remembered her taking her finger and rubbing it over her lips, as if she were putting on makeup. "It's too bad I'll never get a chance to wear makeup. I could have been really pretty." She coughed again; this time she winced and what came out of her was more phlegm, with dark reddish black chunks. "I'm gonna miss you Eagle."

Sam opened his eyes, and realized he was still in the doorway, half inside Simon's room, and half in the green flickering hallway of his past. The air smelled like rotten cherries and lemon-scented bathroom spray but there were no juice boxes here. There was a sour smell coming out of Simon's room, and it reminded Sam of milk that was about to go bad. There was another nurse in the room; Sam had not seen a single doctor. She looked up at him, her eyes were glassy and red, and she looked startled as the words tumbled out of her mouth, like fine beach sand through open fingers. "His face, I'm sorry, it's gotten much worse in the past ..." She checked her watch and then glanced at the clock on the wall; the batteries were all dead. Everything just clicked back and forth in place. "The last half hour or so, it, um, it's all the way to his eyes now."

"Okay. Yeah, his eyes," Sam said this but all he saw was the Little Mermaid's red hair, all he saw was Shannon's mouth, and the way her eyes lit up for a second when she rubbed the blood across her lips.

"And we haven't been able to get the fever down, it's steady at 105 now, but ... it went up to 107.7." She stopped before she continued with, "it was there for over ten minutes, that we have record of. He had a seizure then, and that lasted ..." she looked again at the notes, "a little under four minutes. We sent someone to find you and his mom, but we couldn't. I'm sorry."

"Okay, a fever, a seizure." He closed his eyes and Sam heard a bell; it was down the hallway, but it came closer the longer he stood there. "Do you know if any of the hallways have murals of mermaids in the rooms, and dragons in the hallway?" He said it before he understood his words were aloud.

"Yes, um, not on this floor, those are in pediatric cardiology." The nurse noticed Sam as he looked into the hall; it looked like he heard something, saw something. "Sir, I'm sorry I have to get to my other patients but what I wanted," she scraped her throat, "what I need to tell you is that you should understand, even if Simon were able to get through this and wake up, that he might not be the boy you knew."

"I didn't know him at all." That's not true; he knew that without *knowing* it. He knew the boy loved Shakespeare, he loved pizza day, he knew that he loved his mother and understood her limitations; Sam knew that Simon was lonely, and smart. Sam knew that Simon reminded him of Shannon.

So many *esses* ...

He looked at the plastic tent that Simon was in, and he remembered his legs, tangled with Shannon's in a hospital bed. He remembered her bell that last night, the way he ignored it and chose to sleep. When he walked closer to the bubble, he saw Simon's face for the first time since the morning. He saw the left side of his face was all but gone; it looked burned down to the bone. Sam could see the boy's teeth and upper gums, where just hours ago there had been a cheek that squinched up into a smile at the first words of the Saint Crispin's Day speech. Sam saw skin that had been eaten or melted away. Most of the boy's face was missing up to the corner of the boy's eyelid, the corner of the sclera now peeked out even though the boy's eyes were still closed. Half of the boy's face looked like a pizza, one with too much sauce and not enough cheese.

Sam remembered a sharpened pencil poking him in the eye when he was a kid after a pizza party in second grade . . . he could barely look at the boy, he could only remember the pizza. The party.

Simon's pizza day . . . it was only two days ago now. How could that be possible? How could time move like this when the clocks stayed in place? How could the past two days have felt like a year, yet at the same time Sam could still feel Shannon's bruised legs as they bang up against his while they flip through *The Little Mermaid*. He could feel her legs, yet he could not really remember how it had felt to fuck Melody, less than an hour ago. He looked at Simon, in that bed; he looked smaller than he had yesterday, and it was as if he could see him as he withered before his eyes. His scrawny arms, which had been able to carry a cumbersome bag of books just yesterday, now looked like ice-covered birch branches. His skin taught and almost translucent, it seemed barely to be able to stretch over his delicate bones. Simon's fingers were long and slender, his fingernails were strangely clean; he was an 'indoor' boy, and he had piano hands, like his mother. *Like Sam, like Shannon*. When Sam looked down at his own hands, one of which still clutched George's red flannel shirt, he realized his hands were similar. He could understand why the staff had assumed he was the boy's father.

When Sam uncurled his fingers and released the red shirt onto the chair that was tucked in the corner of the room, he heard his fingers creak, and it startled him. It sounded like a walk in the woods interrupted by the snap of a twig. Sam, too, had grown up as an 'indoor' boy. As he let go of the shirt, the room around him grew darker, the corners of the room seemed to drip with memory. He had the sensation of falling into a well. He could hear the scurrying of time around him, it moved and crept like spiders and the bright green fuzzy caterpillars that always made his skin itch, but Shannon would let them crawl over her arms in childhood ecstasy.

He pulled a stool over to the side of Simon's bed; there was an armhole in the plastic that separated them, Sam could snake him arm through there and then . . . and then what? What could he do? He didn't know, but he put his arm through anyway. Sam's hands were large and seemed overly clumsy once they were close to Simon. The boy was all twigs and wax paper like a poorly done school project. He placed his hand over Simon's, the tips of his fingers touched the bed, but his palm was up like a protective cage. He did not quite touch him; he felt the IV's brush against the inside of his palm instead of feeling the boy's skin.

Sam had wondered when he would get this. Whatever this was. Wasn't that one of the reason's he fucked Melody; he can't say that it wasn't. When he put his cock inside of her, it was like sticking his hand in the fire. He wanted it to burn, he wanted . . .

How had he lived through it all? When he had tried since Shannon's diagnosis to catch up, to be where she was. He was twenty-four years late and knew he could never catch her now.

He pulled his hand out of the armhole, and without understanding why he was doing it, or maybe he did understand, Sam peeled his protective glove off. He flung it to the floor, and it landed with a heaviness as if it had been filled with water. He put his arm back in the tent, and this time he picked up Simon's small hand and placed it inside his palm. It reminded him of a small bird's nest. Instinctively, Simon's hand curled in on itself and his clean small fingernails reminded Sam of eggshells. The boy's hand burned hot, and that was when Sam realized that maybe it was this, this was the fire he had wanted to stick his hand into. He hoped that when he took has hand away, that he would have a burn seared onto his palm, a small fist, the size of an eleven-year old's heart.

Interitus. He took Latin in school. It meant untimely death. It meant rot. It meant this. He had heard the nurses in the hall whispering to the guards, they said that word, and now he held that word cradled in his hand like a gift.

"I'm an asshole." He whispered this; it was a confession. "Sometimes I think I'm good, but I know, I know I'm not." Sam's eyes started to fill with tears, and he wished he could hold George's flannel to his face, he wished he hadn't left it so far away. "You have to know kid, that . . . that . . . I'm not really a whole person, I'm just part of one. I had someone, someone once, she was the better parts of me, she was my heart . . . she was the one to listen after I asked a question; she was the one that remembered everything I forgot. She could always tell when I wasn't listening, even before I realized it myself. She knew I had a hard time reading even before the teacher's knew." As the tears trickled down his face, they pooled in the corner of his mouth before eventually sliding in. They did not taste salty, instead it was sweet, and he was reminded of the thick cherry juice, in that dusty jar on the shelf, before it had all gone bad. "She wasn't perfect, my sister, she could be a bitch, and she, she was smarter than me, and she loved that. Fuck . . . um, sorry . . . I shouldn't swear. But Shannon knew she was smarter; she was smarter than my father was. She would play with us, all of us, and our family did everything she wanted. Not my mom though, she didn't play with her. I asked Shannon once, and she said that mom was like a teacup with a crack in it, that it would not take much for it to break, it was better to leave it alone, even if all it did was take up space." His voice caught in his throat, he made a hiccup sound, and his stomach felt like he swallowed air. ". . . even if all she did was collect dust . . . sorry, fuck I don't know what I'm saying."

He closed his eyes, and he saw the people that loved him. He saw George, with eyes that smiled as they glanced at him through the rearview mirror, he heard George scold him for being late. He saw his mother, the crack in her teacup, which shattered at Shannon's funeral. His father, he didn't see him, he was always just an imposing shadow, a darkness they all skirted to avoid. Mostly, he saw Shannon with dark circles under her eyes, they grew like weeds . . . he remembered the time she snuck into his room one night and said, "Come on, we're gonna play a game, I'm going to pretend you are dying and I'm going to say all the things I wanted to say to you." She had paused then, her eyes were tired, but there was a glint inside of them. "Don't worry, your job is easy, you just have to be in a coma, I'll do the rest."

Too young to be that old.

He pulled his hand out of the armhole, and in a move that he would say was accidental, but he knew he was doing in on purpose; he rubbed his eyes. *Why wasn't he sick?* He felt the clamminess in his hand, the humid sickness; he rubbed that into his eyes. In an instant, the room stopped smelling like rotten Luxardo Cherries, and instead took on a scent of decay, like a rotted mouse, or something larger inside of a wall. Something putrid at first, but soon it would start to smell good; it would smell right. He inhaled deeply and tried to calm himself when he saw it. Simon's hand opened and closed; it was more than a twitch, but less than if he was reaching for something. Sam put his hand back in the plastic bubble. He held the boy by the wrist and rested his hand under his. He watched Simon's fingers as they relaxed against his palm, as if he were floating in water.

Sam remembered that he had seen love, or something like love in someone's eyes . . . it was earlier today, it was aimed at him, from Simon, during the first lines of the Saint Crispin's Day speech. In Sam's head, the words and memories flooded in, until they were the same thing. Love is poetry when you don't have your own words.

He leaned in close to the plastic curtain that separated them. He breathed in, and as he exhaled, he could feel the humidity, the strange personal cloyed air that grew around him. The plastic fogged up in front of his eyes, and his mouth moved against the curtain as he spoke.

"To be, or not to be, that is the question:
Whether 'tis nobler in the mind to suffer
The slings and arrows of outrageous fortune,
Or to take arms against a sea of troubles
And by opposing end them. To die—to sleep,
No more; and by a sleep to say we end"

Simon's eyes, or really an eye, opened a little. His head turned towards Sam, and it was almost imperceptible, it was not life behind the boy's eyes, but there was recognition. When Sam reached with his other hand for the call button to summon the nurse, or summon anyone, he finally looked at what was left of the boy's face. It was the same look he had given him, so many hours before when Sam was at the podium and giving the Saint Crispin's speech just for him. Sam looked at him and understood. He moved his hand away from the call button and he kept going with Hamlet's speech. Though it was faint at first, he finally heard Shannon's bell. It kept a beautiful haunting rhythm with his words. The atmosphere in the room pulsed with other people's words and Simon's pulse. Sam felt it as it hammered though the boy's skin, which had turned thin and delicate like Japanese rice paper. Sam felt the boy's finger, tapping against his palm, like a hummingbird that searched for nectar. Little Simon was tapping in the same steady haunted heartbeat of Shannon's bell.

Simon could hear the bell. His eyes were open now. He was awake.

"Devoutly to be wish'd. To die, to sleep;
To sleep, perchance to dream—ay, there's the rub:
For in that sleep of death what dreams may come,"

The bell was louder now, and Sam could almost feel the breeze coming off the bell, from Shannon's little arm, still so strong. It rang in iambic pentameter. The boy tilted his head back, and made a gagging sound, and Sam wondered again if he should reach for the call button. Certainly, there had to be someone else that would be better for the boy's last moments than Sam was. He thought of the pain he must be in, the tube down his throat, the machine that breathed for him. He shouldn't be awake. Sam looked at the monitors on the other side of the bed, which were blurry because he was looking at them through the plastic sheets that separated them, this sealed-off lonely little world. He could see that Simon's temperature was a little over 107. Simon made a noise in the back of his throat; it was a deep gurgle of a clogged drain. It was a cough, maybe a gag, maybe it was words . . . maybe it was Sam's imagination. Simon had tilted his head up, and when his cheek rubbed against the pillow, a dark mottled puddle of reds and blacks started to form under his face. He was able to tilt his head up and away enough that Sam finally understood at what Simon stared. His one good eye was fixed on the chair in the corner; it stared at the red flannel shirt. When Sam followed his gaze, he could swear that the shirt had moved a little since he had thrown it there before.

Simon did his best to form what he could of a smile underneath the mask and tubes. He continued to stare at it and then Sam realized what the sound was that he had heard come from the back of Simon's throat . . . it was a laugh. Stifled, and painful, but still there. Sam realized he had stopped his speech; his words had fizzled out, like air coming out of a birthday balloon. The bell was louder now; the sound was so close, so insistent. It hurt his ears, and it made the pale scar and the bump on his nose tingle. With his free hand, he reached up and traced the scar on his face. He could barely feel it through the glove he wore. He let go of Simon's hand and was able to peel off the other glove. His finger still traced that scar when he realized the bell had stopped. There were several seconds of silence, and then a wall of sound. The alarms on the machines started to scream like a banshee.

"No, no, no, no, no . . ."

Sam was not sure why he did it, but he pulled the plastic sheets apart. The plastic zippers that held the plastic of Simon's isolation tent together made a sound like someone taking a sharp knife to the air. Everything ripped around him. There was a tear. Inside the tent was death, and where Sam was, outside of it was something that resembled a life. Sam was in both places right now, perhaps he always had been.

"Fuck, fuck, no" His instinct was to cradle the boy's face, the half that remained the way it looked to him just yesterday . . . could it only be yesterday . . . on one side his face was pale but almost flawless like a doll. It hadn't even started the terrible transformation into puberty. But the other side of his face was all but gone. It was even worse than it had been just minutes ago. Sam stared into the boy's one good eye, lifeless, and frozen, but in that frozen state there was a glimmer of recognition, a light leak in a Polaroid photo . . .

A ghost.

Sam placed his hand on Simon's chest; he could feel his ribs on either side of his hand. His chest still moved up and down. The machine did not realize that the boy had died. There was no deep rhythm of a heartbeat anywhere underneath the taught pale skin that seemed to barely make the stretch over his rib cage. The skin seemed to sink down into his spine like collapsed soufflé. He looked at the machines and wished there were a way that he could make the banshees stop howling. He could see the numbers a little more clearly, now that he was one sheet of plastic away from them. They flashed like a railroad warning. At Simon's moment of death, his pulse was 234, his temperature 107.8. His breaths per minute, still being controlled by the machine, were a steady 20. The rest of the numbers blurred as Sam started to sob. He could hear the world outside this room, it pressed into his ears like the pressure he felt deep in his head and the back of his jaw when he drove over mountains. In the hallway, there were other alarms, other sobs.

He was wrong when he thought hospitals smelled like two different kinds of lemon that weren't lemons at all. They smelled like grief. They smelled like the hollow emptiness of all the tomorrows. They smelled like the clock as it finally made its way to midnight and beyond.

Sam was supposed to go to Italy; he was supposed to be far away from all of this by tomorrow or the next day. But everything around him and in his head sounded like a cold wind and he knew he wasn't going anywhere, not for a long time, and maybe not ever.

There were other banshees that had come here tonight. The children's hospital was riddled with them; he could hear the screams from this wing of the hospital, and he could feel them coming up through the foundation all the way from the ER, from the parking garage where he had left George, and from beyond that, he could feel the screams from the city around him.

The air smelled like cherries and sounded like the end of the world.

Sam reached for the red flannel shirt and was able to work one of Simon's arms halfway into it, but nothing worked like he wanted it to. There were too many wires, and no one had come.

"Somebody please help us!" His words came out in broken bursts; his voice was high-pitched and panicked. It sounded like glass shattering due to the cold, as if mismatched puzzle pieces trying to be jammed into a place they didn't fit. He understood it was the way he said *us*. Like Simon belonged to him.

That part didn't fit. He was an 'us,' but she died. He could not be an 'us.' He could not even pretend. There was just a 'him,' and then a phantom limb.

Where was Melody? He looked around for Simon's medical chart; he didn't even know his last name. "Please." It was a whisper, spoken into a storm. For the second time that day, Sam rested his head against that red flannel shirt as he waited and hoped for a heartbeat, and for the second time today, it did not happen.

In the corner of the room, there were two shadows who watched Sam. They looked more like twins than Sam and Shannon did now. Their thin eleven-year-old bodies were similar enough that even though they were just shadows, if anyone had seen them, they would know that now they belonged to each other. Piano hands.

"I'm Shannon." Her voice sounded hoarse to her, unused for so many years and to Sam, it went unheard and blended with the alarms and the distant screams that leaked in from the hallway, and if anything, her voice sounded like the pause between the clangs of a bell.

Chapter/
nineteen

OMELIA

It was thirteen hours past her thirteen days before her temperature finally landed on 103 degrees. There was another six days before it went back to normal and stayed there. Two days into "phase two of her awakening," she would find clarity with more regularity. There were little moments of lucidity in the deep, strange world that were filled with who she was even more than who she is. There were moments that her dreams were consumed by the feeling of being crushed, the sensation of her fleeing in the night from a building gone to ruin. When she would turn back to take one last look at this house she was running from, she always just saw herself. Sitting in front of a camera, she would see the flash go off. She would see a smile. Then, there was nothing.

There were other times that she found herself in her childhood home, where she chased a snow-white cat through the house; it was too thin, and she could see the large fleas crawling through its fur in a beautiful dance.

Sometimes the cat would dart into the basement and then somehow make its way into the walls around her. She could hear it as it scratched … as it tried to get out. There were plaintive mews coming from all around her. The strange kitten cries would build up, like layers of paint, each cry taking the place of the one before. So many layers of green paint. She understood eventually that the cat was crying from inside the walls of her father's bedroom.

She couldn't bring herself to go in there, *could she*? She understood that the cat would starve to death without her help, and her house would be filled with the sweet and awful stench of decay. Horrid at first, but over time she knew she would grow used to it; she would love it. That smell, it would be home.

She had never been allowed to have a cat but had always wanted one. Her father always said no, talked about her allergies, her asthma, he talked about how they didn't have the money for her to get sick. The white cat. This was her chance. She walked up the steep stairs towards the two bedrooms, the third step creaked, and when it did everything around her fell silent. The cat stopped its incessant cries, they always started high-pitched and youthful, but as the minutes and hours passed, they would sound like a song.

When she got to the top of the stairs, she glanced into her room, and it looked too grown up for her. There was a fancy mirror and makeup was scattered in front of it. There were little piles of crushed pigments and an office style garbage can. It was overflowing with makeup wipes and ripped out pages of magazines. She would name the cat Meredith if it were a girl, and Paul if it was a boy. She did not really recognize these names, but they were there, in her head; they belonged to her. There was a stack of books next to the mirror, and in the reflection was someone Nicole did not even know.

She turned to her father's bedroom door; the cat was silent. She thought she could see it, the way it trembled with fright, tucked into the corner under her father's bed. Yes, it was the creak of the stairs that did it. So frightening.

She stood in front of the closed door; it was her father's door, except it wasn't. It had peeling paint and the air smelled stale, but also like urine. No doubt, the cat had been pissing in her father's room. He would be so angry when he got home from work. She wondered what time it was . . . it had been daylight downstairs, but now she could see out of the crooked witch's window in her room that it was night, or almost night. The sky was the color of a bruised apple.

As she opened the door, the white cat jumped out at her and scurried down the stairs; it moved fast, as if it was sliding on ice. The smell of urine was strong, also the smell of death . . . she looked into the room, and she saw his feet, still swaying like a summer rowboat. She heard the creak of beams, and heard the drip of the . . .

She ran down the stairs and realized her dress was too long, too much fabric, she wasn't wearing shoes, but she knew she had to run, to run away from this house, run away from . . . wait what was she running from again? The night air felt like a sealed envelope finally being opened. There was an expectancy to it. An envelope without a letter. She ran until her lungs ached at the bottom, until they felt like a plastic snake that had burrowed inside her had finally been driven out. She turned back to her house, and all she saw was herself, no that's not right, she saw when she was Nicole, her makeup freshly done; it barely covered her eyes, which were haunted and on the verge of tears. The black rotary phone in her lap; the receiver at her ear. It rang once and then—

"911 what's your emergency?"

"My father. He's dead, and I am alone."

"Nicole, Nicole, Nic . . .?" It was the cat talking, the cat was a boy, she named him Paul . . .

Her chest ached; it felt hollowed out, and her breathes were shallow, but they were her own. When she opened her eyes, it hurt, like she walked out of a movie theatre into the afternoon sun. She blinked a few times, and her eyes watered. She felt the tears burn like a hornet's repeated sting as they made their way down one side of her face.

Her face felt tight on one side, and without understanding why she leaned the opposite way from the voice saying her name, saying what *her name was*. She opened her mouth to say something, and when she tried to talk it felt like she was swallowing sand.

"Don't . . . don't say anything. We'll get you some water." Omelia saw her, the frumpy tunic and jangly statement necklace of wife number three. She smelled like sandalwood as she reached across to the table on wheels. The table had a salmon-colored plastic water jug, several crushed paper cups, and three well-loved editions of the "Collected TV Guide Crossword Puzzles."

Ugh, she was so basic.

She tried to move her mouth, but all she could do was open and close it. Her jaw creaked and popped but there were no words, just dry wheezes. That's when she felt it; there was something wrong with the side of her face. Her skin felt tight, and raw. When she moved her mouth, it was as if she could feel threads being plucked apart. She remembered the rag doll her father had given her when she was small, it was a Raggedy Andy, and she played with it until his stitches were loose and the stuffing inside his body separated and balled up in all the wrong places. This is how she felt now: balled up, things were in the wrong places, her stitches were coming loose, and others were too tight. Her hands felt heavy and swollen, and when she tried to move her fingers, they felt the same way boiled hotdogs looked. Wife number three looked blurry on the other side of a plastic curtain . . . it reminded Omelia of a shower curtain.

Water that hit her back. A silk kimono robe. Pipes that clanged, and fingernails that carved gullies in her calves.

It was then, that there was a vague memory that scratched its way back to her. She remembered being in the shower, and she tried to tell her arms to pull her silk kimono robe shut, so Paul would not see her in just her bra. But as much as she tried to make her hands reach for the beautiful, patterned robe to cover herself, she could not make her body behave.

The robe was covered in birds. She had always loved bird patterns, this one was covered in egrets, or were they herons . . . she didn't know, she blamed the man with the parakeet on his shoulder, and all the books.

"I think she's out again." It was wife number three, and Omelia, just to prove her wrong opened her eyes again, and moved her boiled hotdog fingers. She was able to reach out just a little, and her fingers brushed against the plastic shower curtain liner; no, she wasn't in the shower. She was in the hospital. She remembered now, something had happened to her, a small patch on her face, it had looked like Australia as it burned *those poor koalas* . . . "She's fighting to stay awake, maybe we should just let her rest again." *Ugh. She probably just wanted to get back to the TV Guide Crossword puzzles. The answer to 43 across is The Golden Girls, Heather—that's right. Her name was Heather. Like the pretty weeds that grew outside Wuthering Heights.*

"She's not just fighting to stay awake; she's fighting to stay alive. Nic, can you hear me? Do you think you can take some water?" He took the plastic salmon-colored cup from Heather's hands, and a little of it splashed against her beige blouse: she looked like she was lactating. He did not apologize. He held what was left of the water in one hand and unzipped the plastic tent with the other hand. Once he had it open, he leaned in towards her. Omelia had to move her head back in his direction; the air and the stiff cotton pillowcase rubbed against her skin like steel wool on a dirty stove. She felt something wet start to spill out from the corner of her mouth. *Oh, Jesus fuck, am I drooling . . .*

"Easy, easy . . . just open your mouth a little, barely at all, and just see if you can take a little." Paul saw that Nicole's lips were a deep painful red, and there was a crack that ran down the middle of her lower lip. Underneath there was a dark black scab, and it looked like the night sky when he would wake from a nightmare. That scab matched the spindly crack that grew out of the corner of her mouth, as if her skin and veins had turned to root rot under a wisteria tree. Nicole's eyes were the flowers, faded and wilted on the branch.

Her mouth opened and moved, as if she were mouthing the word, "Ukulele." Paul was gentle when he placed the plastic straw, not between her lips, but rested it on the less ruined side of her bottom lip. Omelia did her best to close her mouth around the straw, and as she sucked, she remembered what she had said about Paul so many years ago. Her eyes moved away from his, in a quick back and forth like a typewriter. What she took in was mostly air, but a few drops of water managed to go down as well. It hurt at first and made her have a cough that she tried to contain, until it ended in a low-toned wet gurgle. She sounded like a frozen pipe that had finally burst in the wall. Omelia was thinking about the dream she had; she thought of the cat trapped in the wall, and she remembered a creak, and then a drip. She took another small sip, and this time more liquid than air made its way down.

When she tried to talk, she realized again that her mouth was moving with no noise . . . she took a breath in; it was shallow, but she found that her air could meet the scream she had stifled for as long as she could remember. She could not talk yet, but she could whisper. She saw Heather over Paul's shoulder, a beige wraith, blurry and boring. Omelia used her boiled hotdog fingers to have him lean in a little closer to her.

She wanted to scream.

She wanted to cry.

She wanted to go back to wherever she was when she searched for a lost cat in a wall, wore a gown, and ran from a house, but all she could manage to say was . . .

"My face, there's something wrong with my face . . ."

DAY 128

Vacationing During the End of the world

*How Beautiful is sunset, when the
glow of Heaven descends upon a land
like thee, Thou Paradise of exiles,
Italy!*

Percy Bysshe Shelley

Chapter twenty

Once There Was a Girl Named Omelia

NICOLE

By the middle of February there had been a little over fourteen million deaths worldwide, with more daily. There were another fifty-six million infected with what the CDC had officially called "Herpes Simplex Virus IX – Varicella Zoster Mutation," which was more than the average person could handle saying. It had become more commonly known as "Interitus," which was the Latin term for decay, ruin, and untimely death. Like people with the Herpes Simplex, patients could recover, and then a few weeks or months later, the virus would wake up and burn like fire though their system again. To be fair, *recover* was a word that most who had it would not claim as their status. Though while in remission, the fevers were gone, as well as the knives that seemed to have moved through their veins and come out through their skin. The symptoms in general were gone, but the scars, they were there; they were always there.

Ruin.

Though the first wave of the virus had peaked by November, there were still new cases, and new deaths daily. There was no progress on a vaccine, and there was no real understanding of where this new mutation had come from, and how it had hit so hard and so fast. There were conspiracy theories aplenty; that the virus was a result of a biochemical attack, or medical experiments gone wrong. People blamed China, North Korea; most of the countries in Africa were blamed, as well as Mexico and South America. It all depended on where a person's racism was the most foul—there was no patient zero that anyone could find, during the first few days, and even weeks. In the first wave they were all patient zero.

The few that lived through the first months were given prescriptions for Ganciclovir that were ten times stronger than anything that had been considered normal. It wasn't a cure; it was an attempt to not reawaken the sleeping giant. It was a Band-Aid on a gunshot wound.

As the shock and awe had started to wear off, and people began to process the monumental grief, they also began to grow tired of the constant death tallies and the terrifying uncertainty of this disease and their futures. People tried to get on with their lives in this 'new normal,' but it was hard to do. Everyone was scared that the virus would wake again, and as the CDC had been warning them, the next wave would be deadlier. Carriers of the virus already had weakened immune systems. There was only *so long* that patients could continue to flare and recover, flare, and recover. The human body, and even more so, the human mind could only take so much.

While physically the disease left scars predominately on or near any mucus membrane, it was in the patients faces and in some, their genitals, that the most damage was done. Victims of Interitus were left ruined. Their faces eaten away in places, and dark black vines crawled up from their mouths and near their eyes. Nicole had wished during the months since she first found that red spot on her face that she had been a lucky one; she wished she had died. To her, it would be better to be dead than to live this life. She had become an invisible monster. Every time she looked in the mirror, she was reminded of the soldiers who had returned home from World War

I; their faces ripped apart in battle. The lucky ones, the ones with money, received sculpted and hand-painted face masks they could wear in public. All Nicole had was a pile of generic blue medical masks, and a few special ones that Paul had ordered for her online. They featured some of the covers of her favorite gothic horror novels. Those beautiful women, running from houses—she could not bring herself to wear them. She could not tell Paul about the dream she had right before she had finally woken up.

She had been staying in her old room in Doctor Paul's condo. On the little shelf above her bed, Paul had placed her two tiaras from her teenage beauty pageants, and in between them, a row of her favorite novels. Her makeup and makeup mirror were tucked away, in storage, for safekeeping. Nicole didn't know whether she was there in that condo for herself, or she was there for him. In the early days of her recovery, wife number three, Heather, had also gotten sick. She battled the fever, the blood clots, and cankers for less than twenty-four hours before she died. When she passed away, Paul had said that Heather's face "had become unrecognizable as human. So, see, it could be worse Nicole, your scars aren't that bad." He never made eye contact with her when he said it. He tried his best to cheer her up, and she knew she should have been better to him; after all it was her fault that Heather had gotten sick. Nicole had probably gotten the virus all over the TV Guide Crossword Puzzle books that had been near Nicole's water pitcher.

If Paul blamed her, he kept that tucked away inside, right next to his failed relationship with Meredith, and the reason he never touched alcohol. He never talked about any of those things. He *did* look at her differently than he did before. Not in the *wrong way* she had once accused him of, but instead there was a hollowed-out blankness to him, as if his eyes were replaced by flat paintings, like a dollar store baby doll. Paul, who was now divorced twice, and widowed once, had almost nothing left to give. He spent his days in PPE. He wore goggles over his glasses, and two face masks, underneath a face shield. Predominately, his patients now were all *survivors* of Interitus; he tended to their healing faces the best he could. He injected collagen and

Botox anywhere that was viable. He would come home exhausted; he would eat a frozen Hungry Man dinner and would watch the news. He kept two little notebooks on the coffee table. In the first book, he would write down the updated death count, and the new infection rate in two columns. The other little notebook was filled with temperatures. First line was Paul, and the second line was Nicole. The notebook rested on a pile of TV Guide Crossword Puzzle books; most of them were filled with answers written in blue pen.

Nicole ceased being Omelia the day she saw her new reflection for the first time. Interitus: destroy, rot, ruin; untimely death. Interitus haunted this condo in the shape of Nicole. She slept most of the day, and at night would try to lose herself in fictional worlds; she read and reread the same books over and over again. But often she found that her mind danced in and out of reality; half dreams, half memories. Her life had flashed before her when she had been actively dying, and it has never stopped. Touching the pages of her books, she remembered the way the brittle empty envelope with the postmark from Tampa, Florida felt in her hands; she remembered her school pictures—the ones that happened before she smiled. She remembered a cold wet towel on the back of her neck. She remembered the note, and the creak . . . and the drip.

When sleep could not find her, she would spend countless hours on her phone. She scrolled through pictures of Italy, The Ghost Castle at Lake Como; she scrolled through images of Murano Glass. She searched for a yellow ashtray that looked like the one that had belonged to Meredith. She read about "Virus Island" off the coast of Venice. Poveglia, which had been a plague island in the eighteenth century and had been off limits to people until a few months ago. It had once been known as the most haunted place in the world. Now, people flocked there, all the victims of the virus. Living ghosts haunted that island now. Poveglia had become a cross between Burning Man and a leper colony. It was not the only one. The idea behind these pop-up plague parties was that people could finally be free: no masks, no constant temperature checks, and if they got sick again then they would die happy. She thought about going there. She thought about how it would feel to kiss people that tasted like sunshine. She wondered if she could meet someone; if she could fall in love before she was eventually pulled back into the foggy nightmare of this plague.

She thought about Kim, and when she did there was a dull ache at the back of her throat. This, she knew, was where her grief lived. Kim, who smelled like sunshine, whose love language was "gifts", was probably dead. Nicole had been too scared to Google her. If she didn't know for sure then Kim could always be there; the hope of her, the wish of her. Images flashed through her head of that last night before the world ended, and she wished she had more fun; she had wished she had felt alive, instead of just there.

She looked at the photos she had taken of that night one last time before she deleted them.

Nicole had not come to terms with how the world could have ended, yet still somehow kept going. They still had to go on; everyone just went through the motions of their daily lives. Those who still had jobs worked, people went grocery shopping, they walked their dogs, and they waited; waited for death. She remembered a quote from Isaac Asimov, she had memorized it when she went through her brief Sci-Fi phase. He had said, "Life is pleasant. Death is peaceful. It's the transition that's troublesome."

Yes. Troublesome.

Images of Italy scrolled by on her phone. She could go; she could get on a plane. This had been her thought for the past month. It was the thing that kept her up at night—the airports had started opening again about a month ago, and the Venice airport was one of the few that still saw regular flights daily.

Poveglia.

She hated islands, she thought they were creepy; she blamed this on the one vacation she had been on when she was a kid. Her father had taken her to a little island off the coast of Maine. It was supposed to be haunted.

They had stayed in an old boarding house. The entire place seemed *off* to her and gave her the feeling of walking into a room and seeing the patterns of the wallpaper morph into faces. She remembered coming home from that trip and finding long red hairs for weeks on all her clothes. Her skin had smelled briny, like low tide. That island, Dagger Island, had ruined her, but she had always wanted to see Italy. To go to Venice. She wanted to wear a Venetian Mask, and maybe she would even be happier in one of those. Something with a veil perhaps. A mourning mask. She had wanted to see the rotting door and the royal blue awnings of Palazzo Mocenigo; to see Byron's former home on the Grand Canal. She wanted to see Murano Glass, and a castle with ghosts on the walls; she wanted to see Rome, Florence, Milan. She wanted to run.

She did not know how much longer she would be able to look at Paul's dead eyes and hear his pencil scratching against the paper as he updated the death counts. She pulled up the travel site on her phone, and looked at the flight schedule, she could leave . . .

She tried to think of what she would say to Paul and decided that she would have to write a note. *I'm sorry, I tried, I really did, but I just can't anymore. You look at me wrong.* That would do it. His heart was already broken; it couldn't break again, could it? The alarm went off on her phone, and she knew that meant it was time for her to take her temperature. She knew if she didn't text a photo of the thermometer to Paul in a few minutes that he would be call her in a state of panic. This wasn't a life for him. It may be what he thought he wanted, but it was not what he deserved. He did not need the ghost of Interitus in his condo, no matter how many tiaras were on its shelf. She had clicked the check-out button on the website and was typing in her credit card number with one hand and she reached for the thermometer with her other. She would be on a flight tonight, and well on her way to Boston before Paul was even home from work. He may not even know she was gone until she missed her temperature check in.

And with that thought, the thermometer beeped, and she snapped a photo of it. It was 99.8. Sure it was a little up, but not enough to be too concerned. She snapped a photo of the thermometer and added a little note, and a little lie. "I just had some hot tea, sorry, that's probably why it's up. I wasn't looking at the time. DON'T WORRY!" She hit send, and then she started to pack.

Chapter/
twenty–one

Fly Like an Eagle

SAM

Two weeks after Simon died, and Melody had failed to come back for him, Santo had pulled some strings and Sam had become in charge of the boy's funeral—which was not a funeral at all. Sam, not knowing what to do, had decided to have the boy cremated. He asked that Simon be allowed to wear George's old, faded, red flannel shirt. In Sam's head, it plaited them all together now: Shannon, Simon, and George. Three souls that looked at him and saw that he was—*something*. He was there in the room when they put his body into the cremation furnace. They asked him if he wanted to be the one to press the button, and though he had wanted to say no, to scream it, he could not form the words. There was a ball of sadness like a fist at the back of his throat, and the words, of which there were none, could not even be formed. Instead, he nodded yes, and tears spilled down his face, and pooled in his face mask. They tickled the side of his nose and dripped into his mouth.

Simon's ashes came home with Sam. They were in a small mahogany box and tucked into the top shelf of the bar next to the jar of Luxardo cherries. A few days later Sam had found his well-loved copy of *The Complete Works of William Shakespeare* and leaned it on the other side. Simon would have liked that.

He did not leave the house after that. He hated to admit it, but without a driver he did not really understand how to get places, and even if he could go somewhere, where would he go? Food was delivered, alcohol was delivered, and the three bottles of hidden Adderall were taken from their hiding spots and put back in the medicine cabinet.

The President died several days after Simon was cremated. Santo Anthony Alberti was sworn in as President of the United States in a small, masked ceremony in a hospital hallway. The news footage showed flickering fluorescent lights that made everyone's skin look sallow and bruised. The news footage was the first time Sam had seen his mother in almost a year. She looked like a movie star that had too much plastic surgery. She looked like how he remembered her, but just a little different, as if there was an actress playing her part.

Sam stayed in the brownstone in Back Bay alone. The house became all at once too small, and too big for him. He padded around the house during the day, he drank everything he possibly could, except the gin, which he and Shannon were allergic to. The rehab story, and his banishment from the public eye was a wish never granted. A few hours after little Simon had collapsed at the press conference, the entire world changed as a then-nameless disease slouched towards Bethlehem and waited to be born. No one cared about the 'New JFK' after that.

Sam had not gotten sick, though he had held Simon as he collapsed, and then again as he died. Gretchen claimed she had gotten a *mild case* and was still able to be seen without a mask, at least in private. Her scars were shallow and seemed to look more like the fine lines of a spider's web instead of the hairy, long legs of a tarantula that marked most peoples' faces.

Sam stopped watching the news about a month after Santo had

become the president. He realized that if he had wanted to see his father daily, he would have tried harder to make the man love him. There was something else though, something that made the back of Sam's neck itch, and sent the shivers of long fingernails down his spine. In all the statements, and all the press conferences and photo-ops taken near hospitals and the sick, he had not seen his mother since the ceremony. He knew of course, that she had always been absent, barely more than a haunted painting, but he assumed that at some point she would be there, lingering in the background, like an ice sculpture as it slowly melted without anyone's notice.

Sam waited a little over two months after his news sabbatical before he texted his mother. She did not reply. He searched on the internet; he thought he would find a plethora of chatter about where she was, but it was silent, like those fleeting moments in the middle of a storm when even the insects and wind stop their operatic life.

He texted her again.

Nothing.

Though it was against everything in him, he called his father on his personal cell phone. "Yes?" Santo's voice seemed to come out of nowhere; Sam had not even heard the phone ring.

"It's me."

"I know." Santo paused, as if he were waiting for the next Sam-related crisis. "Is there something wrong, have you done something? Are you sick?"

Sam had hated the order that these questions had come; they were like a letter that was written, ripped up, and then pasted back together in the wrong order. "I was wondering about Mom?"

"Do you mean about her remains?" Santo said. Sam could hear that the phone had been placed down on a desk, so Sam was now on speaker phone. Her heard Santo's fingers click clack on the keyboard, and Sam thought about hearing hail on the tin roof of his Nonna's kitchen when he was a boy. He heard Shannon's laugh, and it sounded like a deep melted gold, and his mother's laugh pierced the air like silver. They had huddled together at the table, and thought the roof would cave in. Their summers in Italy were like postcards and faded photos come to life.

"What do you mean her remains?" There was a lifetime in this pause, and just as Sam was about to speak again, the room smelled like cherries and from the other side of the door of their shared bathroom, he heard the bell. Its notes sang in a slow and even manner, louder than usual. This was not the normal Shannon pattern, this was different. It sounded funereal; the bell seemed to sob, like a little girl with her first broken heart. "She's dead." It was not a question, it was a realization. As Sam said this, he wondered if his father could hear the bell all the way in the Oval Office.

But of course, he could not, he had never heard it, not even when Shannon was alive, not even that night.

The scar on Sam's nose started to sting.

"Gretchen was supposed to call you. I'm sorry, it happened very quickly, and we have been trying to keep quiet about it. We don't need the word spreading too fast, we wanted to wait until after everyone had come to terms with losing the President." Santo cleared his throat, and Sam could hear a milky gurgle in his father's breath. It sounded like cream of mushroom soup coming to a boil. Sam knew he should cry, but he felt like there was nothing left for him to give. Losing his mother felt like nothing more than if he had watched a late day shadow disappear into the gloaming. It was as if she were never there at all.

"You could have called me . . ."

"I've been busy, and I knew I didn't have the time, or the energy to put into some emotional conversation with you when you probably would be high or near blackout drunk— I'm sorry, alright?"

The bell was silent. But the ice clinked in Sam's glass; it sounded like a secret being shared.

"I've decided to go to Italy; I'll be going to Nonna's house, like we had planned."

"You know you don't need to go now, and if you are doing this for attention . . ." Santo breathed in and let out an exhausted sigh, "I just don't have time right now Sam. There are bigger things I need to deal with. What you did to that boy, the things you said, people don't care anymore. Hell, you could run for office again if you wanted to. No one even remembers it."

"I remember it, I remember all of it."

Santo didn't respond, and Sam heard the sound of a fancy pen being dragged across paper; there was a beautiful aggressiveness in the sound, and Sam could tell even without seeing it, that Santo was signing his name. He was working, he was *president-ing*. Whatever that meant right now at the end of the world.

"Your best bet would be to fly into Venice and take the train down. I think Rome is only having incoming flights every few days, and trains aren't stopping there anymore; there are too many dead, the homeless outside the Vatican, the bodies are rotting in the streets, it's a fucking mess, there's no place to put them. Venice would be easier, they are letting people in, and from what I hear they aren't being as strict as they should with the temperature checks either. So . . . if you are sick, and that's why you are leaving, you still may be able to get in."

"I'm not sick."

"Irony, right? At any rate, email your travel details to Gretchen and she will pass them on. I should know where you are, and call when you get there, to Nonna's. I will tell the caretakers to prepare the house. When will you be leaving?"

"Tonight, if I can; if not, then tomorrow." Sam understood that he was already on his way to Italy; he had been on his way since the hospital. Maybe a part of him had never left that hospital, maybe part of him still sat in the greenish hue of the fluorescent lights. He didn't know which hospital room he was in; was it Shannon's room? Was it Simon's? "I should go. Thanks for telling me about Mom." He hung up as he heard his father mumble something. He sounded far away. Sam looked around his bedroom, at the four almost blank walls that cradled his life and he realized that maybe he was never really here at all.

Chapter/
twenty-two

One is the Loneliest Number

NICOLE

N icole had managed to pass every temperature check that she had. Each time she came in just under the highest point of *'normal'*. She had ice water before the Uber picked her up and brought her all the way to Boston's Logan Airport an hour away. It was expensive, but fuck credit card debt. When she got to the airport, she made sure to linger outside; she watched the steam from her warm breath dance and disappear into the low hanging clouds and the stagnant exhaust fumes from the line of taxis out front. Most of which were just idling there, passenger-less. When she got into the airport, there was a temperature checkpoint right away; hers was still just a shade over 99, and was in the *healthy* range. What Nicole didn't tell anyone was that before any of this had happened, her temperature would normally be a little lower than normal; since she was a child, she had always been a chilly 97.6-degree average.

She doubled her dose of Ganciclovir. She chewed an extra one on the Uber ride to Boston. She wished she had moved here; she always loved that the entire city smelled like a tunnel, even if you were above ground.

Nicole did not feel sick, not yet. She had none of the original symptoms; the pain that felt like flesh being branded, or even the cankers that spread and ate away at not just her face, but who she was—who she had become. The virus had done that; it had killed Omelia. Now she was not sure why, but the veil between her memories, and her here and now seemed to be gone most of the time. She felt like she saw and felt her whole life all at once. It played in her head like a slide show; all the moments that made her. Nicole, Omelia, Nicole. Daughter, orphan, foster-daughter, orphan.

Maybe she *was* dying.

She did her makeup, even under the mask, which she knew was both useless but necessary to who she was. When she put on lipstick it felt both foreign and familiar; like trying to read in a dream. There was safety there, in the makeup. She liked the layers of it, a mask under a mask. She spent the most time on her eyes; she used a deep burnished bronze on her lids and created a dramatic smoky eye complete with eyeliner wing. She smudged the eyeliner just little with the tips of her fingers and she had the look of someone who had slept in her makeup; a woman exhausted from last night's party. This was how Omelia had lived her life, and today, Nicole wanted wear the Omelia mask again, even if just for a little while.

On her flight to Venice, the plane was less than a quarter full. She'd been able to stretch out her legs and lean against the window, even way back in the cheap seats by the bathroom. When she closed her eyes, she could taste Scotch, and images flashed in her head like photos that fell from an album; memories already faded and now tossed aside. She heard herself whisper *he looks at me wrong*. The memory startled her awake. She looked at her phone and knew that Paul would have to understand that she was gone by now. She had left the note in his bedroom. His room was stuffy when she walked in, and the air smelled like tears and dirty sheets. She was afraid to taste his sadness if she opened her mouth. She was afraid she would love the way it tasted, and she would never leave. The bed was still neatly made on Heather's former side and pulled to fitful pieces on Paul's. She placed the note on Heather's pillow. As the folded paper had been set down, the room seemed to darken around her, and the paper looked like an origami swan out of the corner of her eyes. She thought it was a strange trick of the light, and she stepped back into the room and saw that it was just her note— still fresh and unread on the pillow.

That was when she heard it, the too familiar sound. The creak . . . the drip . . .

She could still hear it now, on the plane 36,000 feet up. She tried to focus on it and once she did, everything else seemed to be silent. Even the roar of the engine was gone. All there was, was the creak, the drip. When she closed her eyes, she saw his feet, barely two feet off the floor; they still swayed. They always would.

Somewhere in the deepest part of her concentration, when all there was, was the sound of him, she thought she heard a bell ring. The shrill sound seemed to scream though the air. The few passengers in the rows close to her had not heard it, or if they did, they did not react. She closed her eyes again, and as her head leaned into the little divot near the window she heard it again. The sound seemed to be coming from First Class.

Assholes. They ruined everything.

The moisture from the canals blanketed Venice in a low dreamy fog that reminded Nicole of the days she spent in her milky coma in the hospital. The uneven streets and alleys, with their little storybook bridges, were coated with a thin layer of ice that cracked like spider webs as she walked. The glass windows of the darkened shops were frosted over around the edges, and though most places were still closed, there were a few places that were open, and had their lights on. These little shops, which were not much larger than a handicapped restroom stall, mainly sold Absinthe and Limoncello, and for today, that would be fine. She bought a small bottle of each and loved the way the madness green and the bright yellow—the same color as Meredith's Italian ashtray— looked next to each other in the bag. She found a market and bought some bread. The woman behind the register wore a kerchief around the bottom of her face, and it reminded Nicole of a train robber. Before the woman could offer her a bag, Nicole had snatched the bread off the counter and put it in the same bag with the bottles.

As she walked, she reached in and pulled out chunks of still warm but dry bread, and when no one was looking she would take her mask off and eat. Bread had never tasted so good; to her it tasted like finally being able to disappear. Here, in this ephemeral, strange, haunted city, she didn't have to be Omelia, or Nicole, she could be no one. She sipped the Absinthe directly from the bottle. Each sip burned the inside of her throat, and the sides of her tongue started to swell. The inside of her mask smelled like licorice while she wandered the city as it darkened around her.

Every time she took a step on the slick stone streets, she had to catch herself before she slipped. The absinthe had not helped her balance, but it had started to help her. There was something about alcohol that stopped the memories from being able to catch her. The alcohol had helped her to run a little faster, and a little further from her memories. Her feet and fingers had gone numb in the cold, but the strong licorice flavor warmed her from the center of her chest. And though she knew it was only a combination of alcohol and sleep deprivation, she understood that this was what it must feel like to fall in love. She had never been in love or been loved in a romantic way, and now that she was left with a face like a rotted corn husk . . . she doubted she ever would.

She still held out hope though that maybe someday, if she lived to *someday*, that she would fall not necessarily in love, but at least fall out of loneliness. That would be enough for her. It wouldn't be love, but it would be something.

She did not wander too far from her hotel; every turn she took in an attempt to get lost, just led her in a labyrinthine maze that always found her right back on the street of the beautiful pink building on the Grand Canal, just a few blocks from where the bus from the mainland had dropped her off. When she returned to the hotel, she noticed that the lobby was decorated with a beautiful Murano chandelier. It took up most of the ceiling and to her, it looked like a Lovecraftian creature was there to watch over her. The blown glass was the same colors as the alcohol in her bag. There were bulbs that had burned out and most of the glass was covered with cobwebs. The light that filtered from the colored glass seemed to have the strange milky quality of the streets. It made the room look like the foggy night was also a guest here.

The Hotel Bellini was almost deserted, and even though it was one of the few hotels that had remained open, it still felt abandoned. Her room was located up three steep flights of slippery marble stairs, and down a corridor that led to the front of the building. This was the part of the hotel that faced the Grand Canal. When she opened the door to her room, she was in a narrow hallway that had beautiful purple silk-lined walls. It led her past a bathroom with a clawfoot tub on her left before it opened to her bedroom. There were heavy doors that were on the opposite wall; they ran from floor to ceiling, and after she dropped her bag and her mask on the bed she went to the doors. She felt nervous as her hands rested on the door handles. They opened with a deep groan, and they led to a balcony that overlooked the Grand Canal. There were very few water taxis, and the boats that still traveled the canal had to skirt in and around ice. She wondered if the canal would freeze over in the night, and if the boats would have to break though again in the morning. It was an unusual cold snap, and to Nicole it seemed right to be here at this time.

As Nicole stared at the canal from her slippery stone balcony, she thought of Poveglia. She wondered what a life on that island would be like. She imagined that it would be a lot like her Absinthe-laced walk through the city except with loud, electronic music. Now that she was here in this city of ghosts, she began to feel a comfort in the empty streets, and the thought of the Plague Island, with all those people, made her whole body ache with exhaustion and apprehension. She had decided to switch to the Limoncello, but the tart lemon felt like sandpaper on her irritated throat.

She went back into her room and left the door to her balcony open a few inches. She laid on the bed and felt the cool air against her skin; she had never been this far away from home and she found herself homesick and anxious. Her combat boots were still on and covered in a layer of mud, though she could not remember walking through any dirt or sand . . . maybe this was from home . . . there it was again. The homesickness. Manchester already felt like a dream she couldn't wake from. Homesick. Not for a place really, but for a time. Nicole could hear her father's voice as it echoed out of her memory from so many years ago; she heard him tell her to get her dirty winter boots off the sofa. She didn't bother when she was a child, and she didn't bother now.

She let her head fall back on the pillow and felt the shafts of the feathers poke through the pillowcase and scratch at her tender skin. The ceiling of the room had subtle patterns in the plaster; some of them formed screaming, wretched faces, and others looked more like hummingbirds. If she closed her eyes, she thought she could almost sleep. She fought against it, and stared at the ceiling, the faces, and the birds. She did not want to give in to the dreams and the whisper of fear that had started in her head on her way to Boston. The fear of 99.8 degrees, too close to 100. If she fell asleep, she may never wake up. She watched the ceiling faces grow angry and no matter how hard she stared; the hummingbird's wings moved too fast for her to see. She let the steady hum of their wings calm her. Somewhere around 4:30am she drifted off for a little while. She could not fight sleep any longer, and the thought that had started to play on repeat in her mind had finally grown quiet. There was a feeling that quivered around her heart that told her that she no longer wanted to be lonely. That there was a part inside of her that had been bleeding out for years. Since the empty envelope with the postmark from Florida—maybe even before that. For the first time in her life, she wanted a letter in that empty envelope. What would her mother have said?

As she drifted off, she swore to herself that she could hear the same bell that she heard on the plane earlier. It seemed to come from the walls, or even from the empty city itself.

Chapter/ twenty–three

Idiota Ubriaco

SAM

The best part of Italy was that no one batted an eye when Sam drank fizzy wine with his breakfast. It was 6:00am, and after a fitful night of sleep due to his almost blind intoxication and the fact that somehow after years of wishing it would happen . . . Shannon followed him to Italy.

Sam always brought the bell with him; he even had it in college, but it never made a sound. He remembered his college days, leaving bars in Uptown NYC past 3:00am. He was always the kind of blind drunk that made him thankful to be alive the next morning. He still felt that wave of all-encompassing loneliness that he had felt when he was there. He would stare at Shannon's bell and through his tears, he would pray for it to make a sound, he would beg the stale dry air in his apartment for Shannon, he would beg for a sound in the long hours of quiet. She and the bell were silent, always. Until now. Well to be fair, it hadn't made a sound until he was halfway over the Atlantic and had just fallen into what he thought would be a dreamless sleep.

Instead, he paced through First Class off and on throughout the night. Like a colicky baby, the bell was silent as long as he kept moving. The moment he would sit, breathe, and stretch his legs out and close his eyes…it would start again.

By the time he landed in Venice he was half-dead on his feet. He lumbered instead of walked, and the wet, uneven cobblestone of the streets caught under his feet with every step. The air was cold, and he had never been in this part of Italy during winter. He was thankful that the face mask helped to keep him warm as he wandered past the train station.

The Hotel Bellini was a pink nightmare, but it was his nightmare, at least for a night, or maybe two. He needed to figure out how he was going to get to Palermo. He had realized that half the train stations were still closed, and that there was no direct route to get to his Nonna's house. The hotel had an in-house bar, which was closed to the public, but with enough cash, Sam was able to buy a bottle of Jameson to bring back to his room. He opened the bottle and poured an unhealthy four fingers of booze into the dusty water glass that was in the bathroom. It tasted like an attic. The alcohol burned as it slid down his throat. He poured even more into the glass and sipped this one a little slower. He remembered the first time he had mentioned Shannon's bell to a therapist, they had suggested medication; the therapist after that, strongly suggested time away to *"rest."* He told them both the same thing he was telling himself now.

He was not crazy. He was haunted.

It was that thought that bounced around in his head. Sam spent the night in a deep emerald-green velvet chair in his room; he stared at shadows on the wall until they looked like twins. Tangled legs on a hospital bed. He did not sleep, and by 6:00am his skin was sallow and there was a sour smell that radiated out of his pores. It was the smell of a night of whiskey and almost 36 hours of sleepless angst; it was the smell of loneliness and grief. Time. It was the smell of missing Shannon, how he felt her there even when she wasn't. The same way a soldier felt a cold arthritic winter ache in the bones of his long ago blown-off leg. Somewhere in this un-fevered dream, he thought of his mother, and he finally felt the weight of this new loss. It made his eyes heavy, and when he tried to move out of the chair, he found that his legs and arms didn't move, no matter how much he told them to. His eyes closed and he drifted off before he was able to remember the last time he had spoken to his mother. Had he said 'I love you,' had he heard her smile through the phone; did she ask him questions? He didn't know. All he could remember was that when she smiled, she reminded him of winter sun that made the frozen milkweeds at the side of a pond just seem to glow. The light of this memory was so bright that his eyes closed. He slept for a little over an hour and woke as the strange black rotary phone that was next to the bed shrilled into life.

Even when the world ends . . . there is always a goddamn wakeup call.

Meals in the breakfast room were scheduled 45 minutes apart, and if there were other guests in this pink palace, he had no idea. This room was lined with mirrors and made the room seem more expansive than it really was. With a cellphone in one hand, and a paper map of the train routes for Italy in the other, he went to work. They gave him a bottle of Prosecco with breakfast. He drank with the smallest splash of orange juice that he added directly to the bottle. Classy.

Traveling through Rome was out of the question, the stations there were closed, and the city had never come out of their strict lockdown. He would need to take the train from Venice, transfer first in Verona, and then in Milan; from there to Genoa, before heading south to Napoli and then Salerno; and finally, to Palermo, and the solitude of his Nonna's house. He wanted to hear rain on her tin roof. He wanted to remember laughter that sounded like gold and silver. He cried so much these days, and he had little understanding of when it happened.

Sam heard that the trains ran at haphazard times, and sometimes not at all. This journey would probably take him several days. He leaned back in his chair, and he thought of Verona, and *Romeo and Juliet*; he had read it when he was barely ten, and he understood little of it, but there was a rhythm and beauty in the words once he was able to read them. It made the underside of his heart feel lighter. When Shannon was in the hospital the fourth time, he would read it to her. He begged her to do some of the parts with him, so his voice would not get so tired.

She was pale, her hair looked thin, and greasy; her skin looked like an old wartime letter. She was a brittle reminder of how fleeting all of this was. She was a girl who could disintegrate in front of him. First her hair went, and then she lost two fingernails, and her near-skeletal body would bruise when she changed positions in her bed, and *he* complained because his voice was tired. God, he was an asshole, even then.

He poured the last of the prosecco in his glass, and it was then that he realized that he had not bothered to eat. He had piled his plate with runny scrambled eggs, and untoasted rolls of bread. When he glanced up to see the time, he realized his 45 minutes were done. Maybe it was the prosecco, and maybe it was the mirrors, but the room grew fuzzy around him, and he felt medicated and woozy. It was then that he saw it: a red plaid blur, a fuzzy shape in the corner of the room. He was on his feet and stepping away from the table—his heart skittered in his chest. The room around him felt like he was about to tumble down a well. He had knocked the wine glass to the floor where it shattered into pieces; it looked like icy glass snow.

He wasn't crazy.

He was haunted.

"*Idiota ubriaco,*" he heard the woman say, her words barely muffled by her face mask. *Drunken idiot.* She said this under her breath, in a whisper loud enough for the cheap seats to hear. She cleaned up the broken glass, and she never knew that Sam was fluent in Italian. He stumbled a little as he bent down to help her, but she moved away and pressed herself into the wall; she was closer to the street now than she was to him. She shooed him away with her hands, as if he were a stray cat who had come in from the cold to beg. He stood up and took a deep breath. His lungs hurt, not from sickness, but from the panic that squeezed his chest like toothpaste out of a tube. He looked in the mirror again . . . there was no red flannel shirt that he could see, but just because he couldn't see it didn't mean it wasn't there.

He exhaled. He should have eaten. As his hand shook, he grabbed a few hard-boiled eggs and a couple of cold bread rolls and stuffed them in his pockets. He didn't take notice of the woman who waited to get into the breakfast room. All he knew was as he passed her he tried to do his best to keep the social distance, but he stumbled, and his shoulder knocked into the doorjamb. He was already drunk at 7am.

He was still drunk at 7am.

He heard Shannon's bell as it called to him from up the stairs, and it helped him find his way back to his room. At each landing there was a small window; it faced out towards the Grand Canal and the pink sky of a new day. The light made the marble stairs shine in a reddish hue with black vines. It was beautiful and it was awful . . . it looked like a cancer. It looked like Interitus. Each step he took was a technicolor nightmare of all of Shannon's PET Scans and Simon's disintegrated face. By the time he got to his room, the bell had stopped.

He . . . on the other hand, had never cried harder in his life.

Interlude/

I am stronger here; stronger even than I was in that sour room that smelled like bitter medicine and only got early morning sun. The room on the opposite side of that *shared* bathroom.

My room, which smelled like two different kinds of lemon, was my home, it *is* my home. One of those lemon scents was from my Capri Sun juice pouches, the lemonade that didn't so much taste like lemon, but more but like what the idea of lemon was, of what it could be. The yellow of it. The cloudiness of it. After I got sick the juice pouches tasted like the stale air on the bad side of an ocean storm at Nonna's house. Her back yard was filled with lemon trees with no one to pick them or enjoy. The ground under the trees would eventually be filled with darkened yellow rot, and when the wind blew *just right* you could taste something like lemon— something like death, on your tongue.

Capri Sun juice pouches.

They taste like the summer before I got sick. They taste like all the summers.

Now the part of me that can still remember what it is like to have a body stands in a pink building and I hold a shiny almost decaying lemon-colored bell. I held that in my hands when I was . . . when I was who I was before this.

When I was a girl.

Now, I am nothing; I am the lemon scent on stale wind. I am rotten cherries in a dusty jar.

I am a bell that no one hears until now.

I don't know how I am here with him. I have wanted this and not wanted it my whole life. No. No. No. My death. I have wanted it since then. My death. My death. My dying. My…it was twenty-five years ago, but it is still too new for me to understand. I was alive. Now I am dead. Not dying, but dead. Past. I am in the past, yet still, I am here.

His little face—Not as little as mine—was something I understood. His nose was aquiline and too big when we were small. And when he would sleep, after we threw three pre-teen tantrums in a row to convince our parents to let him spend the night at the hospital to be with me, I would stare at him and know that he and his nose would go on living, growing, even after I was gone.

I am a lemonade pouch at my best, and I am the thick lemon that cloys in my nose, and later bled out in scabs. That lemon disinfectant. I am *that* lemon at my worst.

Hospital.

Sweet and Sour.

It would be better for all of us who are, or were, actively dying to not have it be sweet at all, just have it be . . .

Death.

What is the scent of that, what is the scent of my death? Is it lemon? Is it the smell of this bell? Divots in metal that smell like pennies. The wooden handle smells like my skin, but the sound that comes out of it is hope, it's rage, and even though I don't want it . . . the smell that comes out of it is—blame.

Does blame smell like lemon, and late afternoon sun that only shines in my brother's room? Does blame smell like gourmet cherries that stained my fingers a deep red, like the period I never was old enough to get?

Does blame smell like hospital disinfectant that you know people try to scrub away when they leave your room?

Does blame shine on a steep marble staircase, red morning sun on deep black veiny stairs?

No one else had ever heard me until now, until the plane, the hotel, the hope, the wish of me, the painfully beautiful painting of Italy . . . until her. That stranger on the plane who has eyes like old books.

I feel her, and I know Sam doesn't—not yet. All he feels is loss, and he feels sorry for himself. She hears me, and now he does too. Sometimes there are broken things that somehow fit together. Sometimes it is broken china and gold. Sometimes it is strangers . . . and a bell that no one can hear.

Sometimes it's . . .

"Hi."

It's the boy. I have been alone for so long, this is still new, this little stranger that haunts me.

I feel the red flannel he wears before I really see it. The soft fabric touches the side of my arm and all the pale hairs that are really just my imagination stand up on end. It feels like a butterfly kiss. It feels like when my Nonna would blink her eyelashes against my skin.

"Hey." I ring the bell; I am calling to Sam from upstairs. I am helping him find his way back; this is my task. I can hear Eagle stumbling a little up the stairs, his hand on the railing smacks down heavy and pulls him up. His legs are too long for the steep staircase. The boy next to me looks drawn in and hollow the same way I suppose I do. His face is narrow, and his eyes are wide like an owl's, and for some reason half his face is blurry to me. It looks like a memory. He is about my age but smaller. I've seen him before. I was the shadow wearing that same shirt while he was in the hospital. He didn't know that my brother came into his room, smelling like his mother's sex.

But that was a long time ago now. I remember it like it happened yesterday, and like it's happening right now. This boy; his name is Simon, and when he was dying . . . actively dying— he was in and out of his bed . . . in and out of his body. One of the times, I could have sworn he saw me. I tried to introduce myself, but he was already gone.

Just a moth turning to dust.

I ring the bell again, and Simon winces away from its loud clang. I know my brother, and I understand that Eagle doesn't remember what floor his room is on, his home for today, for tonight . . . for the unrecognized hours between rest and running.

"That's my shirt," I say in between the bell ringing. My eyes sneak towards him, the boy, the back of my neck gets hot, and I suddenly wish that I could pull my hair back in a ponytail.

"Oh yeah, I don't know how I have it, I just do . . ." We both look down the stairs and hear Sam's fingernails as they scratch against the wall. He walks with his arms stretched out, a palm on each side of the narrow hallway. He probably thought better of having his hand on the railings.

Too many germs.

"Well, it belonged to me, at least for a little while." I don't know why I am talking about the shirt . . . I have not talked for twenty-five years, and now this.

Flannel shirt obsession.

Maybe I am flirting, but I don't know. I know my neck is hot, and that my brother is drunk, and I think it's not quite seven am. This is bad, even for him.

"I can give it back to you, he gave it to me, or I think he did . . ." Simon rubs the worn fabric near the elbows, the parts that look like damaged window screens, chewed up from a squirrel.

"I just don't know why you're here?" I know I am being a bitch. The air in the hallway starts to smell like cherries.

His little face looks back at me with no answer.

"Why are you haunting him?" I felt strangely possessive of Sam, of my years of being his only ghost; at this rate how many more would show up?

Mom? George? And what about this girl, the one who can hear me?

He was shaking his head, and he said the words right away before he thought better of them, "I think he loved me, probably more than anyone in my life had . . ." He looks uncomfortable now as he turns away from me and he rubs his hands in slow circles on the silk wallpaper. "I know he didn't know me . . ."

When I look at him, I understand it all. I understood the skinny boy, with hands that his body will never grow into, and I understand Eagle. I ring the bell a few more times before Sam finally rounds the last of the stairs before him. He is out of breath; he is beleaguered for a thirty-six-year-old. His eyes are old; he is almost the same age our father was when I died. Too young to be so old.

"He loved me like that too. Did you know that people used to call him the *New JFK?*" I can feel myself smiling, I can feel the stirrings of something like happiness . . . "We can share that shirt. If you want to?"

"Yeah; yeah, I'd like that."

part 11

Chapter/ twenty-four

Her head banged against the train window; its incessant but uneven rhythm made it impossible for her to sleep even with the heavy exhaustion that had climbed into her body. It made her limbs feel as if they were sandbags preparing for a flood. The upper part of her eye socket rested against the dirty side of the window. She wondered for a few seconds when the last time anyone had cleaned this train car . . . days? Weeks? Were there people left to clean the trains? Next to the window looked like an abstract painting; it was smudged with fingerprints. Nicole leaned the good half of her face against the cool surface. It felt sticky, but she only bothered to care for a minute.

Venice was a blur, less than 48 hours of which she slept, four, no, maybe five hours of her time there.

The Vaporetto still ran from 5am until a little after midnight. The captains of these water buses ignored most of the stops now, there was never anyone there. But they were kind to the few people that they did pick up, even the ones that rode the water bus all day. Aimless. Haunted. "I want to see where Byron lived," Nicole said this when she got onto the Vaporetto at a little past seven thirty in the morning. The captain gave her a look that said without words, that he did not know what she was saying. As she tried to get close to him, to point to the photo on her phone, he shooshed her back with his hands clad in brown leather working gloves. The gloves were worn and cracked around the knuckles. Nicole did not understand why but those gloves made her miss her father more than she had in years.

The floor of the boat had bright glow strip yellow tape on the floor; it designated how close you could come to the driver. She tried to shout at him, but it was obvious he was exhausted, and did not know her language, nor did he care. Byron meant nothing to him. Not today. His eyes just looked out at the rotted buildings that lined the canal, this short history of decay. It was cold for Venice and even with his mask on, the captain's breath still gave the inside of his face shield a thin layer of ice that he had to scrape off at every stop, and during the long runs between them, when it was just water, rotted buildings, and damp air.

The boat stopped sometimes, mostly for people in medical scrubs. They kept their heads down and sat as far away as they could from one another. Nicole stayed on the boat, getting off only once to find a dark bar; she paid three euros for a shot of whiskey, and then she used the bathroom. Halfway through the day a different captain took over. Nicole shouted in poorly pronounced and almost comically inflected Italian, "*Puoi mostrarmi dove viveva Byron?*" She had spent the morning and early afternoon learning the phrase, *can you show me where Byron lived?* She thought she must have butchered it. She gestured with her hands like a black and white television show from the fifties. Her words shouted from the safety distance behind the yellow glow tape. The new captain didn't even look at her. She wore two masks. The one closest to her face felt wet, and she wanted to believe that it was sweat except it tasted like pennies and October. In her heart, she knew this taste, it was death, it chased her all the way here.

"*Palazzo Mocenigo?*" His voice sounded like rusty hinges on a door that had been closed for months.

"*Si, Si.*"

He made a motion with his arms like he was guiding a 'Tilt-A-Whirl' ride at an amusement park. When Nicole saw him, she understood that the building was behind them and she would see it on the way back.

"*Grazie* . . . just point to it when you can." Her voice was loud, and she hated the American-ness of shouting to someone who didn't speak her language.

He gave her a thumbs up, and she moved to the furthest side of the Vaporetto. She leaned over the side of the boat; there were two other passengers, and they were far enough away from her that she was able to take off her masks. She wanted to breathe in the cold mist of Venice. It felt like she breathed in history, ghosts, she breathed in other people's stories until there was no room for her own. Her inner mask, as she suspected, was speckled with blood. It was coming from her lungs or from her skin . . . neither were good signs. It looked like a Pollock painting. In her blood she saw a butterfly with a half-torn wing. She leaned her unmasked face over the side of the boat and breathed in the smell of the water; it smelled like every dream she had ever had.

She tucked the mask, darkened with blood, back into her travel purse. She pulled out a new disposable mask and put her cloth mask, with sparkly tiaras, over it. She tasted the city, and the water that made it what it was. It tasted like poetry, ghosts, rotted buildings, and the kind of beautiful sadness that made her feel alive. She wondered what makeup look she would do for this if she could. Mill-yard blues and hints of greens and grays, the colors of the sky, and the icy water. She would use that on her eyes, her eyeliner would be dark and would look like the cracks in the cobblestone. Her lips a deep red, the color of the gondolas that sat moored and alone in the smaller canals. Her face, she would not have to do anything to her face. Her scars were the buildings that were beautiful in their despair, in their rot. These are Omelia's thoughts; they felt like little strangers in Nicole's head.

With the mist on her skin, and wisps of her hair that curled and framed her face, she felt herself as she drifted closer and closer to Nicole, to who she was, who she really was. She closed her eyes and saw a faded green photo album, she saw the sun as it bounced off the steeple of Saint Marie's Church, she began to smell cherries in the air when she heard the words coming at her through a dream turned nightmare and back to dream . . .

"*Ciao, Bella . . . il poeta, la casa di Byron è lì.*"

Nicole recognized the word *bella* before anything else, and for the first time in four months she thought of being Omelia and smiled. She was thankful that part of her was already dead.

She was alert as she saw his fat gloved finger as it pointed to an unassuming white building on the Grand Canal, the colors of the Palazzo going from the beautiful blue and dark greens of rotted wood, to white, to beige, a color that was way too normal for all of this. There were awnings on the windows, they were a brilliant blue. They brought out the mold, the rot . . .

Interitus. The buildings here had it too. She stifled a cough.

She wanted to thank him. Instead, she brought out her phone, and snapped three blurry pictures of the building. They were blurry because her hands shook, not from the cold, but from the normalcy of this moment. They shook because of the beige, because of the rot. She thought of taking a selfie, but that was not her anymore.

She shook because the building was ordinary and ruined from the bottom up. She shook because somewhere inside there had to be something beautiful, something poetic. She thought of Doctor Paul's condo. She thought of the rot that was inside that photo album . . . she thought of it all, and she wished she could take her mask off again. She wanted to lean back and breathe in the subtle moments between monotony.

She wanted to breathe in this moment of her life. The tragic in between. This time, this troublesome time.

If there was a place to exist between the rotten bottom of the Palazzo, with wood turning into seaweed as it ached away . . . and this . . . this hope for the floor above the rot. This hope is her.

The Palazzo and memory fade as the fever inside her burned it down, and then it can be . . .

She opened her eyes again. This fucking train. Her eyes were heavy, and sleep was something she now longed for and feared. as she got older, dreams rarely happen when she slept. They happened in the stolen long blinks of her eyes. Dreams happened in between being woken from a revelry and giving up entirely. Nicole's head hit again, the smeared handprint on the train's wall that rested against her face. That smudge looks like a dance, smudge, smudge, blur, blur, smudge.

She is not alone here on this train as it bullied itself over the rails, as it passed the abandoned buildings that are scattered through Northern Italy. When she looked at the crumbling things that once were . . . she heard a soprano singing. There are creepy trees that look like they were taken from a Dr. Seuss book. The branches reach over the tracks and form a tunnel; they look like the future and the past.

The other person in this train car is another lost soul. A sleeping coffin of a person. He is more alive in flesh than she is probably. Nicole chewed her antiviral medication and pretended she was feeling *fine, just fine.*

Neither of the passengers knew each other. All they felt was the rhythm of the train. They shared this, the fogged-up plexiglass windows; they share the journey.

The handprints that are smeared near the windows know her; they felt like both love and a push away. The train is bumped along, and it made her neck hurt. The rhythm was wrong, and it felt to her what dancing a tango would have felt like if it were done off-time. Too much stop and go. There is a sad accordion that played in the background of her dream. It sounded like a dance that she always wanted to learn, but now it was too late.

Chapter/ twenty-five

Dream a Little Dream

SAM

e tried to leave the pink hotel on the Grand Canal twice during his 48-hour bender. There were times in his room that he could have sworn he looked into the mirror and didn't see himself. He only saw Shannon, and sometimes just Simon. He tried to catch his own reflection out of the corner of his eye, but he could never make it happen. He could never see himself. He didn't know what that meant. In all likelihood, it meant he was drunk; too drunk. He was exhausted, he was haunted, he was not crazy, was he? The bottle of Jameson he got from the downstairs bar was already empty. He did not understand whether this was tomorrow, or if this was still all his yesterdays.

When he did leave the hotel, he managed to make it across the street to a small market. In the refrigerated section they had blocks of soft cheese, and he bought a single sleeve of crackers that were in a dusty box. His dinner would be cheese that tasted like a wet mattress and crackers that bent instead of snapped. Behind the register of the shop there was a small shelf of tourist trinkets. He saw a little porcelain bell with Venezia painted on it. When he held the bell up to the brightest part of the milky winter Venetian sky, he could almost see through it. He slipped it in his pocket. He thought he bought that for Shannon, but part of him knew that any tribute after death was for the mourner, and not the mourned.

He thought he would be able to sit on the wide stone steps of the *Ponte degli Scalzi*, or maybe he would even be brave enough to cross the bridge and leave this part of the canal behind him; he thought he could drop Shannon's new bell in the water like a stone in a wishing well. Sam hoped then that maybe all of them could rest. He thought perhaps he could ignore the invisible rope that he felt tugging him back to his room; ignore the brass bell as it said his name between each ring. It tugged him back to the mirror, tugged him back to something he knew, but didn't know . . .

How was it possible to miss someone more and more the longer they were gone?

He made it as far as the bridge. He walked up four steps, and he tasted the fog that rose from the canal on his lips; it was salty, and old, it was bitter, and intoxicating. He climbed another seven steps before he looked out onto the water on either side. He noticed the thin layer of ice that covered the canal like caramel covering an ice cream cone. There were a few small private boats that tried to chug through the ice, they broke it as they went; every part of it was a beautiful struggle. When he closed his eyes, he saw ducklings in a winter pond . . .

He was eating Frosted Flakes out of a large coffee mug. They were dry, and he poured them in his mouth imitating the way his father drank coffee. There was no one in the kitchen with him, and it was still early; not even seven yet. He chewed with his mouth open. The sugary flakes turned to snowy dust as they sprinkled down the front of his pajamas. Shannon hated when he chewed with his mouth open, so he made sure to do it louder now. He hoped she could hear him all the way in her room, his loud chewing, like a possum. He stopped then, stopped chewing. Stopped everything. He dumped the remaining flakes in the garbage and tossed the mug in the sink where it broke into two clean pieces. He swallowed the rest of the cereal he had left in his mouth. The flakes clumped together and went down slow and painful. He felt it push an air bubble the size of a fist down inside him, past his heart, and it landed in his stomach like a stone.

Sam knew something he should not know. It was something troublesome. The house was too quiet around him, and he waited for it; the moment when everyone in the house would know *it* too. His bare feet had grown cold and stiff on the marble floors. He heard his mother cry out, like a startled bird. The sound was muffled, but nonetheless terrifying. He felt it reverberate down the three floors where it found him. There was a sharp pain in the bottoms of both his feet, like nails. He waited for something else, but there it was again, this wall of silence, this wall of alone. He couldn't hear anything, and all he could smell were cherries.

He heard his father make a sound behind him; it was tears being swallowed. It was a gasp for breath on dry land. It was what Sam would come to understand as sadness. "Did something happen last night?" Santo spoke in a velvety whisper.

"What? No, nothing happened." Nothing had happened, *except it did*; Sam knew, he knew something. "Why?"

"Did you see your sister this morning?" His father's eyes were a trap, a trick, and an accusation. Sam knew something that his father's eyes didn't.

"I didn't check on her. I woke up early, I thought she should sleep. I was hungry. I had cereal—" His voice turned into a whisper. The powdered sugar fell from his pajamas as his entire body started to shake. Santo's eyes landed on the broken coffee mug in the sink. "I'm sorry," Sam stared at his toes; they were pale, bloodless, and they cramped up when he scrunched them in.

"What do you have to be sorry about?"

"Um, I . . . I broke your Harvard mug, I had my cereal in it, and I broke it." These were not lies, Sam had done that, but was he sorry about the mug, no . . . he was sorry about—

"Did Shannon call for you last night, for any of us? Did she ring her bell?"

"No. I mean, I didn't hear anything. If she did ring it . . . Why?" That's *it,* the something, he knows it now, he felt it when he woke up, he felt it last night. The house felt like the gas had been left on; it felt like a storm about to hit. He heard his mother's startled yawp. He did not hear Shannon's bell. "What's going on?" Sam's voice crackled like ice.

"Hey Eagle." Sam had not heard the door open or George walk in. His voice sounded messy; it sounded like mud season. It sounded like sap that ran from trees before it became syrup; it sounded like bitterness turned to love. When George walked in the kitchen, his steps were tender, and his shoulders were up around his ears. He held his red flannel shirt in front of him as if it were a soldier's shield.

"Keep him busy for a few hours." Santo looked at Sam's bare feet, and his thin cotton pajamas; they were sensible navy blue with small yellow polka dots. They were the pajamas of an old man. Santo glanced towards the ceiling. His eyes waged war with his thoughts before he looked back to Sam. "I want you to wear your winter boots and take two scarves at least, and your warmest coat." He stared at him, but no one moved.

"I should put on socks."

Santo looked at George. His eyes were both a plea and a demand.

"Oh, Eagle if you put on socks under those big boots, I know you would complain that your feet were too hot, or the boots were too tight." He smiled, his eyes watered and never quite met Sam's.

"Okay." It sounded like a question, but no one answered him. When Sam turned around to say something to his father, all he saw was a shadow as it disappeared up the back stairs like a black cat; one he always asked for but was never allowed to have. When he turned back, George had Sam's puffy coat and a couple of scarves already in his hands, it was like magic. The red flannel shirt was tucked inside George's interior coat pocket, the bright red fabric peaked out like blood from a deep wound.

Sam hated the way his bare pinky toes felt as they rubbed up against the lamb's wool of his boots. He scrunched his toes in and out as he tried to get the feeling back into them. He had spent too much time on that cold floor; too much time knowing the thing he should not have known. He sat in the backseat of their old Lincoln Town Car, and now that he was alone, he realized the seat was too big. The back of the car was too far away. When he slouched in the seat he tried to reach up, but he couldn't touch the felted top. Shannon had always hated how fidgety he was in the car; his long limbs vibrating with boredom and anxiety.

George drove in silence on a rare light traffic morning from Back Bay to Boston Commons. It took less than twenty minutes, and George had looked in the rearview mirror countless times. Sam never caught his eye, not once. He parked in the Common's Parking Garage and grabbed the half loaf of stale bread from the front seat. Sam waited for George to come around and open his door for him. Sam remembered the broken coffee cup in the sink and wanted to be as good as he could be, especially now, now that Shannon was . . .

Mud season.

Sam's boots almost pulled off his body with each step he took as they trudged over the grass towards the duck pond. Each step made Sam hate the fact that he didn't have socks on more and more. Sam saw the bag of bread in George's hand and understood what was happening. "Shannon loves the ducks."

"She does Eagle, she does."

"I mean loved. She loved the ducks. Right?"

"Yeah Eagle. She loved them."

Sam should have been made to understand this from his parents, but maybe it was better this way; better that he was here with George.

When they got to the edge of the duck pond, they could see that only the edges of the pond were not frozen; everything else had tracks of broken ice that zigzagged their way across the pond and back again. There were baby ducklings that swam through, zigzagging in back of the one in front of them. They made little noises; not a quacking sound but more of a *gurp, gurp, gurp* as they swam. That lead duck broke the ice with every paddle, with every frantic motion.

Sam grabbed the bag of stale bread and dumped it all into the unfrozen part of the pond. The ducklings had to go so far through this broken maze to find their way back to him. Sam tried to throw the plastic bread bag in the water, but it just floated down to his feet. By the time George leaned over to pick it up, Sam was sobbing, and the ducklings were still too far away in their ice maze to care about the bread.

"I'm sorry. I heard it. I heard her bell."

The sounds of George shushing him was soothing, rhythmic, it sounded like . . .

He startled awake. His neck was stiff, and he felt the indentation of his bag against his face. He reached towards his cheek and felt the curvature of the bell where he had leaned against it. He was on the train, which felt like it was bringing him to all his yesterdays and maybe to tomorrow.

Chapter/
twenty-six

Strangers on a Train

NICOLE AND SAM

She tried to sleep and could not. Her head smacked the rim of the window again and again in staccato rhythm. It could be music. If she felt anything, she would have danced with the smudgy fingerprints on the wall. They would press into her temples . . . their fingers would press inside. She could have felt all of that.

Except the world had ended. Now she doesn't feel anything except tired.

Just sleep. Just sleep, just let yourself sleep Nicole. There are worse ways to die.

She willed her eyes to close and all she could see behind her lids were buildings that have turned to blue-green seaweed, and a palace where poetry once lived. She saw masks that were different than hers. She thought of Carnival, Murano Glass, and Poveglia. The train rumbled and she thought it was the bass from terrible electronic music. A party on Plague Island, where people would dance. Where she could kiss a girl that tasted like the sun. Nicole knew that even her Omelia mask would not fit . . . She felt both of those masks hit against the wall as she tried not necessarily to sleep, but to rest.

Four hours of sleep in forty-eight hours. Maybe more—maybe she was awake longer. It was hard to know what day it was.

There was nothing that comforted her more right now than this wall. These fingerprints made her feel a forlorn ache in her stomach. There was exhaustion that weighed heavy in parts of her that she did not understand *could* feel tired.

The tips of her pinky toes.

The upper part of her ear.

These are the places that had only ever felt frostbite or flirtation.

They all burned now, in this place, somewhere between memory and the troublesome time before death.

Now all she felt was this train. All she cared about were these smudged fingerprints.

She was happy to be leaving this city whose streets are filled with ghosts, and masks made for tourists, like Nicole, or Omelia . . . whoever she was right now only wanted to run.

A girl in a long flowing dress—she runs from a house.

Nicole's head vibrated again—she could hear a sad accordion play. Its music echoed through the empty Venetian streets. Her eyes opened. There were abandoned houses that line the train tracks, and they were the most beautiful things she has ever seen. Venice to Verona. Her dreams tumbled along these tracks into Shakespeare. There are ghosts there, too.

She thought of her thermometer; the same one the train stations have. It is tucked in the outer pocket of her weekender bag, and she knew she should take her temperature; she should leave this train at Verona. She looked at the tall man on the other side of the train car. His legs dangled in the aisle. She wondered if her being in here sharing tainted masked air with this stranger would kill him. Unless maybe he was dying too. All she wanted to do was run. Nicole knew she would have to step over his legs if she found herself brave enough to go to the bathroom. Her head banged against the window again. The tango played on in an infinite loop; that fucking accordion, and the dance she was always too scared to learn.

She should get off the train, but she can't. She needed the movement, she wanted to hope. Everything else was troublesome.

Memories are just the dreams she tried to hold onto; no, memories are things that *tap, tap, tap* constantly. Her head hits the glass again and she could swear she wasn't on this train, but instead a wooden roller coaster. Her insides rattled, and her jaw ached. She needed to pee. She should not have thought about it before; she jinxed herself. Nicole had a PTSD issue about having to walk past people she didn't know, like the older kids at the corner store when she was young. She thought they would make fun of her because she was poor, but she also thought the boys, the ones with the long legs that dangle towards the parking lot, would do something to her.

Rape.

Ignore.

Poke fun.

As a child they were all the same. They were all different kinds of *the worst thing*. She looked up the aisle; the guy's legs were still there, and they still blocked her path. Her neck started to heat up. Fever? No, no she's worrying over nothing, maybe this isn't anything. She's not sick, she's scared. Her thoughts are a mess. They are a jumbled tangle of all her yesterdays. This happened to her when she had a fever, or when she was tired. She wanted a damp cloth on the back of her neck. She wanted—

Fuck, why were his legs still in the aisle? How would she be able to walk past him? Step up and over that's how . . . troublesome, these days before death. These days without sleep.

She will stand up, she will walk down the aisle, step over his legs. She could do that. Fear. It's irrational. Yet this same fear had kept her from using the bathroom in school; the thought of walking through the clusters of desks, and past all her classmates made her feel uneasy, even now. In first grade, she started to get kidney infections because she would hold it in all day.

But she's not that girl anymore. She's not *that* Nicole. This Nicole doesn't need to worry about kidney infections; this Nicole is dying. Fear.

She understood this now, even when there was nothing left to understand; that at the end of the world, Nicole knew that no matter how bleak, or deranged it was, that her future leads somewhere over the tall man's legs, and they block the aisle.

She tried to get up a few times, and each time she chickened out. She can't leave her seat even if is just to go to the bathroom. She closed her eyes again; maybe she still was *that* Nicole. She reached up and tucked her fingers under her mask. She traced the scars that felt like zippers and is reminded that she can't be Omelia again. She must be Nicole until she can't be anyone. Troublesome.

Venice was already an hour in her past. The ghosts of that city tried to cling to the train, but they never got in. Her stomach fluttered as the moon moths banged against the walls of a glass jar, and her head vibrated against the glass. The tango played in her head, and all her ghosts are at least an hour away. None of them are here with her now. There are no ghosts on this train. Just a man, with legs in the fucking aisle. She fought to stay awake. In her head she listed the things that made her who she was. All she could come up with was an envelope with a postmark from Clearwater, Florida, and choreography she could still remember from the Miss Maple Pageant; she remembered the miscarriage that didn't mean anything when it happened except it meant something now. She remembered a kiss that tasted like happiness, and she remembered the closed door, the creak, the drip. Those ghosts are in her past. The ghosts of her future are in her long slow blinks as she tried to sleep.

She looked down the aisle again. Legs.

She had to piss, but she didn't want to. She glanced over her shoulder and tucked her masks in place. Her scars are covered. She could feel the new sores on her face; they were small, but mighty. They have already started to make her veins ache.

His legs were not aggressive, but confident in the way they flaunted their relaxation. He was asleep, and she was not. When she tried to remember when she slept last all there was behind her eyes were faded polaroid photos, and the idea that Bryon lived in a palace that turned to seaweed.

All she can see now is beige.

And his legs.

Long, gangly. In her way. Troublesome.

The announcer's voice crackled over the PA system; the voice was garbled, and they echoed and bounced off the walls in the near empty car. The words seem unintelligible but important. They sounded like candy being opened in a darkened theatre. She can't make out all the words, but somewhere in the static she heard Verona.

Her eyes are closed now in resignation. The dirty fingerprint on the wall looked like a butterfly with a torn wing. It looked the way the inside of her mask did yesterday. *Yesterday?* These stains were beautiful in their own way. The walls of this train are more beautiful than Lord Byron's house. When she closed her eyes . . . she thought she could sleep. She just needed to let go of everything. The wooden roller coaster of her memories lull her, soothe her, like a slow hug.

She felt her father place the cold cloth on the back of her neck. The water dripped down her spine. It felt like love. This was it, the memory of her life. If she slept now it would be fine; this, this is how she should go . . .

But then she heard it. Her eyes popped open. *Is that a fucking bell?* The train still barreled forward at high speed as the bell rang in a strange rhythm. It drowned out the sad accordion music. The tango she never learned. That bell was trying to teach her. She wanted to ignore it, but she could not.

The sound was angry, petulant, and it wanted something. It tried to be beautiful, but all it was, was startling. She closed her eyes and hoped never to hear it again. It was silent for what only seemed like 20 seconds. It rang again. It was angry, and loud.

"WHAT THE FUCK?"

Nicole barely lifted her head from the wall. She could feel the dirty smudges against her face; the fingerprints that found their way into her. She cried. She didn't want to, but like an overtired toddler it happened without her control. The tears soaked down to her interior mask. It smelled like an old fountain, green with algae and coins that have been wished on and forgotten. She ignored all of that once she heard his voice.

"What?"

"The bell; that fucking bell." Nicole felt the crook of her mouth split open near her cheek. A ragdoll comes undone. She felt it under her mask. Something dripped into her mouth, it's thicker than blood. She needed to check her temperature at the next train station, there was something not right, she felt—

"You heard the bell?" The train began to slow, and the block letters of the station sign for Verona slip past the windows. The letters are faded and chipped. The man is on his feet. He doesn't need to duck down, but he does out of instinct.

Nicole doesn't answer. It seemed like it was a non-question. Of course she heard that fucking bell. Her head started to throb, and she didn't know when that started. Somewhere between running from ghosts and being one. A dull ache was born behind her eyes. As she stood up, she pulled her sunglasses down from the top of her head. She was slow and deliberate as she moved; she tried not to get dizzy. She didn't want the kids at the store to make fun of her . . .

The doors slid open, but she didn't move. Instead, she closed her eyes again. Maybe she should stay on this train. Wherever you are going, there you are . . . is that a phrase she should care about?

She felt his hand as it wrapped around her wrist, and he tugged her towards the door. She grabbed her bag almost as an afterthought. The sun was bright even through her sunglasses. They were both on the train platform. His dark hair looked like a murder of crows as the wind from the train caught and released it.

The place was bleak, and Nicole could swear she saw an actual tumbleweed that blew across the tracks. Her eyes watered under her sunglasses; it's the sun, and it's the troublesome way that the soon to be dead must live. She is in a place between fever and fear, sleep, and succumbing.

He dropped her wrist and stepped six feet away from her as soon as he was able. He looked at her as she finally said, "Yeah, I heard it, the bell." She scraped her throat and looked down. "It was beautiful." She didn't know why she said that; what she had meant to say was that it was awful. She had meant to say that it was terrifying.

They both looked up at the same time, as an unmarked train heading in the opposite direction left the platform. Had it been there before, had it waited for them and then left them there?

"I think that was my train . . ." He said it without feeling; the way kids in high school read passages of *The Great Gatsby*.

"Mine too I think, I don't know." She dropped her bag, and instead of walking towards the bench she sat on the ground. Her limbs were too tired and heavy to move.

They are the only people there. He wandered in the opposite direction. There are paper train schedules pinned against posts. They are faded, and the edges are brittle. On one side of the post is a map of the train routes; they looked like Polaroids that haven't developed. The different colored lines that zigzagged through the country like veins are now just faded tendrils. They are spindly scars that look like last year's eczema, or stretch marks; even the maps looked like they were sick. On the other side of the post is the schedule, numbers and days in columns like Doctor Paul's death count notebook. The schedule is equally as faded. Whoever had the job of putting new schedules out was probably dead. Maybe it was the same person that was in charge of cleaning the fingerprints off the train car walls.

"Where are you headed?"

"I was trying to get to Rome. But my next connection was in Milan." She moved her sunglasses on top of her head, and out of habit she took out a compact of pressed powder. She tried her best to retouch her makeup from the eyes up. Impending death and sleepless travel are terrible on the complexion. She thought she should write that down in her 'ideas journal,' but then she remembered that there was no point. Those were Omelia's ideas and Omelia had died during a livestream on YouTube.

"Rome's closed, at least the train stations are, no one in or out. They're having a second wave. It came from the homeless, at least that was what I've heard. I think they're having a problem with the dead in the streets, there's just too many of them, and there's no one left to, you know, deal with it." He rubbed hand sanitizer in his hands and then ran his fingers through his hair like it was styling paste. "I was headed through Milan too . . . so . . . yeah . . . I think that was our train."

"Well, it doesn't matter then, I just always wanted to see Rome. I'm Omelia . . . I mean . . ." She stopped, unsure of who she was, who she is . . . "I'm Nicole." Her words stutter. Her name is hers, except it's not. She is who she was and who she hoped to be—and now she is this. It's the end of the world, and it's the end of her. When she said her name, it sounded like a faded empty envelope, it sounded like . . .

"I'm Sam." He reached up to brush his nose and eyes, finding the mask there, he instead goes for his hair again. The same way he did in high school, like it was his was his *go to* move.

It is then that he heard Shannon's bell, off in this distance. It is played against the wind. It is memory, and it is grief. The air around him felt like red flannel, and for the first time in his life he said, "You can call me Eagle."

Nicole laughed, it's awkward, genuine, and painful. She gave an unseen crooked smile under her mask. It is the first time in what felt like forever that she didn't try to stifle it. Her laugh sounded like an old man at a card game. "Um, that's okay. I'll call you Sam." She heard the bell again; this time it really was beautiful, but for some reason it felt all at once that she shouldn't mention it again, at least not right now. She saw him turn around and look behind him. She thought she saw two little shadows as they moved under the creepy trees that tunneled the train tracks, but it must just be the exhaustion and sickness as they finally caught up to her.

Chapter/ twenty–seven

In fair Verona, where we lay our scene.

NICOLE AND SAM

"These schedules are so faded, they're useless." His fingers flicked at the edge of the paper. It was a math equation of aggression and nonchalance. The paper is brittle and a little of it crumbles like cigarette ash onto the ground. "I used to spend my summers here when I was a kid, one time—it wasn't this station, but it looked like this one. A woman lifted her skirt and I saw it, you know, *it*. People think it's just men who do that kind of thing but I'm telling you, I was only nine when it happened. When I told my dad he looked proud. He clapped me on the back like I just scored a goal."

Nicole found herself attracted to him; she didn't get it, she doesn't understand him. "Can you tell whether the train is coming or not?"

"Italian is like Latin, it's all really the same language."

"You're not really answering my question."

"Well Saturdays and Sundays, the words they're almost the same, that's how I remember it, but now I don't know if anyone knows what day it is anymore . . ." His words fade into the wind.

Nicole got up and slung her bag over her shoulder. "I can go try and find out when the next train is coming." Her body is weighed down heavy on one side. It's moments like this that Nicole second guessed herself about packing her books, and one, but not both of her beauty pageant tiaras.

"I can watch your bag if you want."

Nicole thought about her books and the empty envelopes she had tucked inside each of them. Their Florida postmarks were almost as faded as the train schedules. She thought of her bag sitting there on the train platform. Orphaned. She felt vulnerable, exposed, and a little woozy.

"No, it's okay, I should freshen up anyway." She needed to get rid of the masks that were covered in blood and take her meds. Nicole hoped that the bathroom was empty so she could inspect the damage to her face. She knew even with the three doses a day of the strongest antiviral medication possible, Ganciclovir, that there was no cure for this. Each pill just kicked the can down the road a little further; that she was closer to giving up the ghost with each hour. But she had hoped the meds would at least slow it down. Interitus. The rot. She had been home, well, Paul's home, for almost 3 months and she thought until a few days ago that she was doing *okay*, not mentally of course, mentally she was fucked, but physically she had been fine. But then her temperature went up, just a little, and her face—she felt it crack open again as she walked the abandoned Venice streets. She wanted to see Rome, but right now she would settle for seeing anything. She just needed to be well enough to get on the next train. It didn't matter which one, and if one didn't show up, fine, she would see Verona.

Romeo and Juliet. There was something about Sam that made her feel both the hope and the inescapable dread of her future. He had made her laugh, and she could not remember when the last time she laughed was. Normally she would just say, *"That's funny,"* or, *"You're funny."* But he, he had made her laugh. She wanted to laugh again, and she hated herself for it.

She got to the bottom of the stairs that led into the train terminal. She was lost in a dark kaleidoscope of thoughts, and she hoped that when she got back outside that he would still be there; that the train would not have shown up while she was gone. She wanted to ask why he wanted her to call him Eagle—because that was a terrible nickname. She hoped he wasn't some American proud-boy. The end of the world and her slow death certainly did not need that.

"*Controllo della temperatura.*"

Motherfuck. Nicole was already at the bottom of the stairs before she saw the temperature check point. She hoped that the short time she spent outside in the cool air of northern Italy was enough to bring her numbers back down into the normal range. She should have taken off her coat.

The stout woman wore a puffy down jacket and was completely bundled up, even inside. Nicole had been in Italy less than seventy-two hours and had been able to surmise that the Italians were always cold. They wore their leather jackets and overly stylish scarves as if they were armor. She dropped her bag on the floor, and she could not be sure, but it looked like it landed in a dark pool of liquid. She hated that she hoped it was just chewing tobacco spit, and not blood, or worse.

The infrared thermometer was held in front of her forehead; in three seconds it beeped and then the woman spoke. Her words sounded like an old woman shouting from her balcony. It sounded angry and beguiling.

"*Non puoi venire nell atua temperature e 100.6*"

Nicole had heard all she needed to, to be able to understand. She heard *no*, and she heard *100.6*.

"*Grazie.*" Nicole picked up her bag and she did not check the bottom, the new stain, the blood, the tobacco. It didn't matter, did it? She stopped halfway up the stairs and reached into her bag. The interior pocket held two prescription bottles, no refills, some dried out makeup wipes, and a cracked compact mirror. She took the Ganciclovir and two Xanax; she lifted her mask just a little and threw the pills in her mouth and swallowed them dry. She saw that her fingers had come back covered in a light brown watery liquid. She thought of the puddle her bag had been in, and it felt like she looked into a crystal ball. She wondered if she would be met on the platform outside by someone who would not allow her on to the next train, and fuck, she thought about the fact that she still really had to pee.

She hated to piss outside. She was in Verona for fuck's sake, she wasn't camping. Before she looked for Sam, she wandered down a set of tracks that was almost completely overgrown with grass and low-lying vines that crept over everything. This line was tucked in between two windowless buildings. This was the closest thing to a private bathroom she would find until the next train, and even the idea of a next train seemed to be fictional; a thing she believed in once and then outgrew, like Santa, or her favorite jean jacket from sixth grade. The one she covered with antique brooches that she bought at the same flea market she bought her gothic novels. These were the things that she wished had defined her life; sparkling things, and old books that smelled like parakeets and secondhand smoke.

She undid her pants and pulled them down. Her balance was starting to go wonky, so she leaned against the building and right before she closed her eyes, she could have sworn she saw the green vines and the air above and around them start to shimmer. She was tired. It was the Xanax already kicking in, or it was the four days without real sleep; maybe it was her whole life. Maybe she was dying. Maybe she died. Her forehead leaned against the building and it felt so cool, so real. *Why did you have to eat all that raw meat?* She imagined instead of a building it was a damp cloth, and instead of Interitus, it was food poisoning. Instead of dying, it was love. She tried not to fall asleep almost as much as she tried not to piss on her boots.

She was thankful for the old makeup wipes in her bag, and now she was thankful for the cracked compact mirror. With her pants back up, and no one, and no train in sight, she took off her masks. She wiped some loose tobacco from the corners of the mirror; she could not remember the last time she smoked a cigarette. Loose tobacco was the same as glitter, both were impossible to clean up. The little mirror, from the same flea market table as the brooches, had been with her since she was a teenager, and even at her worst, she always loved the version of her she saw in this little round glass. It had broken almost immediately after she bought it, *creak . . . drip . . . she dropped her bag . . .* but the crack in that glass had always made her face make more sense; it showed the before, and the after.

This was a little window into before her father died, and now and all these years later it still showed that part of her. The Nicole, and the Omelia. She hated them both. Her face was red on the left side. The crack on the corner of her mouth had opened again, and she looked like a porcelain doll that had been slammed against a bureau one too many times. Where her face had started to rip, she could see little black lines crawling out, like shattered glass, or a spider's web. The lines were dark black near the root of this new wound, but they faded out to gray and then to little white lines. They crisscrossed and intersected with the still fresh scars that were underneath them. She imagined that this was what the train route would have looked like if the maps hadn't been forgotten and left to bleach and dry out in the sun.

Before she put her mask back on, she reached into the messy front pocket of her bag and popped another of the Ganciclovir; instead of swallowing this one dry, she bit down hard on it and started to chew. She hoped it would make it to her blood stream faster. The pill broke like drywall in her mouth, and it tasted like iron, and reminded her of the yellow Flintstone Vitamins— the ones that were always "Bam-Bam." The pill burned as it went down, and the back of her throat felt hot, and thick with fear. When she swallowed, she was overtaken with the sensation that the back of her tongue, and the inside of her cheeks had been sliced with an X-Acto knife.

She didn't know what was real; was this painful burn just a side effect of the medicine or was it the lack of sleep? Was it the fact that she was actively dying? She thought she would have felt some relief in that, but instead there was a strange newfound urgency to get back to the train platform, and get back to the man named Sam, who asked to be called 'Eagle.'

Though she hated to litter, she tossed the piss-covered old makeup wipe and her soiled disposable mask on the ground. She used the organic peach hand sanitizer that Paul had bought for her at her favorite local boutique before it shuttered its doors for good two-and-a-half months into quarantine. Her hands were shiny and slippery with alcohol and peach, like she had dunked her hands in a Bellini at lunch. For good measure she dabbed a little on the corner of her mouth and rubbed it in; her fingers traced the length of this new wound. It felt like there was a line of brambles from a pricker bush under her skin ready to rip through. She put on a fresh disposable mask, and then her black mask with the cherries over that. She looked in the little broken mirror and smudged what was left of her eye makeup. It looked fresh again.

She smiled under her mask, and a little part of her face split open again. The bramble started to rip through. She remembered why she hated New England summers. Small backyards with long grass, and the insects buzzing well into the night. She picked brambles out of her clothes and hair. She heard her father in the kitchen as he laughed at the rerun of Barney Miller from the old black and white rabbit-eared TV. "I told you not to play near there, I don't understand why you're not happy unless you're getting hurt."

Her father's words weave their way back through the years as she half-stumbled on the overgrown tracks. It's awkward for her to get back on the platform. But no one is looking. *Thank God*. Sam is still a way off, no longer focused on the faded maps. Instead, he stood about ten feet from his suitcase. He did not stare at the tracks expectantly, like people normally did while waiting for a train. Instead, he looked off in the distance past the phone lines at the ditch that separated them from a crumbling and possibly abandoned house. She followed his eyes and looked in that direction and saw several emaciated cows that were near collapse behind a wire fence. There were a few others far enough away that they could almost be sheep or dogs.

The house was beautiful once; now all that it was, was itself. Like the rest of them, it had Interitus. Rot. Ruin. If there were people that lived there, then they probably had it too.

Sam's lips moved as he took off his mask and clutched it in his right hand. Nicole was still too far away to know if they were words, and if they were, she could not hear what was being said. He could be where she was, in this long-waking dream. Maybe he talked to ghosts too. He turned around, and for a brief moment as he fumbled to put his mask back on, she saw his face.

Uninfected.

The perfection of it. His nose was crooked and long. His eyes were sad—but his skin was fine. No scars, no deep black vines, nothing. *It's too bad.* She hated herself; he put his mask back on, and she hated herself.

If he were sick, then there could have been a possible connection here at the end of the world. Without that, she was alone. She pulled her phone out of her jacket pocket. She had not really looked at it when she took the blurred photos in Venice, but now she did. Four days and 29 missed called from Doctor Paul.

She turned the phone off shocked that it still had battery left at all. When she blinked, she almost fell asleep, except her feet were still moving. Her body crept in a lopsided walk. It was heavy on one side from her bag, and the fable of her mother's crooked smile.

Once I was alive, and I hated it. Now I am dying, and I am myself . . . She laughed then. It sounded like an elderly man who fed squirrels in a park, or Golden-Age sidekick on a nighttime talk show. Sam must have heard her coming, he turned and faced her just at the moment the mask covered his face.

She couldn't remember the last time she fucked a man, and it's not that she was gay, and it's not that she was straight. She was whatever it was that made her wish she could have fallen in love with someone who had eyes that held metaphor like a dusty book, or skin that looked like a summer at the beach. The person she could love would have a laugh that sounded like an old photograph.

She could make herself cum. She didn't need anyone for that. What she had always wanted was someone who made her remember, and to feel the parts of her that she killed off just so it didn't hurt so much. There were parts of her that believed in love, believed in herself; the parts of her that screamed inside her head between the *creak, drip* . . . *He looks at me wrong* . . . those part of her were gone. She wanted someone to know her, and to see the dusty envelopes; to understand why she kept them over the years, like relics of a saint. She wanted this. She wanted so many things, but as she walked back towards the bright sun in an Italian winter sky . . . right now she wanted to sleep.

She had never slept next to someone, but she wanted this now, with a stranger; his name was Sam the Eagle.

She could tell he smiled under his mask; there was a crinkle at the corner of his eyes. "What's the word? Are there more trains coming?"

She couldn't say that she didn't make it past the guard. "It's a shit show in there—nothing's updated, it's like out here, except no sun." She tried to smile, but the peach hand sanitizer she rubbed on her face made it feel as if her skin was pinched, the way girls did at slumber parties or in the bottom bunks of group homes to make sure she kept a secret.

"It's fine. I say we take the next train no matter what, good chance it's headed south or west. Worst case we end up back in Venice and start again." She was about ten feet away but could see the crinkle of his eyes. Under his mask was a genuine smile; the eye crinkle, that's how you can tell. That was what happiness looked like. Nicole didn't know if she ever felt that, not really. The closest she came to it was buying a dress only to realize later that it had pockets. Happiness.

She stood far enough away from him for virus safety, but close enough to feel him; he radiated an energy. She understood that even if this train platform had been filled with people that there was something about him, about the way he looked at her, the eye crinkle, the hand sanitizer in his hair—he still would have made her feel like she was the only other person there. He gave everything he had out into this vacated world and then sucked it back in. A train platform. A tumbleweed. Sad cows behind a wire fence. He smiled . . . until he stopped.

It felt like a heartbeat; the kind that skittered and skipped like a stone thrown across the surface of a still pond.

Nicole pressed herself against the metal post on the empty platform. She pressed her hand against it until her fingers were cold. Then she pressed them against her eyelids, and then back on the post to cool down again, and then a few seconds later she placed her hand against the back of her neck.

"Whiskey?" He had a bottle that looked more expensive than she had ever had before.

"We can't drink out of the same bottle, it's not safe." *Unless we are both sick—what was that? A hope? No, no, just a thought. A question no one asked. His face was fine, but maybe he had a fever, or maybe it was someplace else, the rot. The ruin. Interitus: Masculine noun.*

He reached into his bag; his large hands rummaged around the edges and pulled a crinkled plastic water bottle out, and he walked to the edge of the platform and emptied its two-days-old remnants over the edge and onto the overgrown the tracks. The water splashed off the edge of the concrete. It looked like an elementary school diorama of Niagara Falls the *American Side.* The water soaked into all the little cracks that ran down the side of the concrete. The water traveled through these cracks and it reminded Nicole of her face; the black lines reaching up and out from under her mask.

"Where civil blood makes civil hands unclean," Sam said, it sounded like he was reciting lines backstage or delivering a sermon in which he didn't believe. He caught her eye as he was about to pour some whiskey into the water bottle. That was when they both heard it.

The ground rumbled, and neither of them was sure what train it was when it showed up, destination unknown. It was just there. A choice in a Choose Your Own Adventure novel. It was *Dungeons and Dragons*, roll to see if you get on the train or if you go it alone. Sam the Eagle put the empty water bottle back into his bag. The train was unmarked. The first carriage blew past the station and it seemed like it would keep going, just pass them by as if they were not even there. It finally stopped. The doors opened. The choice was theirs.

There was only one door that was within their reach.

"Fuck it, I say let's take this one, we can figure it out from there." Sam the Eagle gave her a little look over his shoulder. It could have been a wink; it felt like friendship. Loneliness had covered her for years in a thick layer of dust, and she felt the dust being brushed off. She didn't know what she was underneath. Nothing? A new person? The rot? The ruin?

"Sounds like a plan." She picked up her bag; it was heavy and grimy with sickness, but light with hope.

Eagle walked onto the train; his eyes crinkled at her over his mask when he looked at her again. Nicole felt like she was about to put her hand in the fire. He disappeared into the darkness. When the train stopped, they were the only ones there, and now it was just her.

There are cows that edge closer to the wire fence. They would taste like tears . . .

Something about this moment felt like that night . . . *creak* . . . *drip* . . . *creak* . . . Nicole whispered, "No," . . . but her words were faraway, and Sam was already on the train. She rushed a little to catch up to him, and she looked one last time over her shoulders at the desolate train station in fair Verona. A chill ran up her spine, and she half expected to see someone behind her, not *somebody*; no, it was *something*. This is why she ran.

The train car was dark, and before her eyes could adjust, the door slid closed behind her. Cool Italian air was replaced by stillness. It was hot and smelled like a rusted stove. Sam looked like a shadow instead of a person; he stood to her left, just there in the aisle. She thought he was moving but he was not, it's the train—Verona, like Venice was another ghost she had left behind.

It's then that she smelled it.

Death.

Chapter/
twenty–eight

Mememto Mori

Once he walked onto the train, it was already too late.

He was frozen in place, and because of his size he had the aisle completely blocked. As the train picked up speed her body lurched forward a few feet, and out of instinct she put up her hands to brace herself. She collided with Sam, and though his size would appear unmovable she bumped him and he stumbled forward a little. His foot slipped in a puddle, and his hand came up and braced himself against a row of seats a couple of feet in front of her.

The air smelled like a mining cave, stagnant and coppery. "I'm sorry, I know we're not supposed to touch—" Her words stopped as she saw it. The light that came in through the window was shattered and red. It looked like stained glass. Blood has more colors than just red; she hadn't understood that before Interitus. It did not register at first, what she saw on the bench. All she noticed was the window and the beautiful and terrifying light. Now she understood—it was smeared with dark red and chunks of what looked like bone, and tissue.

Her eyes moved from the window to the other people that occupied this train car. They were an older couple, in their sixties or seventies. It was hard to tell now. The woman looked to be asleep, except her neck was at a terrible angle. If she slept like that, she would have woken with a terrible crick in her neck. Her mask was soaked through with blood, and half of it had slipped off her face, what's left of her face. The old man next to her still has his mask on, but half his skull is missing. There is a whole in his temple the size of a human heart. In his hand is a gun, the kind a woman would wear in her garter belt in a gangster movie.

"Oh, my fucking God." Nicole backed up a few feet, but Sam was still there, his body stiff, and his shoulders were hunched like he had been punched in the stomach. He was unnervingly still, and in this kaleidoscope of light and the wavering shadows, he looked like a ghost on a castle wall. "Sam?" She reached towards him, and her fingers grazed his back; she was sure he couldn't feel it through his thick wool peacoat. She put a little more force into her hand and pressed down against his shoulder. She looked down and saw that his feet were in a dark pool of blood and what looked like urine. "Sam, come on, we need to move." She tugged a little at his jacket. "You, we, we can't be this close to it, she was sick, really sick . . . and he," she stopped and closed her eyes. She is still so tired, but her heart is racing now.

Creak

Drip

Creak

When she opened her eyes, she realized she was crying, and Sam had turned to face her. The color drained from his face; his eyes are dead. The crinkle is gone. His left hand was covered in dark black blood from when he caught himself on the seat. She saw the little black vines in the liquid; they looked like they were still moving. She dug her hand into the front pocket of her bag and pulled out the remaining dried up makeup wipes. She took his hand and wiped it as clean as she could. She tossed the wipes on floor and pulled him towards her. She made him walk in front because she knew that if she let him stay behind her he would have kept looking back at it.

At them. She knew this because it is what she does, every few feet. She was reminded of the children's Bible she had when she was young, there was a gruesome painting of Lot's wife who turned back to look at the ravening cities of Sodom and Gomorrah. That painting had scared and delighted her. She tried to concentrate on Sam's back; she kept her hand on him and edged him on as her feet seemed to nip at his heels.

"We need to get to another car, far away from this one." Her fingers were intertwined with his, and she felt his fingers as they scratched nervously at the inside of her palm. She could feel his fingernails; they feel sticky with the blood, but his fingers felt cool in her hand, like piano keys.

She wondered what her fever was up to now. She shouldn't be touching him. He opened the doors between the train carriages and the wind battered them; it sounded like they were at the top of Mount Washington in New Hampshire; the wind hits her so hard it felt like her lungs were on fire. They kept moving. They passed through seven unoccupied cars before he slowed down. He let go of her hand and collapsed into a seat on the aisle. She walked up a couple more rows and slid in, her body leaning against the wall, out of his line of vision.

He screamed and punched the seat in front of him; when he ran out of breath, she heard him inhale and do it again.

On his third scream she joined him.

On the fourth scream they both heard the bell.

They didn't scream a fifth time.

Chapter/
twenty-nine

Getting to Know You, Getting to Know All About You

"I'll take that whiskey now if you're still offering?" Her voice seemed disjointed from her body; it might have been because of the mask, or the strange disquietude of not looking at or even being able to see the person you are talking to. He didn't respond to her, but she does hear the squeaky crinkle of an empty plastic water bottle, and the sharp metallic zip of a whiskey bottle's seal as it's broken. The liquid chugs from one container to the next.

"I can trade you some hand sanitizer if you want. Mine smells like peach." He sniffled a little. His jagged breath danced on the edge of balance trying to right itself. Such a fine line between a breath and a sob.

"I have some, it's not peach, but—" He takes a beat. She can feel the energy in the train carriage shift; it is like the light before an eclipse. She could feel real conversation brewing like a storm. So far, their words were nothing but heat lightning. Far away flashes of something coming. But she could feel it now, the rain. "I think mine is hospital scented." His laugh is dry and sounds more like a cough.

It sounds like a defense mechanism.

"Well a hospital has a lot of different smells, there is lemon disinfectant, there's paperwork, there's bleach . . ." The only time she was in the hospital she was dying. All she could smell was herself.

"You can't forget the poop smells, the pee smells, and dirty mop water." She can almost hear him force himself to smile under his mask.

"Well, if yours is poop or pee-smell scented, then please, for the sake of both of us, just take mine. Peach is better than those, it's even better than mop bucket any day." She tried to make her voice light. If she was witty enough maybe then they would be able to forget the pool of blood, and the brain matter on the windows.

"Mine's traditional hospital. I'll stick with that."

"Well, it's a classic; you should."

"Yeah. Coming in—" Sam leaned into the aisle and rapped on the floor until she turned around just in time to see him roll the water bottle, now filled three-quarters with a whiskey that probably cost more than her rent.

"Oh, Jesus, you didn't tell me sports were involved." Nicole was awkward as she leaned into the aisle; her fingers fumbled for the bottle like those plastic claw devices that help old people reach canned goods on a top shelf. She knocked the whiskey-filled water bottle just out of her reach, and it rolled under the seats across the aisle from her. Instead of standing up she stretched herself long across the aisle. "Ow" she said a few times before her fingers finally connected with the bottle and were able to fenagle it into her hand.

Sam laughed, and stopped himself short. He probably hated himself for that. It's too soon to laugh. "I guess I should have just given it to you."

"Well, there was no way for you to know how much I panic if I have to catch anything, or block anything. I feel like I wouldn't be on Xanax if it hadn't been for playing volleyball in high school gym class." *It's a lie. Xanax happened after she opened the door; after the creak, the drip, the creak.*

Xanax and PTSD were the only things that Nicole and Omelia had in common.

Once she was tucked safely back and hunched down out of sight in her seat, she slipped her mask down and took a sip from the water bottle. She should regret not wiping it down with a tissue and sanitizer, but she doesn't. She has less than two weeks' worth of her antiviral medication left, and she already has a fever. It was bad math. She took another sip.

"I didn't do the best job back there; I shouldn't have let you see that. I'm sorry." His remorse made his voice lower; it sounds thicker, and heavier, like a sweater.

"Is it the first time you saw it, how it looks? The Interitus . . . the death?" She stammered and didn't know if either of them should mention the gun, the brain matter, and the splatter on the window that made the light coming in from the window both beautiful and awful.

"No, I saw it before, just once . . . once so far." Sam could still feel Simon's hand in his; he could still hear him say 'pizza day' he still saw the boy's eyes before the virus had started to rot one of them away.

"I'm sorry, was it family, or . . .?"

"No, it was a boy, a young boy I knew. Jesus that sounds creepy, it wasn't creepy . . ." He sipped straight from the whiskey bottle; it tasted like his life, like privilege, repressed emotion, and like money. He wanted to hate it, the taste, and his life, but it was all he ever knew.

"It must have been tough seeing it in a kid, I can't imagine." She sipped the whiskey and thought about taking more medicine. Her fingers traced the raised welts on her face, they felt like angry infected stitches. The edges of something had started to break through her skin like barb wire.

"My twin sister died at the same age he was, and this was—" Sam stopped himself from talking because there was nothing that he could say that expressed it. There were too many tangled pieces in his head. Should he say that when he watched Simon die it was not as hard; should he tell her that Shannon's death was a relief . . . There were no words, just the feeling of a hand that reached inside him and pulled something out. ". . .this was different . . ." He sipped again; his voice was slower now. "What about you? Was this the first time you saw—"

"No, no I've seen it." She wanted to tell him she saw it every time she looked at herself, and when she closed her eyes; she wanted to say that it's her. The disease. The pale rider on a horse, but instead all she could say was, "My favorite former foster father's third wife . . . she could have been like a sister to me." She laughed, and the sound stung, especially when she heard Sam laugh too. "We weren't close, I mean in age we were, but not in life. But, she died, and that . . . that hurt someone that didn't need to be hurt again."

"The foster father?"

"Favorite former foster father. Get the alliteration right." She smiled and the barb wire caterpillar that lived under her skin started to squirm. It was like it could sense her lying and it recoiled from it like a worm in salt.

"Foster father? Why's that?"

"My mom wasn't in the picture; she was always just a crooked smile and a brittle empty envelope with a postmark from Tampa . . . Just old paper that smelled like suntan lotion."

"And dad?" he asked.

"He was amazing, he really was." She sipped more whiskey and even though the bottle was still half full she already knew she would need more. "I have the same smile as my mother . . . eventually that got to be too much for him."

"He left you?"

"No, I mean yes, he, um, he killed himself." She heard the metal cap open again. It is a few rows away, but she felt the jagged edges; they were sharp against the part of her that is dreaming and awake. "He didn't want me to see him, he left a note; he said not to look, but I looked . . . then I did my makeup."

"Jesus, then you really shouldn't have seen what we just did. How did he do it?"

"A belt wrapped around his neck and the beam in his bedroom. I just missed it, really. His body was still moving, he had barely pissed himself before I got there. It was new."The whiskey tasted like old library books; not the ones borrowed, but the ones that were donated and kept in glass cases. "What about you? Your sister?"

"Shannon."

"Shannon. Were you there when she died?"

His answer is yes. He was her twin, but the answer at the core of him, his answer that was his truth was, "No, I mean yes, but no. We brought her home, *they* bought her home. Her room was next to mine—it was twenty-five feet and now it's 25 years . . ." He sipped again. "It's yesterday, and it's here on this train." He waited for the bell; he waited to see a blur of red flannel. Smell lemons and Baby Soft.

It didn't come.

"Speaking of this train . . ." Nicole looked out the window, which was the kind of dirty that made it seem like it's foggy outside. She watched the land fly by. The houses that look like the beautiful ones on the covers of her books. "Do you know where we are going?"

"I saw a kilometer marker for Brescia, but I don't think the train is stopping there." Sam looked out the window in the opposite direction. He watched the landscape freckled with crumbling houses, broken dreams, and the beauty that ached of decay. The land that stretched out for miles. He caught sight of another emaciated cow. This one was tangled in a barb wire fence. The animal stared into the train, into him.

"This got bleak."

"Well, it is the end of the world, right? It was probably always going to get bleak." She doesn't want to mention the brain matter or the skull fragments; she doesn't want to mention the caterpillar with its itchy green fuzz that made her want to scratch a hole in her own face.

"What's your name?"

"I told you, it's Nicole."

"No, I mean your whole name."

"Ugh it's the worst, I haven't gone by my name in years. It sounds like an afterthought, or a single-wide trailer with a shoddy furnace and chipped linoleum floors." She looked at her weekender bag next to her, she bought it at a Big Lots.

"So."

"So, I hate it."

"Just tell me."

She sighed and her breath is trapped under her mask; underneath the whiskey she smells something else. Sickness. It smelled the way a bronchitis cough tasted. "It's Nicole Marie Pelletier."

"What was your other name?"

"Omelia, just Omelia, no one ever really asked for a last name. If anyone had asked, I would have said Omelia Burkhart."

"Like Amelia Earhart?"

"Yeah, my imaginary father was a pilot . . ."

"Were you a stripper, or like a cam girl?" He heard his voice, and there is a judgmental undertone to it; he sounded like his mother, his father, Gretchen. He sounded like money, like fine whiskey, and gourmet cherries. "I mean, if you were, that's cool, no judgement here." *He's an asshole, he knows it. She knows it. Shannon knew it, Simon knew it . . . George, well maybe George didn't know it.*

"No, neither of those things, I wish." Her laugh starts out dry, and then she feels a cough coming out of her lungs; it crawled out at first, she felt its arms, its legs. She tried to hold it in. She pressed her masks closer into her mouth. She felt the blood, or whatever it was that had started to soak the underlayer.

"Oh, well I like Nicole better." His voice was theatrically loud, he talked over her cough. And if he was worried about it then he did a good job masking it with bravado.

"Me too. Not the name, but the person. Omelia she—she was

exhausting to be." The last half of that sentence was barely audible. It was spoken on the tail end of her coughing fit.

Sam had never felt someone's words more profoundly. She could have been talking about him. Sam. The art of being Sam, the *New JFK*, it was a lot. It was too much. He was meant to be a twin after all, there should have always been someone else there to help carry the burden. He took another sip from the bottle, and he realized that his hands were barely shaking now. He wondered at his mind's sense of self-preservation, what he had always been able to compartmentalize away. He closed his eyes and tried to remember what the couple in the last train car had looked like; he tried to see them again, frozen forever in their last moment. The pleasurable terror of it. The blood and the bone, the sickness, and the health.

He couldn't remember it. It was already going or gone. When he closed his eyes, he saw that the blood has transformed to red flannel. "Nicole, has anyone ever told you, that you have a great stage whisper . . ." his voice trailed off.

"I can't say that anyone ever has." She doesn't know why, but she started to cry. She took her mask off and eyed herself in her little broken mirror. The black lines like invasive vines from the corner of her mouth have gotten darker. She dabbed a little bit of concealer on her fingers and taps the area under her eye; she is able to cover the faintest ones. But it is as if she can hear them screaming under her skin when she does this. "And who are you, what's your name?" Her voice is a little stronger now.

"It's Sam, but the birth certificate says Santo Anthony Alberti the third. But Sam was always easiest."

"Ugh Alberti? Like the Vice President? I'm so sorry. That guy is a dick."

"Actually, he is the President now."

"Yeah, yeah of course. But are you? I mean you're not . . . are you?"

"How are you doing on that whiskey? Do you want a refill on that water bottle?" Just like when he and Shannon were young, Sam had mastered the notion of when to offer a refill.

Her voice got muffled again as she put her masks back on; she knew she was far enough away from him that it shouldn't matter, but she doesn't know about the ventilation systems on these old trains. "Are you his son?" There was a pause, and the weight of it felt heavy in her chest. "Aren't you the governor of Massachusetts or a Senator?"

"No, I was just running . . ."

"You were running?"

"Yes." He sighed and thought of pizza day. He remembered sitting with Shannon in her hospital bed, their legs tangled together like a long summer day. He remembered George telling him he should try harder to be on time. He remembered the way worn flannel felt against his cheek as he cried. "I was running."

"Aren't we all?" She laughed a little. "That's what I am doing here, in Italy, on this train." She took a little more of her whiskey. The plastic bottle crinkled under her grip. She saw that her knuckles were turning white. It was a death grip. "I'll have more whiskey if you can spare it." She rolled the bottle back up the aisle towards him. Even though it is crushed on one side and warbled as it rolled, he had no problem leaning over and catching it. "I'm hoping it kicks in, and maybe I can get some sleep." She thought about warning him; telling him not to touch the cap, where her mouth was. She didn't say anything.

"What, and miss this beautiful landscape?"

It's all just weeds growing over buildings outthere, and every once in a while, there were small houses in the distance. They look like campers tied together with rope. They all have too many cars parked all around them, and even with all the obvious signs of life, they look abandoned, but strangely beautiful.

"How long has it been since you slept?" He asked her this, not out of curiosity but out of thoughtfulness. He poured a few more fingers of whiskey in her water bottle. It crinkled in his hands, and he wondered if he would hear this sound years from now and think of this day. Think of blood, and skull splattered on a window like a Pollock painting. He wondered if he would hear this and remember a woman named Nicole Marie Pelletier who he wished he had known before this, before the world started to die.

"I don't really know anymore, it hasn't been much, not since leaving the states. I probably got a couple hours here or there in Venice, but that wasn't really sleep, it was just shutting off." The water bottle rolled back her way, and Nicole did a much better job at catching it this time. "I don't recommend Absinthe and Limoncello with Xanax, I know it sounds like a party but really it's just blurry loneliness. I swear after a while I could start to hear my hair, and it wasn't happy." She waited for him to laugh, but he doesn't.

"You could sleep now, I'll let you know when we get to Milan, I think that's where the train is headed."

"I mean I can try, but I have a hard time sleeping with someone so close."

"So, we're close now . . ."

"No, no you know what I mean."

"Yeah, I get it, but we found dead bodies together, and we might be the last people alive—"

"No don't do that."

"What, do what? Bring up the dead bodies or . . .?"

"It sounds like you're flirting." She stopped and again she waited for a laugh, but it didn't come. "Are you flirting?"

"No, I mean, no, no, it's the whiskey, and the running. It sounds like flirting when you put them together."

"Oh okay. Because if you *were* flirting, I would just say don't; not now."

"It would be a terrible time to flirt with you Nicole Marie Pelletier."

"You have no idea."

"No, I get it, the world's ending. Everyone we love is probably dead. One or both of us is dying for sure in the next couple of months . . . I don't know, ignore me."

"Well, it's just I normally don't fuck men."

"Oh, oh I'm sorry . . ."

"No, it's not that I don't fuck men, it's just I normally don't, it's just easier not to."

"I wouldn't fuck men either if I were you."

"I don't fuck anyone, not now, obviously. . ." Nicole thought about Kim, with her skin that tasted like summer; Kim, whose love language was affirmation and presents. Kim who went to school with her for four years and still didn't recognize her; Kim who was probably dead now. "I appreciate your non-flirting way of flirting. It's been a long time."

"Yeah, for me too, I can't remember the last time I tried to flirt, so, I'm probably bad at it. I was probably always bad at if I'm being honest. I never really had to try very hard, so I didn't." This time when he pulls up his mask to take a sip of the brown smokey liquid, he filled his mouth and just kept it there until it made his gums tingle and the back of his throat almost seize up. He swallowed the alcohol and had to fight to keep it down. "I mean I remember the last time I fucked someone, and it was terrible so . . ."

"You are a charmer. She sounds like a lucky lady."

"She wasn't, lucky . . . No, I mean, the sex was bad, but it was just something that happened, I wanted it to be bad." He rubbed his hands on his eyes. They feel heavy and raw, like he had been swimming in too much chlorine. As his eyes water, he remembered— fuck, don't touch your eyes, idiot. Had he cleaned his hands, really cleaned them since they were in the blood, yes, of course he had . . . right? Hand sanitizer. Hospital scented. How long ago was that now, an hour, two? "Have you ever tried to blow up your life, or just do something shitty just so you feel it, you feel the fucking awfulness of it?"

"I feel like you just read my high school yearbook quote."

They both laugh, and even before they finish, the happiness starts to fade, and it becomes memory. They were like a sepia-toned photo; what happened felt like it was in slow motion but was brutally fleeting, nonetheless.

They were just hummingbird's wings.

"Nicole Marie Pelletier, I wish I had met you before the world ended."

"Oh, you wouldn't have liked me very much . . . or maybe you would have just not remembered me at all. Maybe we did meet. Neither of us will ever know." The whiskey started to taste like old photos in a green album, like a mistake. Nicole reached for her phone which had been buried in her bag, under three days of dirty underwear, and books that smell like green parakeets. The inside of her arm gets a thin cut as it drags against her tiara from the Miss Strawberry Festival. She was always shitty at packing. A tiara, six books, a bunch of old envelopes, three kinds of night cream, but no snacks. "Why did you want me to call you Eagle?" She turned on her phone; the battery was almost dead. She had 14 more missed calls from Doctor Paul. She clicked the phone off again as she tossed it in her makeup bag.

"It was a dumb childhood nickname."

"If it's dumb why did you ask me to call you that?"

"I don't know, it was something that the only people that ever really knew me called me. My sister, and George, he was my driver, it was how they used to tease me, but it was the kind of tease that I hated when it happened but now it feels like love when I remember it."

"You had a driver? I tell you my name sounds like a single-wide trailer and you had a fucking driver." She laughed as she said, "You were right, you are terrible at flirting."

They laugh and it dies out just as the intercom goes off again; garbled static and Italian, they hear the word *Milan*, but it sounded like a whisper through a paper towel roll. It could be from today, or it could be from years ago. But suddenly, the idea of Milan, and sunshine, or another barren wasteland of a train platform seemed like too much. Nicole wished she could just stay here, in this seat, in this car, the furthest place they could run from death.

But that is not how this works.

Nicole got up, and wobbled in the aisle; her hands braced herself on either side, and she pulled herself towards where she hoped the bathroom was. She didn't want to have to piss outside again. She carried her little makeup bag with her; tucked inside the waistband of her leggings was the thermal thermometer.

The bathroom was better than being outside but not by much. She felt the walls press in as the doors closed. There was no air, and the walls felt too tall, brown, metallic, and bleak. Her lung pain started to kick in, and the bottoms of her lungs flicker with the light. When she breathed, she felt herself chug along with the train. None of this worked the way it was meant to.

It was dimmer.

The air was stale.

She took off her masks and hung them on the strange hook that is meant for coats but is somehow too small. The mirror was made of highly reflective plastic and what looked to be a large reflective sticker. In this light her face looked like a green and black bruise; it flickered. She strobed in and out; she was in the bathroom, and she was in the hallway outside her father's room, she was here looking at a warped reflection, and she was on Instagram with thousands of people watching as she made her face look like a gothic queen . . .

There were little veins like train tracks that have traveled up her face. She laughed and didn't know why. It's then, before she could stop herself that she threw up. She didn't make it to the toilet, but instead it splashed in the shallow sink with shitty water pressure. What comes out is mainly whiskey, but she saw the blood, and something else, more solid. She tried to wipe everything down with paper towels and a fresh damp makeup wipe from her bag. She pushed it all down into the bottom of the waste bin, like her high school miscarriage.

As she used the bathroom, she held the infrared thermometer on front of her forehead. It danced in front of her. Her eyes blurred and all the greenish black that she saw in the mirror made this little room look like

Ophelia's drowning moment.

The thermometer beeps, and though it is increasingly more difficult, she focused her eyes to read the numbers. Her fever is 102.2.

Before she left the little bathroom, which was not much larger than an old-fashioned telephone booth, she ran the water until it was as cold as she could get it. It barely came out of the faucet, and she realizes she has cried with more force than this. She placed a few paper towels in the water and tried to straighten them out enough to place on the back of her neck. She took two Aleve and another Ganciclovir. They felt like rocks going down her throat. Nicole took her phone out again and called Paul. He answered after one ring.

"Nic? Are you okay?"

All she does is cry, and she was right, it was with more pressure than the faucet could ever muster.

"Nicole, where are you?"

She can't answer him, he wouldn't understand, and even now, in this bathroom, she doesn't understand. All she can do is whisper, "I was terrible to you, and I'm sorry."

"Don't say that sweetheart."

"I have to, it's true." The air seemed overly quiet, and she was not sure if the call had dropped or if her phone was dead. "Are you still there?"

"Yeah Nic, I'm here."

"I just wanted you to know that you were a really good father. I should have let you be that. You loved me. I should have let you do that too."

"Nicole, if you tell me where you are, I can come and get you." As he said this, the years melt away, and she is 14 again.

"No, no it's okay." She heard him crying now too. He sounded so far away, not just in miles, but in wasted time, years, things unsaid. "I just needed to say goodbye, and say, um, and say . . . I love you." It's quiet again, too quiet. "Paul?"

Her phone is dead, and she was not sure how much he heard, but it was probably enough. She needed it to be enough. She tossed her phone in the trash, and then put the crumpled wet paper towels on top of it. She put her masks back on and left the little room. The light flickered behind her and then it went out.

Chapter/ thirty

What's in a Name?

Sam was waiting outside the bathroom door as she stepped out; if he heard her on the phone, or when she puked, he didn't say anything. He didn't mention her eyes, which were swollen red and blood shot from tears. He carried her bag there. He handed it to her without saying anything. At first her brain got foggy and confused, but then she realized that the train was coming to a stop.

"I thought I was going to have to burst in there and drag you out with your underwear around your ankles." He tried to be light, but it sounded false, like a bad actor in a Noel Coward play.

Words caught in her throat and it reminded her of brambles being pulled off a patchwork skirt she wore as a child. "How many times do I have to tell you to stop flirting with me?" She slung the bag over her shoulder, and then she felt his hand reach out and rest there next to the strap for a minute. She felt him squeeze her shoulder once, but then his hand doesn't move. She could feel the heat from it, the delicious nearness. He took a little of her hair in between his fingers and rubbed it as if it were silk.

Just before the doors in front of them slide open she heard him whisper, "Sorry," before he took his hand away.

To say that the train platforms of Milan Centrale were bustling would have been a lie. But there were a few people far off on other platforms, or asleep up against the shuttered store fronts of cafes and overpriced souvenir shops. All total there were probably only six people that they could see, but they were the only two to get off the train from Verona.

"We should tell someone about the people we found," Nicole mumbled into the wake of wind that the train left as it sped out from the station. The train, like them, was running too.

Sam doesn't respond to that; he just wandered towards a bench and threw his bag on it like he was staking his claim. "It's getting dark, are you going to be warm enough?" He called over his shoulder as he pulled a scarf out of his bag "I have this if you need it."

"Are you kidding, I'm from New Hampshire. I have this puffy jacket and a spare set of mittens in the pocket at all times in case of emergency." Her eyes drift about fifty yards away; she saw a woman, about her age. Nicole first clocked her as another exhausted traveler who was napping on her backpack, but now she saw that the woman was not asleep. Her face rested against a small cloth purse she used as a pillow. The purse, and the shadow around her were soaked in blood. Her forehead and the top parts of her cheeks were tinged blue.

"Let's move a few benches down. I don't know what the wind will do with her germs—and her smell." Nicole gestured towards the woman, already growing numb to this new reality. As they move away from the body, the lights clicked on all around them, as if the timer understood more than they did about how dark it was about to get. There were moths the size of baby birds; they fly slowly in the cold, but still repeatedly hit the large station lights. Their bodies make a sound like pebbles thrown in a dry well. Sam saw her staring at them.

"My first professional theatre role was as Moth in a psychedelic version of *Midsummer Night's Dream*. I was fourteen."

"No offense, but I didn't even know there was a character named 'Moth.'"

"Yeah, one of the lesser fairies, I was no Peaseblossom, obviously, but it still meant the world to me. It was the first thing that was really mine." He placed his bag on the ground and slumped onto a metal bench that was *just far enough* away from the most obvious of the corpses. The way he looked around it seemed as if he were searching for more.

Nicole did the same thing. She tossed her bag on the ground and sat on the same bench, and she pressed herself into the cool metal railing on the opposite side. "Psychedelic *Midsummer Night's Dream* sounds terrible. Like, really bad; was it bad?"

His laughter echoed off the emptiness around them. They could feel the night as it started to lean in like an unexpected kiss. "It was . . . the worst. I had to wear a full body leotard, and it was tie-dye . . . Ugh. The theatre went bankrupt, and the show was cancelled before we ever went on, thank God . . . I mean I was disappointed, but relieved . . . I've never been good at getting out of things I didn't want to do. I always just go with it until it's too late, and then I don't even know who the fuck I am."

"I never had that problem." She waited to see if she had it in her to go on. "I'm good at getting out; at leaving. I always leave . . . even when I don't have to."

He gestures broadly with his arms, "Welcome to Italy."

"Yeah, welcome to Italy." She can see the pale white wisps of her breath creeping out from under her masks. The cool air stung the open wounds on her face even under two layers of protection. She thought about putting on a third mask but is too scared to do it. It would be an admission; a confession of sickness, and she doesn't want that, not now. She doesn't want his eyes to look at her with pity, or disgust. *God, I hope he gets sick too.* The thought is out there in the universe before she could take it back. Nicole realized that she hasn't changed; that she was still the girl who told her social worker that Paul looked at her wrong, still the girl who did her makeup before she called

911 after finding her father. She side-eyed him and watched him sneak a pill under his mask. She didn't see sickness, but she saw something. "Am I supposed to know that you just took something?"

"It's Adderall."

"For ADHD?"

"No, just for fun, or whatever this is. I would offer you one, but you should get some sleep."

"For sleep perchance to dream. That's Shakespeare, right?"

"Yeah, Hamlet."

"Hamlet, of course. You know, I have done Ophelia makeup more times than I care to count. She is one of my favorites. How did an actor become a politician? It's such a gross Ronald Reagan thing to do."

"Well, I was a lawyer first, and then, I don't know how it happened. Shannon, she wanted to work for the ACLU; she wanted to be the first female governor of Massachusetts. She wanted all of it, and for all the right reasons."

"It sounds like you are living someone else's life."

"Says the woman with two names."

"Says the man who wanted me to call him Eagle."

"Well, I mean I just said that I didn't think you would actually . . ."

"Yeah, you were flirting, and it was about birds, and weirdly that is cooler than you think. I have a thing for birds. Parakeets really, and kimono-style robes with egrets on them…maybe they're herons…" He laughs as her voice fades out and then back in again like an old radio station. "Tell me about Eagle . . ."

"Well, what's in a name? That was from Romeo and Juliet . . . in case you didn't know."

"I knew that, I was obsessed with Romeo and Juliet after seeing it on a Brady Bunch rerun when I was a kid, so I read it, a lot."

"Nicole Marie Pelletier . . ." he smiled; she couldn't see it, but she knew it was there. Eye crinkle. He was about to say something flip when the brass bell rang; it startled them both, but then at the same time they both smiled under their masks.

"Can you tell me something? Why Sam the Eagle?"

"I can tell you that my father named me Sam after the Republican Muppet from the Muppet Show, but that my sister convinced me it was because of my nose, and I know you can't see my nose, but it's . . . substantial, and also it has a bump on it from this one time that she hit me with—" He stops himself. "She hit me with . . ." His hand instinctually goes up and traced the small scar that lived in the seam both above and below his mask. He felt the bump on his nose that has been there since that night. "She hit me with a bell, I was being a total shit . . ."

His eyes burned with tears, and even before they spilled over, he felt a knot at the back of his throat. He could hear the bell ringing, and for the first time, he could smell George's flannel shirt; the man's memory danced on the wind. It was a blend of Old Spice and regret; he smelled that in the air. It overpowered the smell of the dead; it was there and then it was gone. Now he could only smell memories. He could only smell love. Maybe it was Shannon wearing George's old shirt. This smell, this sentimental flannel ache that felt like love . . . it was all he had left of the most important person in his life. A person who has been dead for longer than she was alive.

"So this is the bell we keep hearing?"

"You're the only person that ever heard it besides me, just so you know, and it's the first time it didn't happen in our house."

"But what is it?" Nicole straightened up and shook her head. Brain fog. "Not what is it, why is it?"

"It's the worst night of my life . . . and it's in my head. And now you hear it, and I don't know what *that* is. Is it guilt? Is it fucking real? I've never known if I'm crazy or if I'm haunted. Maybe it's both."

Creak

Drip

Creak

"It can be both, I don't know." Nicole wondered if she could hear whatever this was because she had in her infinite wisdom run closer to the edge; this fine line she has been walking since she was a kid: death, life. She always thought there was something else that should have been in there with it. Troublesome. Maybe it was this all along, maybe it was this night that had been haunting her before it even happened. Maybe it was this disease. Maybe it was just the moths that fly slow and hit against the lamps that don't heat up in this weather. Their wings don't burn, so they keep doing it, over and over. Echoes of a stone in an empty well.

A wish. A hope.

Interitus.

The rot.

"So, this bell, it's the worst night of your life?" she said.

"Yeah."

The outer edges of her heart start to itch; it felt like a whispered confession in an empty confessional booth. When she was a kid she always liked to go to confession when there was no priest on duty. Some called that *cheating*, but she never did. No matter what she said, it didn't matter. It was the saying of it that mattered. Her head turned to him; they were three feet apart, and she knows she will never understand what it could feel like to run her hands against his skin; the bump on his nose that until now she never noticed.

He was beautiful in a way that made her hold back tears. He was beautiful in a way that made the back of her jaw ache. He was beautiful in a way that made her regret her life of loneliness. "Confession time, worst night of your life stories. I'll tell you mine if you tell me yours." Her voice was getting lower, huskier. The bottoms of her lungs felt like they were filling with mud.

They both heard sirens going off, outside the city limits of Milan. They sound like fire alarms, and underneath that was a sudden wave of ambulances; then deeper and fainter than that, was a bell.

"After you, my lady." The smile was gone from his eyes.

Chapter/
thirty-one

I'll Show You Mine

NICOLE

66My mom left when I wasn't yet two. It's fine. Some people shouldn't be
moms, she probably didn't have it in her, no matter what she thought she
wanted." The exhaustion that Nicole had felt for the past few days was
gone now; it had been replaced by a nervous energy that made her want to
laugh and cry. She was filled with regret. She thought of her conversation
with Kim; the building that she had wanted to crush her. This story, *this* was
the building. It was years of not smiling. It was years that she had refused to
be loved; it all rushed in her ears like the wind between the train cars.

"She was beautiful; my dad said she looked like Rita Hayworth but
with sadder eyes. So, she was gone, I didn't know her. She moved to Florida;
that was the story. I never would have believed it except he kept all these
envelopes." She reached into her bag, and she took her copies of *Conjure
Wife*, and *the Ghost I Had Been*, and slipped the envelopes out of them. They
felt like dried leaves in her hands. No one understood how beautiful an old

envelope could be. "I'm sure he kept the letters, but I never saw them. All I saw were these." She pulled out a few more envelopes and fanned them out in her hand like a she was doing a card trick. "Tampa, Clearwater, one from Miami, then back to Tampa. The dates were all close at first but then the last few were spread out."

Sam's arms were long, and though they were on the opposite ends of this bench his fingertips were able to graze her shoulder blade. Through her puffy coat his fingers felt like the wings of a moth. The ones in the air, and the one he was supposed to be onstage. Nicole was hunched over; she never hunched before this, before the world ended. Maybe she was still tired. Maybe she always had been.

She should have smiled more when she had the chance.

"He never showed the letters to me. I don't know what she said, and I didn't know her enough to even try to imagine. I just knew they weren't mine. But he gave me the envelopes, and to me, they smelled like sunshine, and look how brittle they are. They look like sunburned skin that you peel off in sheets." She thought of her mother who was mostly imaginary; she thought of Meredith in a bikini, and Kim who smelled like sunshine. Florida . . .

"I had to think she was happier than we were; there was no other reason for her to leave, right? Don't answer that. There's that saying, something about every happy family is happy the same way, and every unhappy family is unhappy in their own way. I used to know who said that, now I can't remember. Is it Shakespeare?"

"It's Tolstoy. *Anna Karenina*." His fingers pressed a little harder into her shoulder blade, and the moth wings turned into bee stings. She wanted to flinch away from the pain but instead she leaned into it a little more. It was real.

"He gave me these envelopes, and I loved them, this brittle paper. It was better than loving a person. A person you could hurt, and they can be fine, but these envelopes, they were fragile. They were old even when we got them. They are empty and cruel." She straightened them out and tucked them back in her bag, all of them slid into her copy of *Night of the Visitor*. "They are probably a lot like her. She's probably dead. Maybe she died before all of this. I should feel something about that, but I just can't."

She doesn't say anything, she just waited and listened to him as he breathed. She thought he would say something, but he didn't. He just looked at her. "I have her smile, it's a *compliment,* except it's not. I never smile in photos, to this day I don't do it. But I did once . . . It was eighth grade when I was finally allowed to wear makeup to school, and this photographer, fuck, he was really kind of a creeper when I look back on it, but . . . he made me smile. And I laughed. And when I did, it felt like sun peeking out from a cloud, but then the flash went off— it was too late.

"I brought the photo home a couple weeks later. We never had the extra money to buy wallet sized and 8x10's, but the school gave us a complimentary 5x7 every year. My father always hung it on the wall in the kitchen. Right over the old coffee can filled with pencils and pens and a couple of screwdrivers. He didn't hang this one. He looked at it and he smiled a little and just put in on top of the pile of old Union Leader Newspapers. He thought I didn't notice but I did.

"That night before I went to bed, I put one of his razor blades, two Flintstone Vitamins, the rest of my mother's old Midol she left in the medicine cabinet, and some Tylenol in a Ziplock bag. I hid it under the mattress and then before I left for school in the morning, I tucked it in a Japanese box that he gave me . . . The next morning was normal, he went to work, I went to school . . . but maybe he left early, maybe he never went, maybe he just drove around until I was gone. There is so much of my own life that I don't know.

"When I came home there was a note. He told me not to look, he told me just to call the cops. But I did look. When I opened the door, it was still so new. His body was still swaying there, belt around his neck . . . the piss hadn't even stopped dripping from his leg.

"He must have gone to work; worked a full day. It was timed so perfectly. He did everything right, except I fucked it up—I looked after he told me not to. I dropped my bag; I had a little mirror in it, which broke. It was more than seven years of bad luck." She wanted to reach in her bag and show him, show him the mirror that had the two different Nicole's reflected in it, but when she tried to move her hands again, she realized how much everything had started to hurt.

"I didn't call 911 right away. I dragged my bag into my room. My little mirror was broken, my eyeshadow palette that I snuck around with was broken. I was broken. I didn't know what to do so I did my makeup. When I was done, I didn't look like me, I looked like …"

"Omelia," he finished.

"Yeah, I looked like Omelia, and she doesn't even exist. She never did. She was the worst version of me, and I *chose* to be her. Because it was easier than having to feel everything all the time, all of that hurt."

"And foster care?"

"I was lucky, it was good . . . until it wasn't. That was my fault too." Nicole pressed her fingers to her eyes to stop the tears; she thought they smelled like the train; metallic and dirty. But she was wrong, they smelled like blood, and she is lucky that the light in the sky went from bruised to blackened in such a short time. She was lucky he couldn't see her face.

"It wasn't your fault."

"Sure, yeah. That's what my shrink said too," she sniffled. "Now show me yours …" There was still some whiskey left in the water bottle. She turned away from him and felt his hand slip away from her. It felt like it was already goodbye. It felt like it was already tomorrow. She drank as much of the warm whiskey that she could in one gulp.

She didn't think it would help.

Chapter/ thirty–two

SAM

"**Y**ou need to know that Shannon was everything that was good and bad inside of me. When I was angry, she was furious. When I was funny, she was hilarious. When I tried hard, well she didn't even have to try, and when I was cruel . . . she could be vicious. Even with all the bad parts of me . . . she was loved anyway, somehow, she was loved even more for it. She was born 2 minutes before me, but she was always 20 years older than I was. She had the eyes of an owl; she was the oldest 9-year-old I had ever met." He waited and expected to hear her bell in the distance, but maybe she was right there with him, maybe she had sat to listen. He never talked about her, and he had especially never talked about this. Maybe she could tell. Maybe she wanted to hear it too. A ghost story around a campfire.

He thought of Simon, but he couldn't go there, not yet. Shannon was a wound that would never heal but it had on occasion scabbed over. His guilt about Shannon was ice that formed on a winter river or a duck pond.

your bones ache and your skin burn. A memory so dark it hurt his eyes like the sun ring around an eclipse. He closed his eyes and he saw half a bag of stale bread dumped into winter water. George's face was already fading, his mother's face was gone even before this. Everyone who had ever been willing to love him was dead.

"I wish I could say that when Shannon got sick that it broke our family, but that's not true. We were broken already; I don't remember a time when we weren't. We were more like a painting of a family rather than something that was real. No one talked, no one said things that mattered. They just laughed politely, played cribbage, and jingled ice in their glass if they wanted a refill." He reached up to rub at his eyes, but then thought better of it, and instead ran his hand through his hair. "When she got sick, we were almost 10, and I assumed I would get sick too. There had been nothing in our lives at that point that was one of ours and not both of ours. Our memories were the same, the way we laughed was the same, the faces we made when we cried were the same. She was in every memory I had. And then she wasn't. Things were different before I had a chance to know that they would be. She was in the hospital and I was home. Maybe that's when *I* broke. I'd never been an I. We were always a *we*. I was so angry at her for finally being able to be her own person. I didn't care that she was dying. I was jealous; jealous that she was doing something that wasn't about us. About me."

He stopped talking then, but there was still an electricity around him. The air held an anticipation of an unfinished thought. He rested his elbows on his knees and leaned forward. He felt his mask get a little loose against his face and it felt like a hand being removed from over his mouth. He stared at the ground. He wanted to look at Nicole but knew if he did, he would start to sob. He would probably wrap his arms around her and never let go. There was a sharp knife that dug into the bottom of his heart. The pain was real, but then it turned to dust. This was the pain of wanting to touch someone but not being able to. "She had a brass bell, which she used when she was able to come home. It was for emergencies, or if she needed something. My room was closest, so I always heard it first. She wasn't perfect. Dying didn't make her a saint. She had been a real bitch for days, I could tell she was hurting and scared, but I just felt like she was trying to get attention, and she already had *all* the attention. We got into a fight; I took her bell and was ringing it and sort of mocked her. She grabbed it out of my hand and smacked me in the face with it, right across my nose." His finger traced the bump that barely showed above his mask. He knew it was nothing more than a faint white scar that looked like nothing more than a cat scratch. But even though it was such a little thing he could feel it through his whole body.

"I called her a 'fucking bitch.' It was the first time I ever said that word aloud. *Fucking*." He whispered it even now; this was when the tears came. They fell from his eyes in slow motion; when they hit the dirty train platform, they looked like blood. A thousand little cuts. "I put the bell back on her nightstand, and I left the room, I made sure to slam her door and then my door. I wanted her to know how mad I was. Everything was quiet for a while, but then she started to ring her bell." He looked up at Nicole for the first time since he started talking. "I don't know why no one else heard it. But I heard it, and I did nothing." He pulled the top of the whiskey bottle, faced away from Nicole and took a long slow sip. "It stopped after a while and then it started up again, it was slower, weaker. It went on almost all night." His voice caught in his throat as he said, "I never did anything. The last thing I said to her was that she was a fucking bitch." He turned away from her now; his eyes scanned the darkness around them and noticed the strange stillness of the other people on this platform, like extras in a play.

Without second guessing herself, Nicole scootched towards him and rested the right side of her cheek against the back of his shoulder. The heavy wool of his peacoat felt like a kiss from dry lips against her temple. His hand reached over and found hers without even looking, as if his hand had reached for her for years and finally found her. He rested his hand on top of hers and just left it there. He didn't hold her, but she could tell he wanted to. This felt like home. "This the bell I keep hearing?" It was a question, except it wasn't. Nicole was scared to hear the answer to it. What did it mean that she could hear her?

"Yeah, it is." His hand left hers and he put in on the back of her head; his hand was in her hair. His fingertips touched her scalp like she was made of old paper. Brittle, but precious. His fingers moved in her hair like they were touching velvet. "No one besides me has ever heard it, and it's been twenty-five years. Even then, I could only hear it when I was back home. Every time I left that house, the bell was gone. I hated them; the bell, and Shannon, but I needed them. It's all I had left; it's my connection to her, that fucking bell . . . it's like asking questions in a letter, it's useless, but it's necessary." He leaned his head over, and through his mask he kissed the top of Nicole's head. His mouth was still in her hair, and she could feel his words more than she could hear them. "But you heard her bell, and I don't know what that means, but I know it means something."

Nicole wanted it to mean something, she wanted it to mean that Shannon was looking out for them, but in her heart, in her stomach, in her lungs, that felt heavier and heavier the longer she sat here. The fever inside her that she knew had crept closer to 103 . . . she knew she heard it because she was dying. She has had one hand in the fire since before she left for the airport. All her years of wanting to stare into the darkness and have it see her, have it say her name . . . it's happened. This darkness: Shannon's bell, it has called her home. She felt sleep as it tugged at her. Her head is on Sam's back and she knew if she just let go, she would be gone.

She was more tired than she thought she was.

There are moths that hit the station lights in slow motion, and there is an echo that has reached out of a nightmare from her childhood; *creak . . . drip . . . creak*. She can't cover her face with makeup, she can't be Omelia and change what has happened. There was a fight inside of her, and when she got up from the bench, she was not sure if she has won or lost. His hand stayed in her hair for as long as it could. When it fell against the back of her puffy coat it made a sound like those moths with their slow wings as they battered themselves against glass and light until they were exhausted but not dead. She walked to the train maps; they were not as faded as Verona, and she could trace the route lines the way a lover would trace the blue veins that are just underneath the thin pale skin over her heart. Her finger moved up the map, north from Milan, the opposite direction that Sam was going.

"I don't know if there will be anymore trains tonight, but if there is one headed north, I think I could get to Lake Como from here, it's close, just an hour and a half." She looked at him and smiled. She realized like Shannon's bell, and questions in a letter, that it was useless, but necessary. She hoped that he understood that this was going to be goodbye.

"What's in Lake Como?"

She pulled her *Lonely Planet Pocket Italy* travel guide out of her pocket and flipped to a page that had a bright pink post it note sticking out of it. "There's a castle there, with ghost sculptures on the walls, just staring out to sea. They're beautiful." Her tears move in the opposite direction of this train line. Her tears move south, towards Palermo, where Sam and Shannon spent their summers. She kept staring at the map, her finger stayed put on Lake Como; her ghost castle . . . the perfect end to her story. A girl running from a house, from a life, from a disease . . . She wished she could do her makeup and dress up one last time; she could picture herself in a flowing gown, a mask . . . she can see herself running from this until she was nothing, not even a memory. She would run until she was a ghost, forgotten. A sculpture on the side of a castle she may not live to see.

"Or instead of that, you come to Palermo with me."

"Oh, for fuck's sake . . ."

Chapter/
thirty-three

"**W**hat?"
She laughed the way she would when she would tell someone she didn't want to see them again. She laughed to hurt him before she was hurt. "You are not serious."

"I am." He had to shout this, as there was a train that was barreling into the station one track away.

"It's a terrible idea. You don't know me, and I don't know you. Whiskey isn't knowing someone, even if the world is ending." She shouted back to him as the wind kicked up before the train was even in eyeshot. They both looked at the one person, a man, not much older if at all than either of them, who stood at the edge of the platform. That was a man who knew where he was going. The train came into view; it still sped without any indication that it would stop. The man, a stranger, had his toes dangling off the edge of the concrete. Nicole and Sam could feel it, it was two hundred yards away, but it felt the same as the death train they travelled here on. It wasn't a question that made the air electric; it was different. The man's bags were still tucked next to the building, and from this distance you could almost believe he was wearing a red mask, but Nicole knew; she understood that he had taken it off.

Everyone is unhappy in different ways. *Anna Karenina.* The train.

"Sam turn around, don't look at it." She spoke too late.

The stranger dove in front of the train; Sam stared at in resignation and despair. They could not hear his body thud against the tracks, and they could not hear the sound, whatever that would be of a train destroying what was left of a life. The only thing they did know was that the train didn't stop, and wherever it was going, it was going alone.

"Oh, my fucking God, my fucking God." Nicole held onto the post where the train map was posted. Everything spun around her and the black veins thick with sickened blood began to pound in her ears.

"Come to Palermo with me," he whispered. "We'll figure it out, we'll get there somehow. We can't stay out here; this isn't a life." Even Sam didn't know what he meant by that. He had never cared about being alone, and he had grown accustomed to loneliness; it was just the green moss growing over the walls that surrounded him. He had been lonely since Shannon, and now there was hope . . . and it scared him. "Please, please, Nicole Marie Pelletier . . . come with me."

The bell rang. It was angry, but its sound grew tired easily, and it echoed off the darkness. The lampposts burned too bright. Troublesome. And all at once the exhausted moon moths, with bodies like baby birds, all fell to the ground. The world ends. Beauty dies. When Nicole heard the bell, she flinched, not away, but inside. "You don't know me."

"But I could know you. And you, you already know me more than anyone else ever has . . ."

"And now you want me to go meet your grandmother, and then what?" When Nicole laughed, she felt a little more of her face split open. Ragdoll. She turned away from him and just wandered the platform, unable to look at him. She took the infrared thermometer out of her inner pocket and held it in front of her forehead. Her hand, which she swore still moved like waves, looked like a beach vacation; her hand moved in and out of now— and her memories, in and out of photos of people who smiled before she knew them. Her hand moved like letters she was never allowed to read. Her hand moved from Florida; her hand moved like paper, her hand moved like learning to dance and sing. Her hand moved like Meredith's moods, and the bright blue ribbon of her first beauty pageant sash. It moved like a wave. It moved like water and time. It moved like regret, and grief, anger, and love. It moved like affirmation, like Kim's love language. It moved like loneliness. It moved like—

103.1

She threw the thermometer on the tracks in front of her; the plastic hit the metal rails and it cracked like a porcelain doll. These train lines already look overgrown with weeds; it looked like nothing would come here, like nothing would come to bring her to her castle of ghost. Nothing to bring them to grandmother's house.

"My grandmother, my Nonna, she's dead. They're all dead. Everyone in my life that I loved, that loved me, they're all gone . . . It's the end of the world and there was nothing. I was fine with nothing, and then there was you. I wish the world didn't have to end so we could meet." Sam's eyes darted from the corpse on the train tracks back to Nicole and then back again to the corpse. The heat from the train made it smell like meat. "Please."

There are some words that don't echo, no matter the empty space. They land heavy. Every syllable is felt.

"You could be sick . . . I don't know." She wanted to smile, but she knew with the mask it was useless, and she couldn't fake a smile all the way to her eyes. "Or I could be sick—" Her voice was quieter now and it sounded like a sharpened pencil writing in cursive. Letters written but not seen. Old paper. These words are a letter a daughter has never read.

"Come to Palermo." It's not a question. Sam said this as if it were a decision already made. His words were a photo album never opened. His words were a crooked smile never given. They could be hope. "We can make a life there . . ."

"Can we? How can we make a life? WE'RE DYING—" Nicole's arms flailed out in random gestures towards the sleeping corpses a few hundred yards away, their hoods and masks pulled up over them like they are castle ghosts . . . her arms gesture towards the man, so freshly dead that they are only now hearing the rats and critters starting to scurry out from the places in a train station where wet and shadow meet . . .

"I'll show you mine if you show me yours." Sam's hand reached up and removed the ear loop from one side of his mask. "I'll show you mine, if you show me yours . . ." He still holds the fabric in front of his face, but she already knows what she would see. She saw him earlier when he didn't know she was there.

The long endless day has been the closest thing to happiness that Nicole had ever known, and because of that, that fear, that hand in the fire kind of pain— pain, that was brittle like envelope of love . . . she reached up too. She knew when he sees her face, it will all be different. Her face way she looks like the raw pieces of hamburger that made her sick as a child . . . she knew this. If she took her mask down it would be the easiest way to run.

If you show someone a monster, they will run. They must.

"You don't need to be a ghost in a castle . . . not yet."

She hated him for saying that. Under the hate was what? What else was she feeling? She didn't know. "Okay then count it down."

In unison, as if they were lifelong friends, or an old married couple. "Three, two, one . . ."

His mask was down a little before one, she saw his face. It was strong and beautiful, there was a bump on his nose with a little scar. Uninfected.

He was a dream. A hope. A wish. She saw that and tugged the rest of her mask down anyway.

There was no mistaking death when it stared him in the face; it gripped his gut and pulled it in every direction. There was a sound like a howling wind. There was a brass bell, it rang all around them. There was a breeze, which had been stale before, and now it moved like delicate fingers against her exposed skin.

It felt like a flannel shirt and smelled like two kinds of lemons. It smelled like old books and parakeets; underneath it all, cherries.

She smiled, and it was crooked, like her mother's.

There were pieces of her once beautifully imperfect face stuck to her mask like an underexposed polaroid film on a plastic sheet.

Someone screamed, it was Sam; maybe it was her. It felt like the end of the world, but it was just the end of her.

She said, "I'm sorry," and she knew he didn't hear her. All there was, was a howling wind; it screamed in her head, and in all her silent thoughts. This wind: this scream, it was inside every thought she has ever had, the ones that are not grief; every thought that's not her regret, or anger. When Sam screamed it was that sound, the same one she knew since she was a child.

She heard that sound, it was guttural; like liquid and stone, a scream that was a banshee, but more personal . . . and then there was nothing. Silence.

Drip

Creak

Drip

"Nicole Marie Pelletier." His arms were around her, she tried to move her ever deteriorating face away from him, but she could not. She felt his chin on her head, and then his mouth in her hair, his breath were the wings of the dead moths, and his words were shapes against her ever-rotting self.

"Come to Palermo . . . don't haunt a castle in Lake Como . . . haunt me." The words were drowned out as a train came into the station. She felt his lips against her hair, and against the part of her skin that was still held together. The rest of her spilled away, 103 to 104.

"I'm dying. I'll probably be dead before we ever make it there."

"Then haunt me."

A train stopped in front of them. Headed south to Palermo.

She held onto his hand, he put her masks back on for her. His fingers were delicate against her skin; she felt like antique lace. Her feet moved without thought. He kissed her temple again. He did not let go of her face, even as the deep brown blood trickled down his arm.

"Haunt me."

Nicole closed her eyes and felt everything fade away. She could sleep. He was everything she never knew she could have.

"Haunt me."

"Haunt me."

"Haunt me."

"Haunt me."

"Haunt me."

"Haunt me."

They both heard a brass bell; it was everything they needed, nothing they wanted, and then there was nothing at all. They were on the train, their bodies tumbled into the closest seats. She rested her head against him, and even though they were moving, she didn't feel like she was running. She closed her eyes, and then she felt sleep as it moved in, like an anticipated reunion.

"Haunt me . . ."

"Haunt…"

𝕿𝖍𝖊 𝕰𝖓𝖉

Acknowledgements

It truly does take a village to get a book out there into the world. I have to start first with my amazing research assistant Patty. I will always be grateful for all of our disgusting texts while you helped me discover what the virsu was that I was dealing with in this book. Thank you for giving this mysterious monster a name!

Thank you to my beta readers Bill, Lauri, Michelle, Allison, Roman, and of course my friends at Sci Fi Saturday night, Cam and Dome. Thank you all for understanding my work and being excited for it every time.

Thank you to the Vox Vomitus Vixens, Allison and Trisha. Thanks for hosting the show with me and for listening to me talk about this book when even I didn't want to talk about it anymore.

Thank you to Patty from Seeing Eye Editing for the initial round of edits, and then (again) to Allison for working with me to get the book into the best shape it could be in.

Thank you Diane Zinna for inspriring me, teaching me how to write about grief and for helping me unlock what was going on in my character's heads.

Thank you to Julie and the Team at Books and Moods for all of the design help. Thank you to the bookstagrammers and bloggers.

Thank you to the best publicist in the world Mickey Mikkelson with Creative Edge Publicity.

Thank you to my agent Paula Munier at Talcott Notch.

Thank you to all my friends and fans who have bought the book and spread the word.

Thank you to my mom and my dad, though he is no longer with us.

Most of all thank you to my husband Roman, who has been nothing less than perfect. Thank you for giving me the time and space I needed to write this book. Thanks for always being my first reader. Thank you for playing with Lord Tubby when I was too busy. I love you.

About the Author

Jennifer Anne Gordon is a gothic horror/literary fiction novelist. Her work includes *Beautiful, Frightening and Silent* which won the Kindle Award for Best Horror/Suspense for 2020, won Best Horror 2020 from Authors on the Air, was a Finalist for American Book Fest's Best Book Award- Horror, 2020. It also received the Platinum 5 Star Review from Reader's Choice as well as the Gold Seal from Book View. Her second Novel, *From Daylight to Madness (The Hotel* Book 1*)* received the Gold Seal from Book View, as well as The Platinum Seal from Reader's Favorite, her third novel *When the Sleeping Dead Still Talk (The Hotel* Book 2*)* was released in late 2020.

Jennifer also had a collection of her artwork published *Victoriana: The Mixed Media Art of Jennifer Gordon.*

Jennifer is one of the hosts as well as the creator of Vox Vomitus, a video podcast on the Global Authors on the Air Network, as well as a Co-Host of the podcast Writers Showcase. As a podcast host Jennifer has interviewed authors such as V.C Andrews, James Rollins, Paul Tremblay, Sarah Langan, Mary Rollins, Josh Malerman, Carol Goodman, Paula Munier, Wendy Webb, and Matt Ruff. She had been a contributor to Ladies of Horror Fiction, Horror Tree, Writers After Dark, Reader's Entertainment Magazine, Nerd Daily, and Ginger Nuts of Horror.

She is a member of the Horror Writers Association where she sits on one of the juries for the Bram Stoker Awards. She is also a member of New England Horror Writers.

Jennifer is a pale curly haired ginger, obsessed with horror, ghosts, abandoned buildings, and her dog "Lord Tubby".

She graduated from the New Hampshire Institute of Art, where she studied Acting. She also studied at the University of New Hampshire with a concentration in Art History and English.

She has made her living as an actress, a magician's assistant, a "gallerina", a comic book dealer, a painter, and burlesque performer and has been an award-winning professional ballroom dancer, performer, instructor, and choreographer since 2010.

When not writing she enjoys traveling with her husband and dance partner, teaching her dog ridiculous tricks (like 'give me a kiss' and 'what hand is the treat in?' ok these are not great tricks) as well as taking photos of abandoned buildings and haunted locations.

She is a Leo, so at the end of the day she just thinks about her hair.

For more information and benevolent stalking, please visit her website at www.JenniferAnneGordon.com _

For media and interview requests please contact Mickey Mikkelson at Creative Edge Publicity – mickey.creativeedge@gmail.com

CPSIA information can be obtained
at www.ICGtesting.com
Printed in the USA
LVHW080312080721
691865LV00009B/133

9 781735 402185